I0789010

Every Time We Meet

A. M. Leibowitz

Supposed Crimes LLC • Matthews, North Carolina

Published in the United States.

ISBN: 978-1-952150-03-6

www.supposedcrimes.com

This book is typeset in Goudy Old Style.

For perfectionists everywhere, with love from your kin

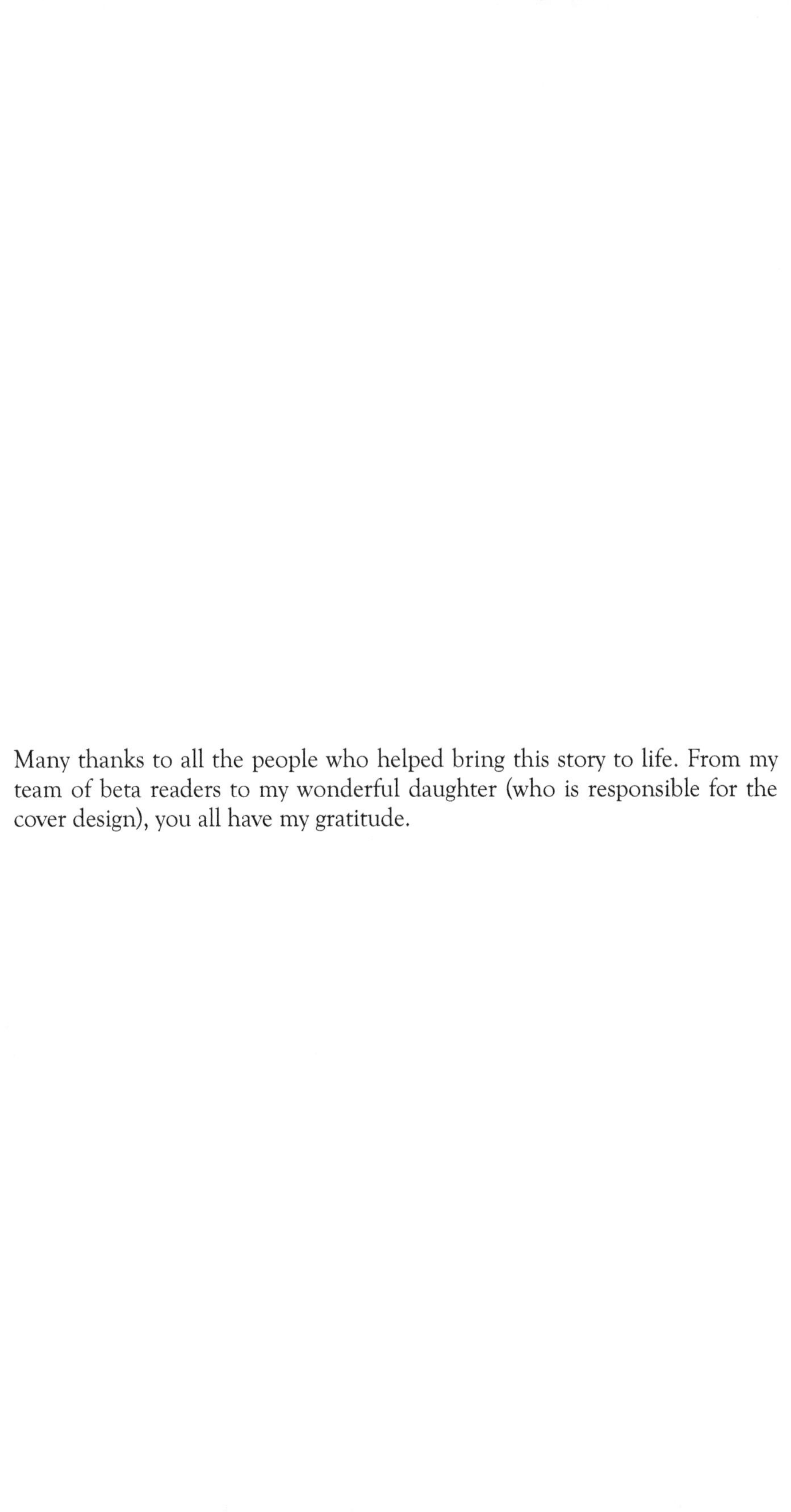

Many thanks to all the people who helped bring this story to life. From my team of beta readers to my wonderful daughter (who is responsible for the cover design), you all have my gratitude.

DAY ONE

I

The smell of coffee from the automatic pot woke Heidi from a deep sleep. She stirred restlessly, vaguely recalling that she'd been dreaming—something about her long-term partner. They'd been together for two years, so it wasn't surprising Cass would feature in her imagination.

Heidi squinted and peered around. Gray light filtered in around the curtains. She blinked, trying to clear the sleep from her eyes, then opened them fully.

Instantly, she regretted that decision. Her head hurt, no doubt from last night's celebration with her friends. She screwed her eyes shut then rubbed them. After several attempts, she was able to keep them open. She switched on the radio on her bedside table, wanting to wake up more slowly while listening to her favorite station.

"Goooooood morning, Rochester!" It was the cheerful voice of Angel Flores. She was one of the usual morning commute co-hosts on WNDR 95.5. "We're live here at the Lilac Festival, where the parade begins in less than a half hour!"

That was when it hit Heidi what day it was.

She threw off the covers and dashed around, yanking clothes off hangers and out of drawers. Her alarm hadn't been set properly, or maybe she'd shut it off instead of hitting snooze. Either way, she was late. There was only enough time to throw on clothes, leave a note for her kids, and grab her coffee to go. She had to be at Highland Park by ten-thirty, and it was five past now. Not even enough time for a shower.

She yanked on her jeans, threw on a white T-shirt, and added a deep violet flannel button-up. Her standard uniform when she wasn't working at the hospital. She had to search for socks of the same size, and even then, they didn't match. No time to care.

At her dresser, she fluffed her hair in the mirror and shoved a tube of lip gloss in one pocket. Also a Heidi-standard. Taking a deep, cleansing breath, she fished around in the top drawer among her lacy underwear to find it. The ring. If she couldn't be dressed up, then she'd at least have the best piece of jewelry she could afford when she proposed to Cass underneath the huge magnolia tree right at the top of the hill.

She carefully put the velvet box into her shirt pocket, but it fell out the minute she bent down to pick up her shoes. She replaced it and and buttoned the pocket this time. No sense losing it or all her plans would go awry. She left her bed unmade and went into the kitchen to get that much-deserved—and needed—cup of coffee.

Kate, her oldest daughter, was already at the table. She had cards and envelopes laid out and was filling them in with her careful, neat handwriting. She looked up when Heidi entered.

"What's all this?" Heidi asked.

Kate's mouth hung open for a full five seconds. She closed it and glowered. "Mom. Graduation? You know, that thing I'm doing in six weeks? These have to go out as soon as possible."

"Oh, damn. I'm sorry, sweetie. I totally forgot. I'll be home to take them to the post office as soon as I do this one thing."

A sly grin blossomed on Kate's face. "You mean Cass? Today's the big day."

"Yep. Ah, crap. I have to go. You're getting Max to and from play rehearsal, right? Jilly has her viola recital this afternoon."

Another open-mouthed stare. "Again, Mom. You know I can't bring him home. I have a game, and then I'm going dress shopping for the prom with Bre and Amber. It's in two weeks, remember?"

Heidi didn't hold back on her swears this time. "Fine. I'll call Dad."

"Thanks, Mom. And don't worry about the invitations. I'll drop them off on the way to the game. See you there?"

"I wouldn't miss it." Heidi bent and kissed the top of Kate's head. "I'll catch up later, with good news, I hope."

Kate wished her luck, and Heidi dashed out the door. On the way, she phoned Evan, her ex. Divorce wasn't glamorous, if the last five years of her existence were any indication. She had escaped more fortunate than some, but that didn't make it any easier. For any number of reasons, she found it difficult to remain civil around Evan, even for the sake of their children. He knew her buttons, and he seemed to take pleasure in pushing every single one of them. Their arguments usually revolved around something with the children: Who was taking time to do what with whom, who would pay for their extracurriculars, whether or not they should be involved in certain activities, who was responsible when the school called with a problem. It was tedious and draining, to say the least.

After more than ten years of marriage, everything had come unraveled. Then there had been several years of trying to make it work, but by the time Jilly was four, Heidi had finally failed. The last straw was when she found evidence that Evan had been cheating on her. She had endured his long hours at work, believing that they would eventually make it past that hurdle. After all, he was establishing himself. He had finally completed his degree, and he had earned a position with his company. For the time being, it provided a stable job. She had breathed a sigh of relief at that point, thinking that perhaps for the first time in their relationship they would not have to struggle.

They had been far too young to be married. In fact, there had really been no good reason for them to take that step, she speculated. Lots of young couples had babies and didn't bother with all that baggage. Perhaps they should have tried co-parenting, or perhaps Evan would have faded into the background as mere white noise in their daughter's life. What on earth had they been thinking?

Heidi knew the answer to that question. Evan had always been the kind of person who wanted desperately to do the right thing. It didn't matter to him that they barely knew each other or that they had only just graduated from high school. It only mattered that he wanted to be the best father he could be the minute Heidi said she was keeping the baby.

That shouldn't have come as any kind of shock to her. Evan, as far as her teenage self had been concerned, was nearly perfect. He was a star athlete, running cross-country in the fall and track in the winter and spring. He was the sort of good-looking guy who appealed to any adolescent girls who weren't attached, uninterested in boys, or nuns in training. He was a decent student, although not obsessive about academics. On top of everything else, he was *nice*.

"Was" being the key word there. He hadn't been nice in a long time. She'd had a particularly infuriating conversation with Evan the previous night, mostly about making sure that Max got to the school on time for the upcoming play. There were four performances, but because of her work schedule, she could only get Max there for two of them. She had asked Evan to take care of getting him there and back, to which he had initially agreed. At the last minute, he called to tell her that his wife was not amenable to the schedule and she would have to make other arrangements at least one of those days. Seething and probably intoxicated, Heidi had called late at night to let Evan know exactly what she thought of the new Mrs. Page and her inability to think about someone other than her precious two-year-old. Evan, in turn, had called Heidi a bitter wench and hung up on her.

It had only taken a few phone calls to sort Max out for the play, but she was still seething at Evan's casual dismissal of their son's needs. Today, she had to beg him for more help because she'd gotten too involved in her plans with Cass to remember everyone's activities. Now look who was calling the kettle black.

"Morning, sunshine," Evan said when he answered.

It left Heidi more irritated than she already was, given that the weather was definitely not cooperating. It hovered on the edge of rain. "Hey. I need a really huge fav—"

"No," Evan said. "Our niece's baptism is today, and we're getting ready for it. We talked about this. You can't depend on me for every last thing when you're not organized enough. Whatever you need, get Kate's help or do without."

"Evan. They're your kids too, and you hardly see them."

"I have them every weekend that you're working, and I do the best I can the rest of the time. But you only ever seem to see me as their other parent when you don't have your own shit together. Goodbye, Heidi."

He ended the call, and Heidi threw her phone onto the passenger seat. She screamed. Well, she'd show him. Nothing said she couldn't get to the park, pop the question, and be done in time to watch Kate's game, pick up Max from rehearsal, and have Jilly at her recital. Then she'd be free and clear to get back to the park for the rest of her date with Cass to see the opening concert at the festival. Easy-peasy, right? Right.

***

II

Traffic by the park was horrible. There was no other word for it. Heidi hadn't exactly forgotten the parade, but she hadn't exactly remembered it, either. She drummed her fingers on her steering wheel while she sat in the line of cars being redirected around the parade route. In hindsight, she should've taken the shuttle. She was late either way, and at least then she'd have been assured of a parking spot.

She finally snagged one at the back of the Al Sigl Center lot, paying several times what she would've to take the shuttle. She emerged from her car and slammed the door, darting away and locking it simultaneously like a pro. She checked the time. Nearly an hour late. She mentally crossed and uncrossed her fingers that Cass would be there when she arrived.

Just as she got to the bottom of the hill, her phone buzzed in her pocket. She drew it out. "Hey, honey," she said. "I'm almost there. Just give me another five minutes to climb the hill, okay?"

There was an audible sigh on Cass's end. "You're out of breath. Have you been running all the way here?"

"Yeah. I woke up late. Sorry about that. I really am almost there." Heidi's feet hit the pavement of the path up.

"Look, I need to get going. I have a lot to do before the recital. Maybe we can reschedule."

Panic rose in Heidi. She'd planned everything out, and now Cass was leaving. "But I—"

"I'm really sorry," Cass said, not sounding authentic. "How about you come with me to set up for the recital? You can bring Jilly, and—"

"I have to get my other kids to and from all over creation. Kate's got softball, and Max has a rehearsal." Heidi deflated. Cass wasn't a whole lot of help with them on average, though Heidi didn't feel as if she had the right to expect it of her. Cass had so much to do today herself, but maybe she had a little time free first. "I hate to ask, but I have to be in multiple places at once because I miscalculated. Are you free to have a quick lunch before Kate's game?"

She didn't even get the whole phrase out before she heard Cass's exasperated huff. "That's the trouble, Heidi. I'm always trying to fit into your plans. Even this morning, you knew I had a full day, but you still asked me to show up. And you're late, which I guess shouldn't surprise me. You seem to think the world should run on Heidi Time."

"That's not fair. You know I'm juggling kids, work, and Evan."

There was a long pause before Cass said, "I do know." She sounded resigned.

"This morning didn't work out, and we're both busy all afternoon. But we're still on for dinner and the concert after the recital, right?"

Another silence. "Um…yeah, sure we are. I'll meet you in this same spot at five. But, Heidi?"

"Yeah?"

"Try to be on time, okay?"

Cass ended the call before Heidi could reply. She supposed that's what she got for being so late. She'd already ruined the moment she'd wanted. Now she was going to have to wait until later to propose. It wasn't all bad. They'd still get to enjoy festival food, the kind of thing they didn't eat the rest of the year, and then explore the vendor booths a bit before the concert. Maybe proposing over Red Osier or a Garbage Plate from a tent wasn't the most romantic, but they'd make the most of it. The good news was, Heidi had time to make sure everyone was where they were supposed to be ahead of time.

She looked around. No use wasting the money she'd spent on parking by going home now. A walk would do her good, get her head on right and help her relax. She set off in the direction of the Conservatory.

It took a while to get there, given that Heidi couldn't cross the road until the parade went past. So she stopped to watch. She wondered where along the route the radio stations were set up to broadcast. She assumed closer to the beginning, not where she stood by Highland Avenue. It was packed, with nowhere particularly good to watch from. She wedged herself between a big, muscular man with a handlebar mustache and a woman with a purple flag. She craned her neck to watch whatever school's marching band was on its way past.

It wasn't a hot day, not this early in May with the threat of rain hanging over them. Even so, Heidi was rapidly growing too warm in her flannel and jeans. It didn't help that she seemed to be absorbing the body heat of everyone around her. She tried to focus on the parade, but her head spun. She had to get out of there.

Moving was going to take some effort. People had crowded in behind her. By the time she wriggled her way to the back, she was a wrinkled, sweaty mess. She brushed off her shirt the best she could and carefully made her way behind the people still watching the parade.

It was almost at the end. She saw the last float as it came around the corner. Once it passed, she was going to have to make a dash for it or get squashed by the entire population of Rochester attempting to cross Highland after the parade ended. She looked for a break in the crowd and braced herself.

Sure enough, there was a wave of people crossing right after the end of the parade. Heidi took aim for the other side of the street and ran. Thankfully, she made it without more than a couple of jostles from either side. She shook herself out and looked up the hill. After everything she'd done to get there, it looked like an enormous effort to get up the steep incline. At least she wouldn't have to try to squeeze in a trip to the gym. Her calves would be in excellent shape after today.

She decided to bypass the top of the hill and head right for the Conservatory. She wasn't in the mood to think about the missed opportunity to make her proposal romantic, surrounded by the scent of barely-blooming lilacs. They would probably peak next week. She would've waited, but she was working, and there was Max's play, and...

Now she was thinking about her wasted morning again. She pushed those thoughts aside and focused on her mission to enjoy some damn lilacs, whether they were fully blooming yet or not.

And that was exactly when it started to rain buckets.

Heidi shrieked and made a beeline for the Conservatory. It was the only building nearby where she could hunker down and wait. There was an entry fee, which she happily paid for the purpose of not having to stand out in the downpour. Not that it mattered; she was completely soaked.

So were all the other shivering people huddled in the Conservatory. Little puddles dotted the floor where wet people had stood looking at the plants. Heidi shook herself like a dog and wandered around. She soon warmed up and dried out a little, and eventually the rain let up. It slowed to a fine drizzle, enough that she thought she would take a risk and head out.

She had to make it to Kate's game. When she pulled out her phone—mercifully enclosed in a waterproof case—she growled. Late again. Cursing both the parade and the rain under her breath, she at least remembered to thank the woman at the desk before leaving the Conservatory. Then she prayed her aching calves would hold up for one more run through the park to her car.

***

III

It was still drizzling when Heidi pulled into the parking lot at the ball field. She grabbed the umbrella out of the map holder and slammed the car door, getting her shirt caught in it. She swore under her breath as she fought with her key to unlock the door, pull her shirt out, and close it again.

She jogged to the bleachers, her already-wet shoes squelching in the grass and her umbrella threatening to take off like Mary Poppins. It finally gave out about fifty yards from the team tent, the wind whipping it inside out and breaking the metal rods. she wrestled with it until she more or less got it closed, lumpy and deformed.

Under the tent, she shivered and curled her lip in disgust at the cheap, broken umbrella. All the other parents were huddled at the edge of the enclosure, watching the action on the field. The game was well underway. It must not've rained as hard in this part of town, as the field looked all right. Heidi mentally kicked herself for wasting time hiding out in the Conservatory instead of heading to her car after the parade. She already had to miss the end of the game in order to pick up Max. She hadn't realized she'd said anything out loud until the man next to her turned to look.

She almost groaned in embarrassment when she made eye contact. It was Hot Tom. She didn't even know which girl was his daughter, only that he was the talk of the moms' gossip. Tom was a single father, which meant a fair number of the women—single or not—thought he was eligible. One or two of the dads too, and the rest always seemed a little envious of him.

Tom was extraordinarily attractive. His hair was dark, with a classy bit of silver on the sides. He had striking blue eyes and a charming smile, the kind that made a person feel as if their words were the most important thing to Tom in any conversation. He was tall, broad, and muscular, in a way that suggested he was BFFs with the trainer at the gym. His smooth skin was naturally golden tan all year round, and his scent was what Heidi could only describe as "expensive." She didn't know enough about men's fragrance to know what he wore, only that it was never too much and was as elegant as the rest of him.

He turned that mega-watt smile on her now. "How's it going?"

"G-good," she said, feeling a little faint. She tried to pat her hair into something presentable, even though she knew her bedraggled whirly-curls were a lost cause.

"Kate's having a great game," he told her.

Heidi gaped at him. She'd had no idea Tom even knew who she was, let alone which kid belonged to her. "Th-thanks," she stammered. "And how's...um..."

"Nevaeh?" he supplied.

"Yes. Nevaeh. How's she doing?"

"She's the pitcher. She's up right now."

"Oh. Right." Heidi peered out of the tent. Then she shivered violently.

Tom frowned. "Are you cold? Do you need a jacket?"

It took her a moment to react. "I got a little wet on the way over." She cringed at how completely inane that sounded. He probably saw she was soaked through.

"Here." Tom reached into a bag and pulled out a sweatshirt with the team's logo on it. "These came in, and there were a few extras."

"I'll give it back," Heidi told him as she set down the broken umbrella and pulled the shirt over her head.

"No need. Keep it." Tom flashed that smile again.

For a moment, she thought he was flirting. But then she saw the cooler for the drinks and orange wedges next to him. He was the parent chaperone this time around. Guilt twisted in Heidi's stomach. She hadn't signed up yet to be the game parent, mostly due to the chaos of the kids' schedules and her work.

"How much do I owe you?" she asked as a way of keeping her mind off all the things she was messing up.

"On the house. Like I said, there were extras."

They watched the game in silence for a few minutes. Heidi wanted to bring up the sweatshirt again, to tell Tom she didn't need his charity. She knew very little about him, but she always assumed he provided well for...Nevaeh. She really should try harder to remember the girl's name in the future. Tom seemed to have the impression Heidi couldn't manage, maybe clued in by how late she was to the game or how inappropriately she was dressed for the current weather. Which, she noticed, was now clearing up. The drizzle had slowed to a few drops, and the sun was turning the clouds a warm, pale yellow in a few places.

She had lost track of the action for a moment. There was some yelling, and then a flurry of running. Someone had hit a home run. Heidi craned to see, and sure enough, there was Kate, rounding the bases. The group of parents hiding under the tent emerged almost as one cluster, whooping and cheering.

Heidi wanted to rush over and congratulate Kate, but of course, she couldn't. She'd have to be sure to tell Kate the minute she got home that she'd seen it. She pulled out her phone, wishing she'd thought to take a picture. When she saw the time, she shoved her phone back in her pocket. If she didn't leave immediately, she would be late to get Max and then even later to get Jilly and her viola. If she played her cards right, she'd have time to freshen up before the recital.

"I'm really sorry," she told Tom. "I have to go."

"No problem. We'll look after Kate." Another grin.

"Thanks!" Heidi called as she rushed out of the tent.

The rain had fully stopped now, and she tossed the broken umbrella in the trash on the way to the car. At the door, she paused long enough to pull off the sweatshirt. When she opened the door, she flung it into the back seat and almost threw herself inside as well. Taking care of kid number two? No problem at all.

***

IV

Heidi checked herself in her visor mirror before exiting her car. She scowled at her limp, frizzled hair and attempted to fluff it with her fingers, only succeeding in making it worse. She applied her lip gloss, but that didn't do a whole lot either. There wasn't anything else to try, so she climbed out of the car and headed for the school.

She waited outside the auditorium with the other parents, impatiently tapping her foot. She was sure she looked unfriendly, which was why the other adults were keeping their distance. A little girl kept peering around her mother's legs, making eye contact with Heidi and then turning to hide her face in her mother's long sweater.

Max was in the ensemble. He'd told her a bit about what he got to do in the show. Heidi imagined his parts were identified by labels like "Zebra No. 2" and "Hyena Chorus" and "Blade of Grass." She couldn't be sure, as she'd never looked at his script.

There was gossip, of course. There was always gossip. The adults were often as bad or worse than the middle schoolers. Heidi didn't have time to join in. Today, she gathered that there was tension between the kids who had lead roles and the rest of the cast. Who knew for sure? Max never talked about it or complained.

One of the other parents came up next to her. "Max's mom, right?"

"Yeah. Um...yes, I'm Heidi." She remembered her manners and stuck out a hand.

The other woman chuckled. "Benji. Kayla's mom?"

"Right. I think Max and Kayla hang out during rehearsals."

Benji nodded. "Kayla's always talking about him." She tilted her chin briefly at the cluster of parents. "In a good way, I mean."

Heidi hid her quiet laughter behind her hand. "Same." It was nice not to be alone in her distaste for theater politics.

She glanced sideways at Benji. She had never had much of a type, but she did appreciate how attractive Benji was. Taller than Heidi, with short, blond hair. Like Heidi, she seemed to be a jeans-and-flannel kind of person, but somehow, she wore it differently. She had a weathered, brown leather jacket over her blue and green checked shirt. Heidi wanted to touch it and see if it was as soft as it looked. She cringed at her own thoughts and returned her gaze to the theater door as if no such thing had crossed her mind.

"Is it always like this?" she asked. "Max is usually done when I get here, so I don't hang around." She didn't add that it was because she was often running behind.

"Pretty much, yeah. Same song, different day." Benji didn't mean it literally; she kept her voice low as she continued. "It's always the same people, regardless."

Heidi peered around her. "This is the first time we've done anything like this. Max's first play."

"I've got two older ones, both adults now. They were into theater in high school, but they've moved on to other things."

"Does it get better?" Heidi eyed the other parents.

"Not a bit." Benji grinned. "Max says he has an older sister. So she's not into all this?"

"No way," Heidi said. "She plays softball. That's where I just came from. There's a bit of an age gap between the kids. Five years."

"Same here. Kayla was my surprise baby. Ten years between her and the next one up."

"That was my oldest. The surprise, I mean." Heidi scrunched her nose and muttered, "And why I don't recommend marrying your baby daddy when you're both only eighteen."

"Oh, god." Benji laughed. "Yeah, been there and done that. Kayla came along right before the divorce."

"You too? Jilly was planned, but we thought that would hold it all together. We loved being parents together back then." Heidi sighed. She missed that side of Evan.

"At least you had something like that. A common goal. Not so much for us."

"I'm sorry," Heidi said. "I know how tough it is when you can't make it work."

"It's hard when you want very different things."

"Don't I know it!" Heidi thought back to all the arguments about Evan spending time away from home, advancing his career.

Something told her she could trust Benji, though she couldn't have said what gave her that impression so quickly. Maybe it was the shared bond of single parenting. Maybe it was how easily Benji opened up to her. In any case, she was happy to have an ally among the theater parents.

Benji arched an eyebrow. "I'm going to guess one of your differences wasn't that you were more interested in your husband's sister than in him."

Heidi clapped a hand over her mouth and then slowly lowered it. "Uh.

No? But I'm also guessing your husband wasn't having an affair with his committee co-chair."

"Yikes, no. Our split was amicable, despite my crush. His sister isn't interested in women, sadly." Benji laughed.

"Yeah, well, ours was not so amicable. And my husband married her. They have a toddler with a pretentious name now."

"I'd say you win, but really, is there any winning here?"

"Probably not."

They fell silent. Faint singing came from inside, and Heidi's impatience returned now that she wasn't absorbed in conversation. She had to get to Jilly's recital. It was bad enough she'd missed the majority of Kate's game. Now she was going to be late to see Jilly perform.

"Somewhere to be?" Benji asked.

"My daughter's viola recital. My girlfriend...my partner is her teacher."

Benji's eyebrows shot up. "Ah, I see. Do you need me to take Max home?"

It had occurred to Heidi she should try to make some friends among Max's cast mates. Maybe she'd be able to trade some rides on days she didn't have to work. Or didn't have to get to three kids' separate activities all happening nearly simultaneously. Somehow, though, she'd never reached out to any of them. She didn't have an easy time making new friends, with everything else she had to balance. It was miraculous she found time for Cass, especially since Heidi had to go to her place most of the time. Now she wanted to get to know Benji better, to have someone to talk to who got it about messy exes and single parenthood.

She was about to accept Benji's offer, but she decided the extra few minutes it would buy her wouldn't matter anyway. "No, I've got it, thanks. We have to go get his sister after this. But maybe another time?"

"Sure," Benji said. "How about I give you my number?"

They made the exchange, and the way Benji smiled at her made her flush. She had a feeling this might've been about more than offering an occasional ride. Surprising, given how bedraggled Heidi was at the moment. No time to think about it or do anything. Her current mission was to get Max, watch Jilly play, and be back in the park to propose to Cass for real this time.

The doors finally opened, and a flood of middle school actors exited. It took forever and a half for Max to finally work his way over to Heidi, Kayla in tow. The two of them were going on excitedly about something from rehearsal, but Heidi was too distracted to say much more than to ask Max to tell her in the car.

"But, Mom! It's important. We need some costume stuff. I have to go to the store, and Kayla—"

"We'll do it tomorrow, okay? I promise." Heidi took the coat Max handed her and wondered why he couldn't take it himself.

"You always say that," Max muttered.

Benji cut in. "I could take him with us," she offered. "Kayla and I are off to get hers, and they need the same things. It's mostly just colored shirts."

"Mom, can I?" Max was nearly bouncing.

Heidi shook her head. "I didn't bring any money. We'll do it on our own."

Max looked furious. Kayla looked confused, and Benji gave Heidi a sympathetic pat on the shoulder.

"It's rough," she said. "Having to plan for so many things at once. I meant it, though. Call me if you need anything. I was there too."

Heidi sighed. "I wish I had more help some days, but I manage okay. This is a tough one, with three kids in three different places all overlapping."

Max and Kayla had moved away from them and had their heads together, whispering and giggling at something on Kayla's phone. Heidi turned back to Benji, and the two of them exchanged an amused glance.

"The two of them have been buddied up for a while," Benji explained. "Kayla keeps asking if he can spend the night like one of the girls."

"I'm glad they haven't lost that innocence yet," Heidi remarked. "He's asked about it too, but I keep putting off explaining to him why it's not quite the same."

"At their age, it's still not all that different. I don't know. I struggle to know what to do with her, especially because my others are older. Things have changed even in that short a time."

"They sure have." Heidi checked the time again. "Damn. I need to go. Catch you later." She yelled to Max, who returned to her side somewhat resentfully.

She didn't have time to process it with him. She said goodbye to Benji and Kayla and then urged Max toward the outer door. In the car, he buckled in and stared out the window. Heidi knew he was mad about not getting to go with Kayla. She might've tried to talk to him, but he wasn't going to budge and neither was she. So she drove home with his silent simmering, taking the time to plan out her steps to get Jilly to her recital with minimal damage to the schedule.

***

V

At home, Heidi barely had time to freshen up before she was rushing Jilly to the car. Because Max's rehearsal had gone late, and then she'd stood around talking to Benji afterward, they would never make it across town on time. Jilly was already in her dress with her viola and music in hand when Heidi and Max arrived.

"Mom!" Jilly cried. "We're so late! Cass is gonna be worried."

"Don't worry. We'll be there. I'll text Cass so she knows." Heidi pulled out her phone and sent the message. "There."

She stepped into the bathroom, and Jilly followed her. She stood in the doorway while Heidi combed out her hair and adjusted her clothes. She'd dried out, and there wasn't time to change, so she straightened everything and put on more lip gloss.

"Hurry!" Jilly urged.

"Okay, okay. I'm ready."

"Finally," Jilly said. "I wanted to hear my friends play, and now I won't."

Ignoring her, Heidi grabbed a fresh sweatshirt from the coat rack. Max, who had been watching them rush around, disappeared into his room.

Heidi called over her shoulder, "Do some homework! You're not spending all day on your electronics!"

Then she and Jilly stepped out, racing to the car. Heidi pulled out of the parking lot and headed for the city. According to her car's clock, they would be about twenty-five minutes late. Jilly might have to go last, but she'd still have time to play. Afterward, Heidi would help Cass clean up, then she'd take Jilly home and head back to the park for their date. Maybe not ideal, but she still had time to rescue this upside down day.

On the drive there, Heidi had time to reflect on how far they'd come. She'd met Cass by way of signing Jilly up for private lessons. This was long before she'd considered dating again, and Cass was still married at the time anyway. Jilly had always been a precocious child, the kind of kid with a Life Plan almost the moment she was out of the womb. She'd been adamant that she wanted to play the viola, starting from the first time Heidi and Evan had taken all three of their kids to see the Rochester Philharmonic. Jilly was three.

Then came the divorce and all the baggage, so Jilly hadn't gotten her coveted viola lessons for another three years. She could've waited another couple until she was old enough to learn at school, but Heidi knew she'd kept Jilly waiting long enough. When the kids were at the YMCA for summer camp, one of the other parents recommended Cass's studio. Her minimum age was six, which worked out perfectly. Jilly was with her for two solid years before Heidi worked up the courage to ask Cass for a date.

Cass was exactly the sort of person Heidi easily fell for. Kind, hardworking, gentle. Evan had once been like that, before he and his new wife got together. Maybe she had a type after all. In any case, she'd overcome her nerves and asked if Cass wanted to spend time together outside Jilly's lessons.

At first, Cass had been reluctant. For one thing, Heidi was a student's parent. While there wasn't anything stopping them—Cass ran her own studio—she'd still felt it might be inappropriate. Then there was the matter of Heidi's ex. Cass had never been the type to treat her like she was one step away from leaving Cass for a man. But she wasn't keen on adding that dimension to a relationship, one where she had to regularly deal with Heidi's contentious relationship with Evan.

Part of it may have been that Cass and her ex-wife never had children. They'd never wanted any as a couple. Nothing tied Cass to her ex aside from a few mutual friends, which left her free and clear. Heidi, on the other hand, still needed to work out issues with visitation and who paid for what when it came to all the extras.

Still, Heidi had been persuasive. Not pushy, or at least she hoped not. Instead, she'd waited. They'd built a friendship, and Cass had ultimately said yes when she asked again. Today, Heidi was hoping for a yes of a different kind. She hadn't even been able to have her moment to propose yet, let alone have the response she wanted. Well, that was going to change once they got through this recital and had their date.

Heidi pulled into the driveway of Cass's Park Avenue studio. It was a converted house, much like several of the businesses on that same section of the street. If she was ever bored while waiting for Jilly at the studio, she could go three doors down and get a piercing, or she could wander next door for a tattoo. She never had, choosing instead to stay in the lounge outside the practice room.

There was a tiny parking lot in the back, enough room for the parents who were there to see their children. Heidi still didn't understand why Cass had picked a date during the Lilac Festival, but she wasn't in charge of the decisions. Traffic was still somewhat congested, even in this part of the city. And of course, she was already late as it was. At last she pulled into the lot, parked in the only available spot, and hurried with Jilly into the building.

They hovered outside the room, waiting until the tiny girl at the front finished and the audience politely applauded her. Then Heidi and Jilly slipped inside, and Jilly crept along the wall toward where the students were sitting. Cass turned around and shot Heidi an irritated glance. Heidi slouched in her seat. She wouldn't have been nearly so late if she hadn't kept talking to Benji. Even worse, the reason she'd talked to her was that Benji was attractive and attentive.

She tried to clear her head. She sat up straighter and shifted her gaze to the front of the room. That's when she noticed Evan, Jen, and their toddler. They were several rows up, and Evan had his phone out to record Jilly. Heidi slid sideways in hopes they wouldn't look back and see her.

Jilly hadn't even had time to take out her viola or have Cass help her tune. Instead, she was rushing to do it now, off to the side of the piano. Heidi couldn't tell how many other kids had already played, but it looked like they were nearing the end of the recital.

Cass stood. "We have just one more student before we go in the other room and enjoy the refreshments you all brought."

Heidi almost groaned. She'd forgotten. Not left it at home but entirely forgot she was supposed to bring something. Too late now. She focused up front, where Jilly was taking out her viola. It took a few minutes for Cass to have her ready, but then she stood facing the audience, and Cass motioned to the accompanist. Jilly began her piece. She sounded nervous at first, but then she gained confidence and made it through her song. Heidi was both relieved and proud.

Afterward, she mingled with the other adults while the kids ate cookies and chattered. Evan and Jen thanked Cass and then took their toddler home. They didn't even speak to Heidi. That may have been a good thing; She had no idea what she would say to them anyway. They'd sat through however long—Heidi wasn't sure of the time—waiting to see Jilly, who should've been farther up in the program. At least she'd been able to play.

Jilly was at her side. "I missed Megan."

"She left already?"

"No, but I wanted to hear her play."

"Maybe next time, sweetheart. I'm sorry."

Jilly huffed. "Megan's older. She's, like, Kate's age. She's not going to play next time."

"I'm sorry," Heidi said again.

"Also, we forgot snacks."

"I know. C'mon, let's go talk to Miss Cass and I'll apologize."

She let Jilly lead her over to Cass, who was congratulating other parents. Ahead of them in line was a teenage girl and a man who must've been her father. He was a little rumpled, not unlike Heidi. He had tightly curled iron-gray hair and a lot of laugh lines around his eyes and mouth. Jilly tapped the girl's shoulder, and she turned around. When she saw Jilly, she gave her a huge smile and a hug.

"You were so good!"

"Thanks." Jilly blushed. "I'm sorry I missed you."

"It's okay." The girl, who Heidi now assumed was the famous Megan, whispered, "I wasn't my best today."

Jilly giggled. "I bet you were amazing."

"Hi," the man said to Heidi. "I guess the girls know each other. I'm Dominic."

"Nice to meet you. Heidi, and this is Jilly." Heidi tilted her chin at the teenage girl. "Megan?"

"That's right." The man smiled. He had extremely white, straight teeth.

"She must be about the same age as my other daughter. Jilly says she's graduating?"

"Time flies, right?"

"Sure does. You have other kids?"

Dominic nodded. "My son's a freshman. I'm glad I have a couple more years before I'm on my own."

Heidi didn't ask what he meant. There wasn't time because the line moved, and Megan was already greeting Cass. Around them, the room emptied out while Heidi waited her turn. Jilly had gotten bored and wandered off to hang out with the remaining few kids.

"Hey," Heidi said when she finally reached Cass.

"Hello, Heidi." Cass sounded so formal, so distant.

"I'm really—"

Cass put up a hand. "Don't say it. I know you're sorry. You always are."

"I had to get Max from rehearsal. It ran over."

"He couldn't have had a ride from one of the other kids?"

Heidi sighed. "I don't really know them that well. I'm doing the best I can, but there's only one of me. I'd love it if I could singlehandedly attend a game, a rehearsal, and a recital, but something has to give. I only went to part of Kate's game, and I didn't help out with Max's rehearsal. And now I'm late here. But I've managed at least part of every single one of those. Doesn't that count for something?"

Cass put her hand on Heidi's arm. "The thing is, you don't have to do it all by yourself."

Heidi didn't correct her. She didn't remind Cass that she wasn't an active, involved almost-stepparent. She didn't explain about Evan and Jen and how focused they were on their own child. She didn't talk about how she'd been doing all this mostly on her own since Jilly was four.

"I'll try to do better," Heidi promised. "I know you all deserve my best."

Cass looked like she wanted to say more, but one of the other parents waved to her. She waved back and then said to Heidi, "I'll see you later, okay?"

"For dinner?"

"Sure." Cass sighed. "I have to clean up here first, but I'll be there. Five-thirty at the main stage."

Heidi kissed her cheek. "Love you."

"You too." And off Cass went to talk to someone else.

Heidi watched her, frowning. She was still distant, and Heidi knew somehow she had to make it up to Cass. Dinner had to be perfect because god knew, nothing else about that day had been. And then Heidi had to work out how she could get it all right, juggling work and her kids' activities.

"Jilly? You ready?" Heidi called.

Jilly skipped over with her viola and music in hand, and Heidi led her out of the building. There probably wasn't enough time to change, but she could at least freshen up a little, swap out her T-shirt for a clean one and change her pants. Determined to stay on schedule, Heidi headed for home.

***

VI

She met Cass near the main stage, and they bought dinner inside the large food tent where local restaurants had set up shop. There were some tables inside, but they headed outside. They sat at one end of a picnic table already occupied by a family with a baby and a preschooler. One of the parents was wrestling to get the preschooler into a stroller, despite the child's loud protests. The other was wrangling with a jar of baby food while the little one opened and closed their mouth like a baby bird.

Any other time, Heidi would've had to hide her amusement. She'd been there and done that, and usually had a third child in tow as well. By the time she'd had both Max and Jilly, Kate had been old enough to be "helpful," which is to say, not very helpful at all in that situation. Even now, Heidi thought fondly of the times she and Evan had done that sort of thing. They'd herded kids for the sake of being out of the house and introducing them to new experiences.

Well, they'd done a damn good job. Kate was ready to fly off into the world on her own. Max was confident on stage, and Jilly had been wonderful at the recital. Heidi thought that would be a good place to start, a way to break the ice. She knew Cass was still frustrated with her, but Heidi wasn't going to let a whirlwind day stop her from moving the two of them forward.

"Hey," she said, putting her hand on top of Cass's.

Cass shifted her gaze from the family next to them back to Heidi. "Hm?"

"The recital was great. You're so good with those kids." Heidi smiled and rubbed Cass's hand with her thumb.

"Thank you." Cass visibly relaxed. Heidi was sure putting together the recital must've been stressful, so it was nice to see Cass beginning to let the tension go.

This was her moment. "I wanted to ask you something." Heidi looked down at her Red Osier sandwich, cooling in its box. So romantic.

"Oh?" Cass withdrew her hand and picked up her fork. She'd settled on Indian food from a different booth. On reflection, Heidi wished she'd done the same.

Feeling in her pocket, Heidi sucked in her breath when her hand landed flat. Where was the box she'd so carefully put in this morning? She looked down and saw the button was gone too, probably ripped off during one of her mad dashes from one place to another. Trying to calm down, Heidi told herself she didn't need a fancy ring to propose. It didn't help.

"What's wrong?" Cass asked.

"I..." Heidi deflated and let go of her shirt. "I was going to make it all romantic and everything. I wanted to do it this morning, before the entire day ended up as a heap of chaos. But I was late, and then you couldn't stay, and the ball game and play practice and the recital..."

Cass's eyebrows shot up. "What do you mean?"

"I wanted to ask you to marry me. But now I've even lost the ring." Heidi closed her eyes. When she opened them, the woman at the other end of the table was smiling at the two of them.

Cass was silent for long enough Heidi didn't have to hear her answer. At last she said quietly, "I don't think getting married is a good idea for us right now."

Heidi knew it was coming, knew the minute Cass didn't jump into her arms and hug her and tell her the ring didn't matter. That didn't make the rejection hurt any less.

"I had a feeling." Heidi kept her gaze on her unappetizing meal, trying to keep the burning in her eyes from becoming fully formed tears.

"It's not—" Cass stopped. "I was going to say 'it's not you,' but that would've been a lie. I love you, Heidi. I do. But I can't live with the constant dramatics and messes. Today shouldn't have been about needing to wait for you at every turn. I even had to move Jilly around on the program for you, and it's not my fault you couldn't be up in time to meet me. I just...can't do this. Not on a permanent basis."

She stood, and that was it. There was nothing more to be said between them. Heidi wasn't sure if Cass was breaking up with her or simply saying they shouldn't get married or something halfway in between. It didn't matter. Either they were done and would exchange terse smiles at Jilly's lessons from now on, or they would slowly stop reaching out to each other. Maybe Heidi should consider hiring a new teacher.

She watched Cass go, and the woman at the other end of the table, now finished feeding her infant, gave Heidi a sympathetic look. Maybe she'd been there too before meeting the man who was hitching a backpack higher on his shoulders. Heidi stood and grabbed her uneaten food and the rest of Cass's trash. She tossed them in the nearest barrel and wandered along the path toward the other vendor booths.

By then, the band had started to play. Leather Anvil. She and Evan both liked them, but Heidi remembered Cass wasn't a fan. She'd only agreed to the concert because Heidi liked them, and they were opening for a band Cass wanted to see. Heidi remembered now who it was: Generation Xerox, an up-and-coming local 90s grunge cover band.

She ducked in and out of foot traffic, occasionally stopping to look in a booth. Ahead, she saw exactly the one she wanted. They were selling Leather Anvil CDs. Heidi thought to get one, since she was missing them now. Their latest, *Sonic Pixie Dream Girls*, was great. Heidi'd gotten a couple tracks online already.

As she reached the booth, someone shoved her hard from behind. She lost her balance and flew sideways, crashing right into the tent. She hit the table, rattling it and causing CDs and other merchandise to slide. There was no way to stop gravity; Heidi landed on the grass right next to a pile of Leather Anvil keychains, banging her head on the table leg so hard her ears rang.

In an instant, someone was down next to her. "Are you okay?"

Heidi blinked. She felt all her limbs. The top of her head hurt where she'd smashed it, but otherwise, she was okay. She'd had presence of mind enough to know not to put her hands out, so no broken wrists. She didn't even see any blood.

"Yeah," she said. "I think so."

"Can you stand?" The other person held out a hand.

Heidi took it and braced her hand on the table. Once she was upright, she scanned her body. Everything seemed to be in order.

"Thanks," she told the stranger, and then her mouth dropped open.

This was the first she'd gotten a good look. It was definitely her. Angel Flores. Heidi had seen her face plastered on city buses with her morning co-host. There was no mistaking it.

She had a knitted rainbow beanie covering her dark hair and just showing the full row of earrings down each ear. Instead of the casual-but-professional outfit visible on the side of the bus, she had on a black Leather Anvil T-shirt and jeans. Heidi wasn't surprised to see a branching tattoo that began at her wrist and ended somewhere up under the T-shirt's sleeve.

Her matte purple lips curved into a smile, and Heidi realized she'd been staring. She flushed, and now Angel laughed.

"Come on," she said. "Let's get you to a bench. I'll grab some water."

She reached into a barrel full of ice and Wegmans bottled water, pulling out two. Heidi couldn't hear the exchange, but Angel said something to the other two people in the tent, who were cleaning up Leather Anvil merch. They waved Heidi and Angel off.

There was a place to sit near the stage where all the children's events were held. Some group was there now, one Heidi didn't recognize because she no longer had kids young enough to bring them. As she sat, she realized she was a little dizzy. Whether it was from the fall or from being so close to Angel was anyone's guess.

Angel opened one water and handed it to Heidi. She took the other herself and sipped it, silently watching the kids' concert. After a few minutes, she turned her attention to Heidi.

"I'm Angel," she said. "But I take it you knew that."

"Heidi, and yep. From the radio." Heidi giggled nervously. "I listen to you every day on my way to work."

"Yeah? Where do you work?"

"Twenty-three-hour surgery at General. I'm a nurse's aide." Heidi took a big gulp of water, closing her eyes and enjoying the feel of the cool liquid sliding down her throat. The throbbing in her head eased, and she opened her eyes to look at Angel. "So you also moonlight selling Leather Anvil gear?"

"Something like that." Angel laughed. "Being a morning show host is great. My dream job. But I also do some publicity stuff for Leather Anvil. I've known Martina my whole life."

"The lead singer? No way!" Heidi shook her head. "I love them. I was on my way to get one of the CDs when...well, you saw what happened."

"People are so rude. That guy definitely didn't need to shove you to get through." Angel put a hand on Heidi's arm. "Are you really okay?"

"I am." Heidi flashed her a grin to reassure her. "Physically, anyway. Not so sure about the rest." She deflated, thinking about how horrible the day had been.

"No need to worry," Angel said. "The others have it under control back at the booth. I was just there to hang out. No harm done, as far as I could tell. Even the table." She elbowed Heidi, but that cute half-smile was back, the one that told Heidi that Angel was amused.

Angel had it wrong. Sure, Heidi was a little embarrassed about her mishap. And she was definitely a little warm in Angel's presence. But it was everything else, all the way up to and including dinner with Cass, that had her heart sinking. She had to go home soon and tell the kids what happened. They all loved Cass.

Heidi had thought *she* loved Cass.

"It's not that," Heidi said before she could think about what was coming out of her mouth. Maybe she'd been hit on the head hard enough to lose her inhibitions. "I proposed to my girlfriend, and she said no. Which was the perfect end to this perfectly sucky day." Heidi set the water next to her and put her head in her hands. Even the music from the kids' concert seemed to be mocking her.

"Aw, I'm sorry." Angel patted her back, and for some reason, it made Heidi's emotions contort themselves so she was laughing and crying at the same time.

"I just wish," Heidi said, sitting up and wiping her eyes, "that I could have it all to do over again, you know? Not make the same mistakes."

"Do you?"

"Do I what?" Heidi frowned.

"Wish you could have the day back."

"Yeah. I'd get it all right, and everything would be perfect."

Dejected, Heidi lowered her head again. There was a small bunch of lilacs on the grass by her feet, probably discarded by a grabby child who had pulled it off one of the trees. Remarkably, no one had trampled it, and it looked fresh.

Angel saw it too and picked it up. She handed it to Heidi. "Make your wish," she suggested.

Heidi laughed. "That's dandelions, not lilacs."

Angel shrugged. "I think it works with lilacs too. Especially on the first day of the festival."

Still chuckling, Heidi closed her eyes. She willed away her rotten day and all her failed attempts to be everything to everyone. All she wanted was to be the kind of parent who could manage three kids' schedules and the kind of girlfriend who lived up to her partner's expectations. Or maybe just her own. She opened her eyes again.

"You make your wish?" Angel asked. When Heidi nodded, she said, "Now, blow on it, or it won't come true."

Heidi felt silly, but she did as she was told. Nothing happened, not even blossoms falling off the lilac sprig. Heidi shrugged and instead inhaled the sweet fragrance of the pale purple blossoms.

Angel stood. "I should go back to the booth. Come on. I'll give you one of those CDs." She winked. "I happen to have connections."

***

VII

By the time Heidi arrived at home, all of her children were there. Kate had reheated the previous night's chicken enchiladas and generously shared them with the younger two. All Heidi wanted was to collapse into bed and sleep, possibly for the rest of forever. She definitely did not want to talk about Cass's rejection or pathetically sitting on a bench in Highland Park until *the* Angel Flores took pity on her. No way was she admitting she blubbered all over her about the day's events. And as for that silly wish, it could stay in Heidi's "embarrassing moments not to share" drawer for eternity.

Heidi sifted through the day's mail. There wasn't much, just a few ads for takeout places, a credit card bill, and a statement from the orthodontist reviewing last month's charges for Max's braces. Heidi tossed the ads and put the other things on the kitchen table. She would take them up to her desk later, where they would probably sit until they were past due.

As Heidi began emptying the dishwasher and refilling it, she heard a soft sound behind her. Turning, she was surprised to see Max, arms crossed. He looked upset about something.

"What's up?" Heidi asked, trying to keep her tone light.

"We still need those costume parts," he said. "I have to have them by Monday."

"So we'll go tomorrow."

"That's what you said last time. And then I still had to borrow stuff."

"This late at night isn't the best time to tell me. Remind me in the morning, and we'll do it." Because of course Max wouldn't ask Evan. Or Evan wouldn't help even if Max asked him. Heidi could call, but Evan would only accuse her of being a mess again and tell her to get it together. "I'd have taken you today, but Jilly had her recital."

"I could've gone with Kayla and her mom today. She said she'd take me if I had the money. I told you about it last week, and Mrs. Sherman sent an email too. You always say we'll do this stuff, but you get busy or we can't or something."

"We will this time, I promise."

"Yeah, right."

Max walked away, shoulders slumped. Heidi finished the dishes and sat down at the table to collect her thoughts. Kate was already there, and it was clear she'd heard the entire conversation with Max.

Heidi sidestepped whatever Kate might've been about to say on the subject. "Hey, honey. How was dress shopping? Did you find something?"

"It was okay." She didn't sound any happier than Heidi felt.

That surprised her. Kate was a lot different than Heidi had been at her age. Heidi had needed persuading to go to her own senior prom, and she preferred not to think about the fact that Kate was the result of giving in. In contrast, Kate was excited to go with her group of friends. Heidi wondered what had happened to cause Kate to look like she'd rather discuss any other subject.

Heidi struggled not to ask. She had come to understand that pressing Kate on anything usually left her more moody and sullen than she'd been to start. It wasn't exactly that Kate didn't like to talk about her feelings. It was more that Heidi was her mother and everything about that created at least a small degree of drama. If Heidi asked, Kate would see it as a personal attack on her choices. So Heidi sat patiently, waiting to see if Kate would add anything else. The suspense was making her itch.

She finally gave in. "And what about the game?"

"It was great. I hit a home run. But you missed it, as usual." After emphasizing a sigh, Kate continued. "I'm just sick of feeling like I'm the least important thing in your life."

Heidi tried to stop herself from feeling defensive and failed. She knew she'd screwed up. Her entire day was full of the same. But after what happened with Cass, her resistance was low.

"I'm doing my best," she said. "There's one of me and three of you. Today, everyone had somewhere to be. I can't be everywhere at once."

"Exactly!" Kate glowered at her. "Our activities are more important than we are."

"Is it so bad I want to give you advantages I never had? You'll be off at college in a few months, and I'm trying to plan for all of your futures." Too bad she hadn't been so successful at planning for her own.

"That's just it," Kate said. "You're really good at 'planning for our futures,'" she made air quotes, "but you suck at doing things that matter right now. You schedule us so hard you can't even show up. And I'm not even sure I want to *go* to college." Kate wasn't looking at Heidi anymore.

It was all Heidi could do not to screech, "*What?!*" in Kate's ear. As it was, she had to take several slow, deep breaths through her nose to keep from saying anything they would both regret. Closing her eyes against the storm of fear and anger building inside her, Heidi leaned forward and put her elbows on the table and her head in her hands.

"You're mad. I knew you would be mad."

Heidi opened her eyes and turned to look at Kate. "I'm not—okay, yes. I'm mad. You have a full scholarship, between your grades and softball. How could you not take that opportunity?"

"I knew it. This is my decision, Mom. Not yours. You can't make me go just because you wish you had."

"That's not—"

"Yes it is! You're always telling us that we're going to regret our choices. All you ever do is push us to plan ahead, never make decisions because it feels right. And then you miss things because you were thinking six months ahead and not a week from now. Just because you were stupid at my age doesn't mean that I am!"

Kate got up from the table and stormed off to her room, slamming the door shut behind her. Heidi stayed where she was, still stinging from Kate's words. Was that true? Was she always telling her children to be careful that they didn't regret their decisions?

Jilly, having been booted from their shared room by Kate, crept out to the living room with her sketchbook. She eyed Heidi warily before sitting in the recliner to doodle. Heidi waited for Kid Number Three's accusation, but Jilly gave her the silent treatment. Maybe she'd already said her piece at the recital.

By ten o'clock, when Heidi went to check on Max, he was fast asleep with his tablet on his chest, headphones still on. Heidi gently took them off and set them on his bedside table with the tablet then tucked him in. He briefly stirred but didn't wake. Jilly had already gone to bed, and all three kids were finally settled for the night. No one had asked how it went with Cass, but Heidi figured they were all more concerned with their own part in the day's endlessly burning dumpster fire. She would tell them in the morning that it was over, likely for good.

Heidi heated some milk, added a tea bag, and plunked herself down on the sofa with the cup. She turned on the television and flipped through channels, but she wasn't interested in anything that was on. She let her mind wander back to her conversation with Angel.

If she hadn't been so foolish, everything would be different. But one decision changes everything, and a person can spend a lifetime wishing for a do-over.

Heidi would know.

Once upon a fairytale prom date and a summer in love, Heidi'd had big dreams. Her future was planned out, her college education ahead of her. And then, on a hot July night under the stars—figuratively, as they'd been in Evan's bedroom while his parents were away—her entire world had shifted. One night, one stupid decision not to make sure it didn't happen. Heidi was very much aware of how to use birth control, but when it came down to it, she simply...hadn't.

She was not going to let her kids make spur-of-the-moment decisions based on failing to look ahead. Maybe she didn't have every last detail worked out, but softball and theater and viola and good grades were a head start on setting themselves up for success. Once they'd finished their education, they'd be adults and could do as they liked. But Heidi wasn't letting any foolish mistakes stand in their way before then.

Otherwise, any of them could end up nearly thirty-seven, divorced, and parenting an eighteen-year-old, a thirteen-year-old, and a ten-year-old on their own. Living in a tunnel of regret.

Heidi gave up on television. She went to the kitchen and picked up the bag with the CD Angel had given her. Leather Anvil's *Sonic Pixie Dream Girls*. She opened it to play it and saw a lilac-colored business card tucked into it. Angel Flores, Lilac City Social Media Management. The font for her name was a delicate script, a deeper purple than the card, and the logo was a sprig of lilacs with angel wings. Beneath the phone number, Angel had written, "Call me sometime."

Trembling with nerves, Heidi sat on her couch, staring at the numbers. Was it too late to call? Angel worked early mornings, but only during the week. Would she still be up at almost ten-thirty on a Saturday night? It felt rude to try, so instead, Heidi entered the number in her phone and then shut it off so she wouldn't be tempted. Maybe she'd try in the morning.

With a stretch and a sigh, Heidi forced herself off the couch and down the hallway to bed.

Day Two

I

The smell of coffee from the automatic pot woke Heidi from a deep sleep. She stirred restlessly, vaguely recalling that she'd been dreaming—something about a woman with light brown hair and hazel eyes. Cass, Jilly's viola teacher. That was odd, not being able to fully call her to mind. She squinted and peered around. Gray light filtered in around the curtains. She blinked, trying to clear the sleep from her eyes, then opened them fully.

Instantly, she regretted that decision. Her head hurt, no doubt from last night's celebration with her friends. Heidi screwed her eyes shut then rubbed them. After several attempts, she was able to keep them open. She switched on the radio on her bedside table, wanting to wake up more slowly while listening to her favorite station.

"Gooooooood morning, Rochester!" It was the cheerful voice of Angel Flores of WNDR morning radio show fame. "We're live here at the Lilac Festival, where the parade begins in less than a half hour!"

That was when it hit Heidi what day it was.

She threw off the covers and dashed around, yanking clothes off hangers and out of drawers. Her alarm hadn't been set properly, or maybe she'd shut it off instead of hitting snooze. Either way, she was late. There was only enough time to throw on clothes, leave a note for her kids, and grab her coffee to go. She had to be at Highland Park by ten-thirty, and it was five past now. Not even enough time for a shower.

She yanked on her jeans, threw on a white T-shirt, and added a deep violet flannel button-up. Her standard uniform when she wasn't working at the hospital. She had to search for socks of the same size, and even then, they didn't match. No time to care.

At her dresser, she fluffed her hair in the mirror and shoved a tube of lip gloss in one pocket. She left her hand there for a moment, feeling slightly off-kilter. She chalked it up to her unwise decision to celebrate her engagement before it happened, even though her coworkers had insisted. Taking a deep, cleansing breath, she fished around in the top drawer among her lacy underwear to find it. The ring. If she couldn't be dressed up, then she'd at least have the best piece of jewelry she could afford when she proposed underneath the huge magnolia tree right at the top of the hill.

Heidi carefully put the velvet box into her shirt pocket and buttoned it. No sense losing it or all her plans would go awry. She left her bed unmade and went into the kitchen to get that much-deserved—and needed—cup of coffee.

Kate was already at the table. She had cards and envelopes laid out and was filling them in with her careful, neat handwriting. She looked up when Heidi entered.

"What's all this?" Heidi asked.

Kate's mouth hung open for a full five seconds. She closed it and glowered. "Mom. Graduation? You know, that thing I'm doing in six weeks? These have to go out as soon as possible."

"Oh, damn. I'm sorry, sweetie. I totally forgot. I'll be home to take them to the post office as soon as I do this one thing." Heidi frowned. She had a weird sensation of having had this conversation before, which only made her more frustrated with herself that she'd forgotten.

A sly grin blossomed on Kate's face. "You mean Tom? Today's the big day. Totally cool that I have such a feminist mom."

Tom...from softball. Why was she a feminist again? Heidi tried to clear her mind and remember what day it was and what was going on. Images of proposing to the man all the single women referred to as "Hot Tom" popped into her head. Right, that's what this was about. When had she even started dating Tom, let alone asking him to marry her? She must've had a lot more alcohol last night than she'd intended if she couldn't remember that. She decided to go with Kate's flow.

"Yep." She looked at the time again. "Ah, crap. I have to go. You're taking Max to and from play rehearsal, right? Jilly has her viola recital this afternoon."

Another open-mouthed stare. "Again, Mom. You know I can't bring him home. I have a game, and then I'm going dress shopping with Bre and Amber for the prom. It's in two weeks, remember?"

Heidi didn't hold back on her swears this time. She also knew without a doubt they'd exchanged the same words, but she couldn't for the life of her recall when. "Fine. I'll call Dad." Which sounded like a bad idea, but she didn't have a choice.

"Thanks, Mom. And don't worry about the invitations. I'll drop them off on the way to the game. See you there?"

"I wouldn't miss it." Heidi bent and kissed the top of Kate's head. "I'll catch up later, with good news, I hope."

Kate wished her luck, and Heidi dashed out the door. On the way, she phoned Evan. She wasn't looking forward to talking to him, especially after the heated argument the previous night. Maybe she shouldn't have called him after having too much to drink. She definitely shouldn't have accused Evan's wife of only being interested in her own progeny, but Evan shouldn't have called her a bitter wench, either. On the other hand, now here she was, asking him for more favors, this time due to her own poor planning. Kettle, meet pot.

"Morning, sunshine," Evan said when he answered.

It left Heidi more irritated than she already was, given that the weather was definitely not cooperating. It hovered on the edge of rain. "Hey. I need a really huge fav—"

"No," Evan said. "Our niece's baptism is today, and we're getting ready for it. We talked about this. You can't depend on me for every last thing when you're not organized enough. Whatever you need, get Kate's help or do without."

"Evan. They're your kids too, and you hardly see them." Why did it always feel like she was having the same exchanges with him ad infinitum?

"I have them every weekend that you're working, and I do the best I can the rest of the time. But you only ever seem to see me as their other parent when you don't have your own shit together. Goodbye, Heidi."

He ended the call, and Heidi threw her phone onto the passenger seat. She screamed. Well, she'd show him. Nothing said she couldn't get to the park, pop the question, and be done in time to watch Kate's game, pick up Max from rehearsal, and have Jilly at her recital. Then she'd be free and clear to get back to the park for the rest of her date with…Tom, apparently, to see the opening concert at the festival. She had everything under control, just like always.

***

II

Traffic by the park was horrible. Heidi groaned and dropped her head to the steering wheel. The parade. How had she forgotten? Angel Flores had even announced it on the radio less than half an hour ago. Heidi lifted her head and huffed at the line of cars being redirected around the parade route. She definitely should've taken the shuttle. She still would've been late, but maybe less late and with a decent parking spot.

She finally found one at the back of the Al Sigl Center lot, paying several times what she would've to take the shuttle. She emerged from her car and slammed the door, darting away and locking it simultaneously like a pro. She was nearly an hour late and the sky looked threatening. Crossing and uncrossing her fingers several times, she hoped the rain would hold off long enough to find Tom.

Just as she got to the bottom of the hill, her phone buzzed in her pocket. She drew it out. "Hey, honey," she said. "I'm almost there. Just give me another five minutes to climb the hill, okay?" She held the phone away from her ear, frowning at how familiar that sounded. Had she and Tom had this conversation before?

There was a long silence on Tom's end. Then, "You sound a little distracted. Everything okay?"

"Yeah. I woke up late. I'm so sorry." Heidi's feet hit the pavement of the path up.

"I need to go. I'm bringing the snacks for the game this afternoon, remember? We'll see each other there."

Panic rose in Heidi. Was this in the plan? She didn't even recall how she and Tom had ended up dating, let alone what she was supposed to do other than propose at the top of the hill. If that went sideways, what did that mean for the rest of her day? "But I—"

"Sweetheart, it's all right," Tom assured her. "We could go somewhere after the game if you like."

"I have to get my other kids to and from all over creation. Max has a rehearsal, and Jilly's recital is today." Heidi deflated. Like always, she was the one making sure everyone got where they should be on time. Except herself, it seemed. "Maybe you could give me a hand, and then we can still have dinner after the recital."

She didn't even get the whole phrase out before she knew she'd said the wrong thing. Tom's sigh sounded resigned. "Heidi, I knew when we got together that the kids always came first. I'm the same way. But it seems by 'first' you mostly mean only *your* kids, and we have to fit into *your* plans."

"That's not fair. You know I'm stretched thin and getting very little help from my ex."

"My ex isn't great about it either. Look, I think there's probably something we should talk about later. But I'll see you at the game, all right? Just...try to be on time for that."

Heidi was close to crying by then. She couldn't figure out why this felt both so familiar and so wrong at the same time. She certainly had no idea what it was Tom wanted to talk about, but from the sounds of it, they were through. He wouldn't have accepted her proposal even if she'd managed to orchestrate it right.

Trying to hide her tears, she said, "Sure. See you."

She ended the call before Tom could reply. She supposed that's what she got for being so late and ruining the moment.

She looked around. No use wasting the money she'd spent on parking by going home now. A walk would do her good, get her head on right and help her relax. She set off in the direction of the Conservatory.

She stopped to watch the parade, and it was strange: she knew which floats were coming. She even knew the Somewhere-or-Other High School marching band was about to play a cover of "Bad Romance," with bagpipes. In addition to wondering how she knew that, she was also curious where the radio stations were set up to broadcast. For some reason, she wished she knew what Angel Flores was saying about the band. Heidi was on Highland Avenue, nowhere near the broadcast booths. If she saw Angel, she'd have to remember to ask her.

That stopped Heidi in her tracks, wedged between a big, muscular man with a handlebar mustache and a woman with a purple flag. Heidi ignored the parade in favor of trying to work out why she had any interest in talking to Angel at all. It wasn't as if Heidi knew her, though she had the oddest feeling they'd met. Maybe it was only that she'd seen Angel's face on the side of a city bus, but that didn't seem right. Angel-on-the-bus was polished and pretty, made up for the camera. Angel-in-person was tiny and cute with a soft butch aesthetic. At least, that's how she appeared in Heidi's mind.

The day wasn't hot, but between the body heat of the crowd and the flush brought on by Heidi's thoughts, she was far too warm in her long sleeves and jeans. She had to get out of this pocket of people before she passed out.

She wriggled her way to the back of the crowd, turning herself into a rumpled mess with sweat beading on her forehead and seeping into her shirt. She straightened herself out as much as she could and slipped along the outer perimeter of the crowd.

Heidi saw the last float as it came around the corner. As soon as it passed, she made a break for it. Unscathed, she stood on the opposite side of the street, looking up the big hill. She'd been so close to her goal, but being late ruined it. The lilacs weren't even fully blooming yet, completing her misery.

That was the moment Heidi realized her mistake. She wasn't anywhere near as miserable as she became thirty seconds later when her memory of being soaked collided with the reality of being caught in the downpour.

Heidi shrieked and cursed whatever déjà vu gods had failed to give her recall soon enough to seek shelter. She decided it was no more trouble to run back to her car than to try to make it to the Conservatory. By the time she made it there, the rain had slowed. She shook herself off and climbed in, wishing she had a towel. She turned on the car and blasted the heat in a poor attempt to dry herself off.

When she pulled out her phone—mercifully enclosed in a waterproof case—she growled. Late again, and she'd forgotten about seeing Tom at the game. She supposed he'd seen her look worse than rain-soaked, and if this was a deal-breaker, then it was a good thing she hadn't been able to propose yet. Heidi pulled out of the parking lot and headed for the game, still shivering.

***

III

Mercifully, Heidi's memory seemed to be coming back. She'd woken up having forgotten she was dating Tom, let alone proposing to him. That was it, she was absolutely never, ever again getting wasted with her work friends. Worst idea in the history of bad ideas. She'd found an emergency stash of meds for her headache and a bottle of water in her glove compartment, and she was returning to normal now. Therefore, she had better recollection of her relationship, too.

It was odd, though. The memories were disorienting. Sometimes they seemed far away, as if she were watching them on television with a degree of separation between herself and the feelings. Other times, like with her dream about Jilly's viola teacher, they seemed to belong in some other life. She figured it was a bad side effect of the first hangover she'd had since college and nothing to worry about. Certainly nothing demanding her attention on such a busy day.

It was still drizzling when Heidi pulled into the parking lot at the ball field. She grabbed the umbrella out of the map holder and slammed the car door, getting her shirt caught in it. Another wave of déjà vu hit her, as if she'd done this very thing on some other rainy day at the ball field.

One wet, soggy jog across the field in her already-soaked shoes, and she was under the tent with the other parents. Tom rushed over and handed her a team sweatshirt.

"Here. Put this on."

She pulled it over her head, and Tom ran his hands vigorously up and down her arms to warm her. She shivered, and he turned her to face the field, wrapping his arms around her from behind. God, he was so warm. And he smelled nice, the pricey cologne he always wore. One of those distorted memories popped into her head, of Tom giving her an expensive necklace for her birthday and the kids oohing and ahing over it. Was that the sort of thing Heidi even wore?

"Better?" Tom asked.

"Much, thanks." Heidi smiled in spite of herself. She'd picked a good one, for sure.

She spotted a few of the other women eyeing her suspiciously, but she turned to face the game with Tom's arms still around her. The field was relatively dry, which means it hadn't reached past misting rain here. They'd have called the game otherwise. Tom's daughter was at bat. Heidi felt like she should remember the girl's name, given however long she and Tom had been together. She frowned in concentration. Nevaeh, that was it. She and Kate weren't close, despite being nearly stepsisters and on the same team. Friendly, but not besties. Heidi wondered why they didn't all spend more time together. Hopefully that would change once she and Tom were engaged.

They watched the game in silence for a few minutes. The drizzle slowed and then stopped, and the sun peeked out. Heidi had once heard a radio host say that the weather was always "sunny and eighty" in Hawaii. Rochester's weather was, if not the polar opposite in temperature, definitely the opposite in sun factor. She didn't really need the forecast to tell her that at least some part of the day would be overcast. Having any tiny amount of sun on a dreary day felt nice. She could certainly get used to everything she was experiencing right now.

Tom planted a kiss on her forehead and let go. She wanted to tell him she was still cold, but the sweatshirt and his body heat had warmed her nicely. It was probably for the best that they not have too much PDA during their daughters' game anyway. Tom went to open the cooler and hand out water, and Heidi wandered to the edge of the tent to keep her eye on the game.

When she glanced back at Tom, he was laughing with one of the other parents. Wilhelm. Heidi only knew that because he and his twin girls had moved to the US only a few years ago. And also because Wilhelm was one of the men who referred to Heidi's nearly-fiancé as "Hot Tom." He had his hand on Tom's arm. It didn't look exactly flirtatious, or not the way some of the women still shamelessly batted their eyelashes at Tom. But it caught Heidi's attention nonetheless.

She had lost track of the game and only tuned in again when she heard yelling from the girls on the field. Something had happened, and she was confused until one of the other moms rushed over.

"Oh, my god! Did you see that? Kate's home run!"

Damn it. She'd missed it. She didn't admit to that, though. "Wild, right?" she said.

When things had calmed down, Heidi looked at her phone. Crap. She had to hurry or she wouldn't be there in time to get Max. Why did she feel somehow like she was about to mess things up again?

She hurried over to Tom. "I have to go get Max. Tell Kate I said good job, okay?"

"Sure." Tom kissed her cheek, but it felt distracted.

"Are you coming to Jilly's recital?"

"I have to get Nevaeh home and do some stuff before our date tonight. That okay?"

"No problem. I'll see you then."

Heidi headed out of the tent. She turned back to give Tom a promising smile, but he was already back to talking with Wilhelm. Heidi shook her head and jogged back to her car. She'd forgotten to throw away the broken umbrella on her way, so she threw it into the back seat. She'd also forgotten to either pay for or return the team sweatshirt. Thank goodness Tom was one of the regular volunteers. She'd just give it to him later. She threw it into the back seat with the umbrella, climbed in, and took off to get Max.

***

IV

Heidi checked herself in her visor mirror and scowled. Her hair was a limp, frizzled mess that wouldn't cooperate with any amount of finger-combing. She gave up and applied her lip gloss, which only served to amplify her messy appearance. She wiped it off again and exited the car.

Outside the auditorium, she tuned out the random bits of adult gossip around her. How could middle school parents produce more drama than their kids did on stage? Blah blah about who were the favorites and who should be the next lead and what things the director was doing all wrong. Heidi was intense, but not about that. Or not intentionally, anyway. She didn't care what part Max had or didn't have, but she was definitely invested in making sure he was there every week.

The other parents seemed to be ignoring Heidi too, which was just as well. A couple actively avoided her, leaving her wondering if she'd accidentally said something rude once.

Eventually, one of the other parents came up next to her. "Max's mom, right?"

"Yeah. Um...yes, I'm Heidi." She remembered her manners and stuck out a hand. The woman looked familiar, but Heidi assumed that was from all the weeks of rehearsals or possibly last year's show.

"Benji. Kayla's mom?"

Ah, that explained it. Max's best friend from the shows. "Yes, now I remember. Max talks about Kayla a lot."

Benji nodded. "Kayla's always talking about him too." She tilted her chin briefly at the cluster of parents. "In a good way, I mean."

Something pinched Heidi's mind, like she'd had the same exchange before. She forced a smile to cover for her confusion. "Same."

Benji was attractive, in a leather-and-denim kind of way. She was tall, broad, and blond, the kind of woman Heidi thought of as handsome. Heidi shook herself. There was no time to get distracted by good-looking women, especially when Heidi didn't know if Benji was interested in other women. Besides, there was Hot Tom. Heidi wondered why he wasn't her first thought in stopping her distraction in its tracks.

They fell silent. Faint singing came from inside, and Heidi's impatience returned now that she wasn't absorbed in conversation. She had to get to Jilly's recital. It was bad enough she'd missed the majority of Kate's game.

Now she was going to be late to see Jilly perform.

"Somewhere to be?" Benji asked.

"My daughter's viola recital."

Benji's eyebrows shot up. "Ah, I see. Do you need me to take Max home?"

That would solve one problem, at least. Heidi waffled. Benji seemed nice, and Kayla was Max's friend. Why not take her up on the offer?

"Actually, that would really help. I have to go home anyway, but if they're going to be a while..."

"They might be another five or ten minutes."

"Is it stupid to ask you to do that? I mean, I already need to get his sister from our apartment."

Benji shook her head. "No. Go do what you need to." She smiled. "You know, it would be fun to get the kids together outside this. Kayla's doing a camp this summer, and she wanted me to talk to you to see if Max might want to go too."

"A...camp?" Max was interested in camp? When had that happened?" Heidi shook herself. "Sure. Um...you've definitely got this?"

"I do. Oh, and I can take them shopping for those costume pieces they still need. Tights, I think, and some shoes. If you give me some money, I'll get the stuff for you."

"Oh. I...can't today. But thank you anyway."

"No problem. Hey, let me give you my number."

She entered it into Heidi's phone, and then Heidi took off without another goodbye. She had an odd feeling she and Benji had talked before, but she couldn't recall anything about it. No matter. There wasn't time to dwell on why that felt familiar. She raced to her car and sped toward home. With a little luck, she'd make it just in time.

***

V

At home, Heidi barely had time to freshen up before she was rushing Jilly to the car. They were still late, but not as bad as it could've been.

"Mom!" Jilly cried. "Miss Cass is gonna be worried."

"Don't worry. We'll be there. Here." She handed Jilly her phone. "Text her while I drive and tell her we're on the way."

Jilly had been taking lessons from Cass since she was six, the youngest age she taught. Four years in, and Jilly was doing very well. She was already talking about learning some other instruments, although through school and not more private lessons. Heidi was incredibly proud of her.

And also worried they wouldn't make it for the start of the recital. She felt like her body was racing as fast as her car, hoping against hope to get Jilly there on time. She would miss the warm-ups, but Jilly would be okay. She always was.

"Mom," Jilly said, breaking into Heidi's thoughts.

"Yes?"

"I missed the warm-ups."

"I know, sweetie. I'm sorry."

Jilly huffed and slouched in the seat behind Heidi. "I'm gonna miss Megan's song."

"No, you're not. See? We're only going to be five minutes late. You'll hear almost everyone."

Heidi pulled into the driveway of Cass's Park Avenue studio, fuming about Lilac Festival traffic. Cass had planned this as some kind of Mother's Day thing, but she hadn't wanted to do it right on Mother's Day because of family plans. She'd possibly forgotten this was during the Festival or else didn't care.

Heidi and Jilly squeaked in just as one of the kids finished a painful rendition of *Minuet in G*. Heidi clapped politely while shuffling Jilly in and up the side aisle. She grabbed a seat at the back. Evan and Jen were a few rows from the front, and Evan turned to eye Heidi critically. She scowled at him and he turned back around.

Jilly performed beautifully, of course. Heidi was proud of the work she'd put into practicing and polishing her piece, Isaac Albeinz's *Tango*. Heidi wished she'd recorded it, but she was glad to see Evan had.

When Jilly finished, Cass stood. "We have just one more student before we go in the other room and enjoy the refreshments you all brought."

Heidi groaned inwardly. She'd forgotten. Everyone was supposed to bring something to share, and she'd been so wrapped up in the rest of her day that she hadn't done it. Jen glanced over her shoulder with a smug look, and Heidi glared daggers at her. Of course Perfect Jen would've brought Perfect Treats to share.

Afterward, Heidi mingled with the other adults while the kids ate cookies and chattered. Evan and Jen disappeared without talking to Heidi, which was just as well. Heidi would probably have said something they all regretted.

Jilly was at her side. "At least I got to see Megan. But we forgot snacks."

"I know. C'mon, let's go talk to Miss Cass and I'll apologize."

She let Jilly lead her over to Cass, who was congratulating other parents. Ahead of them in line was a teenage girl and a man who must've been her father. The two of them looked familiar, but Heidi was certain they'd never met before. Jilly tapped the girl's shoulder, and she turned around. When she saw Jilly, she gave her a huge smile and a hug.

"You were so good!"

"Thanks." Jilly blushed. "You too."

The girl, who Heidi now assumed was the famous Megan, whispered, "I wasn't my best today."

Jilly giggled. "Naw, you were the best."

"Aw, thank you." Megan grinned.

"Hi," the man said to Heidi. "I guess the girls know each other. I'm Dominic."

"Nice to meet you. Heidi, and this is Jilly." Heidi tilted her chin at the teenage girl. "Megan?"

"That's right."

The man smiled, and Heidi's legs wobbled. He had a sort of rumpled-attractive look that Heidi found charming on some men, if they had the personality to match. Somehow, she imagined Dominic did. More distractions Heidi did not need today, so she put those thoughts out of her mind.

"Megan must be about the same age as my other daughter. Jilly says she's graduating?"

"Time flies, right?"

Heidi frowned at the familiarity of this conversation. Had they done this at a previous recital? She didn't think so. Cass didn't often have all her students play on the same day, and Megan was much older.

"Is Megan your only child?"

Dominic shook his head. "My son's a freshman. I'm glad I have a couple more years before I'm on my own."

Heidi had no time to ask him anything else because she'd reached the front of the line. Jilly had wandered off with the other kids.

"Hi," Heidi said when she finally reached Cass.

"Welcome." Cass sounded so formal, so distant. It bothered Heidi in a way she couldn't explain, as if that was not how this moment was supposed to go.

"I'm really sorry we were late."

Cass put up a hand. "I understand. You have a lot going on."

"No, but...well...Kate. And Max. And...I just..." Heidi was at a loss for words, frustrated that she wanted to explain everything to Cass even though she was only the woman teaching Jilly's lessons and not Heidi's friend.

Cass put her hand on Heidi's arm. "The thing is, you don't have to do it all by yourself. I have a lot of parents who feel all this pressure to give their kids the best, and they struggle a lot like you are."

Heidi wanted to snap at Cass that she was fine, thank you very much. She had to figure out how to play Schedule Tetris, that was all. Fit everything in. Plan around stuff. She was so good at long-range goals, but she wasn't much use with the individual pieces. Tom wasn't a whole lot more help than Evan was, leaving Heidi constantly harried and frustrated.

"I'll try to do better," Heidi promised. "I know Jilly deserves my best."

Cass looked like she wanted to say more, but one of the other parents waved to her. "Thanks for coming. Jilly did fantastic."

Heidi would've replied, but Cass was already heading for the other side of the room. Heidi sighed. Even her kid's teacher saw how bad she was at keeping up.

"Jilly? You ready?" Heidi called.

Jilly skipped over with her viola and music in hand, and Heidi led her out of the building. She had to get home, freshen up, and make it back to the park. There probably wasn't enough time to change, but she could at least swap out her T-shirt for a clean one and change her pants. Determined to stay on schedule, Heidi headed for home.

***

VI

Heidi met Tom at the food tent, and they took their dinner outside. When they sat, Heidi frowned at her meal. When did she start liking curry? She tasted it, and it wasn't bad, but she was still confused about why she felt so compelled to order from that booth. She glanced up to see a family with a baby and a toddler. They looked vaguely familiar. Heidi had been to so many places over the course of the day, she might've seen them and simply not registered.

Watching as the young mother fed the baby and her partner wrangled their toddler, Heidi was reminded uncomfortably of the years she and Evan spent doing exactly that. By the time they had two youngsters close in age, Kate was old enough to help. But by then, it was the beginning of the end. Heidi hoped this family would have more good years ahead of them than she'd had with Evan.

Which brought her back to Tom, who was eyeing her, his fork stalled with a bite of food on it. She shook herself a little as she returned to the present.

"You okay?" Tom asked.

"I'm good." Heidi put her hand on his. "You said earlier we should talk. We didn't have time at the game."

Tom nodded and dropped his fork back into the compartmented takeout container. "This might not be the best place." He motioned around.

"All right. Want to finish up and take a walk?"

"I meant being here, at the festival. It's not exactly private."

"Wow," Heidi said. "This must be something important."

Tom nodded. "I've been doing a lot of...soul-searching. And talking with Wilhelm."

"Oh." Heidi frowned, and then it dawned on her. She remembered the way Tom and Wilhelm almost had a secret code. "Ohhhh. Oh, god."

"It's not what you think!" Tom reached out with his other hand so hers was sandwiched between his. "But I have to consider what would be best for me while I'm working through all this."

"You. And Wilhelm..." Heidi trailed off, feeling faint.

"Nothing like that," Tom said. "At least, not the way I think you mean it."

Heidi stared down at her uneaten food. "I was going to ask you to marry me," she mumbled. It felt strange saying it, as if she'd already known it wasn't right.

Tom stared at her. Hot Tom, the man almost every unmarried woman—and a fair share of the married ones, plus at least Wilhelm and who knew which others of the men—wanted. Somehow, Heidi had been lucky enough to be the Chosen One, and yet here she was, listening to her would-be fiancé telling her he was...what? Interested in Wilhelm?

"Okay, look." Tom withdrew his hands. "I love you, Heidi. But it's a good thing you were running late today. It made me realize we're not suited to make our lives fit together."

"And you think Wilhelm might be—"

Tom huffed. "No. Well, I suppose it's possible, but that's not what this is about. Nothing is going on between us. He was only helping me to understand something I didn't want to admit."

With that, Heidi grew angry. "You knew about me right from the start, that gender isn't a factor to who I love." She was always up front with anyone she dated, mostly to avoid the people who were hateful about it. "Why did you think you couldn't trust me?"

"Because of exactly that!" Tom exclaimed. "You're so confident. You told me there's never been a time in your life when you weren't able to be honest, even with your ex. I didn't think you'd understand what it's like to hide something so important."

"I don't live in some perfect world, you know," Heidi said. "Jilly's viola teacher doesn't speak to her parents. Having support is why I'm so passionate about making everyone feel safe."

Tom was silent for a long time, not looking Heidi in the eye. Eventually he raised his head and said, "I don't think you realize how difficult it is to get you to slow down long enough to have this kind of conversation. Did it really take festival food at a picnic table to finally make some time?"

"I—" Heidi didn't know how to answer him. He wasn't wrong. Today was one of many in which she was stretched to her limit. Between work and kid things, and Tom having his daughter every other week, they hadn't been spending time together lately. "You're right," she admitted.

"I need space to figure myself out. You need to work out your priorities."

Tom stood, gathered his garbage, and walked away. Heidi watched him go. That was it. They were done, and Heidi felt...odd. Relieved, confused, disappointed. She couldn't separate them out. The woman at the other end of the table, now finished feeding her infant, gave Heidi a sympathetic look. Heidi suspected she'd never had a partner leave her so publicly or for the same reasons, but at the moment, it didn't matter much.

Leather Anvil was on stage, playing their first song. Heidi and Evan both liked them, but Tom hadn't known who they were when Heidi suggested the concert. She'd introduced him to them; she had a hazy memory of playing one of their songs and then making love on Tom's couch. She sighed, recalling how Tom never seemed to want to spend time at her place or get to know Max and Jilly or even Kate, who he saw regularly at the games. She should've known they weren't meant to last.

Heidi frowned. None of that sounded right. For some reason, she couldn't shake the feeling it hadn't been Tom on her couch, listening to Leather Anvil or refusing to stay overnight. And how had she known that about Jilly's viola teacher? She didn't remember having such a conversation.

Come to think of it, she was having trouble with a lot of her memories and had been all day. She definitely needed to be more careful not to go out drinking with her coworkers. It wasn't directly related, but her head ached again.

She stood and gathered her trash, pitching it in the nearest bin. Tom was long gone, and she was at loose ends. She still wanted to hear Leather Anvil, but she had to clear her head first. From where she stood, she could either wander over to the grassy hill by the stage, or she could head in the other direction and check out vendor booths. She opted for the vendors.

The first one was a lot of eclectic jewelry. Heidi examined the beautiful earrings and noticed a collection of hand-painted plugs. She frowned when an image of Angel Flores popped into her head. Did Angel wear tunnels? Heidi concentrated on the photo of her from the city bus, but she couldn't remember the details.

Impulsively, Heidi purchased a pair. She had no idea what she was going to do with them yet, but something told her she needed them. Back outside the vendor tent, Heidi thought to put the ring from her pocket into the bag. But when she reached in to extract it, the ring wasn't there.

Heidi's heart raced. Where had she lost it? The ring could've fallen out anywhere from home to where she stood now. There was no point in looking for it. Panic led Heidi to wriggle her way as quickly as she could through the crowd. She was going the wrong way for the concert, but she didn't care. She put her head down and slipped between people and around strollers and dogs.

She wasn't looking where she was going, and before she knew it, she was colliding with a big, burly man. He yelled something at her, but she was already down, her head smacking the concrete hard enough to make her dizzy. She yelped and rolled to the side to avoid being trampled.

Strong hands gripped her, and Heidi felt the grit of the pavement on her skin as she was dragged to the side. On the grass, she lay back, panting, and flung an arm over her eyes. Once her pulse slowed, she sat up and looked around. Crouched next to her, wearing a worried expression, was none other than Angel Flores.

"Hey," Angel said. "Are you okay?"

Heidi felt her head and examined the scrape on her side. No blood, though it hurt like hell. "Yeah," she said. "I think so."

"Can you stand?" Angel rose to her feet and held out a hand.

Heidi took it and let Angel haul her up. Then Heidi took a good look at Angel. She had a knitted rainbow beanie covering her dark hair and just showing the full row of earrings down each ear. Sure enough, the lowest ones in her lobes were tunnels. Instead of the casual-but-professional outfit visible on the side of the bus, she had on a black Leather Anvil T-shirt and jeans. Heidi wasn't surprised to see a branching tattoo that began at her wrist and ended somewhere up under the T-shirt's sleeve.

Her matte purple lips curved into a smile, and Heidi realized she'd been staring. She flushed, and now Angel laughed.

"Come on," she said. "Let's get you to a bench. I'll grab some water."

This felt familiar, as if Heidi had once before bashed her head and needed *the* Angel Flores to take care of her. Except that was impossible. Heidi was sure she had never met Angel before, let alone needed her help with anything.

Angel reached into a barrel full of ice and Wegmans bottled water, pulling out two. Heidi couldn't hear the exchange, but Angel said something to the other two people in the tent, who nodded in response. They waved Heidi and Angel off.

There was a place to sit near the stage where all the children's events were held. Some group was there now, one Heidi didn't recognize because she no longer had kids young enough to bring them. As she sat, she realized she was a little dizzy. Whether it was from the fall or from being so close to Angel was anyone's guess.

Angel opened one water and handed it to Heidi. She took the other herself and sipped it, silently watching the kids' concert. After a few minutes, she turned her attention to Heidi.

"I'm Angel," she said. "But I take it you knew that."

"Heidi, and yep. From the radio." Heidi giggled nervously. "I listen to you every day on my way to..." She trailed off, feeling strangely as if she'd had this conversation before.

"On your way to..." Angel motioned for Heidi to finish.

"Work. I listen while I'm driving in."

"Yeah? Where do you work?"

"I'm a nurse's aide at RGH." Heidi drank some water, hoping it would clear the buzzing in her head. "You're working at that booth? Or just a Leather Anvil fan?"

"Martina is one of my friends. We've known each other for years. I help her out sometimes with this stuff." Angel smiled. "I wish I could manage them full-time, but it wouldn't pay my bills. And anyway, I like being a radio host."

"You know the lead singer?"

"Like I said, for a long time. Are you a fan?"

"Yeah." Heidi sighed. "My ex and I used to love them."

"Ex...oh. Recent?"

"You could say that. Well, no, I guess I have two now. I was married, but I've been divorced for six years. And I just broke up with the person I was about to propose to." Heidi cringed. "Sorry for dumping that on you right after we met."

"It's okay." Angel giggled. "I think I have that kind of face. People tell me stuff they otherwise wouldn't say out loud."

"Really?" Heidi looked over at her. "Yeah, I suppose I can see that."

Angel gave her a playful shove. "What's that supposed to mean?"

"You have a nice face." Heidi's cheeks instantly burned. "I mean—"

"Don't worry about it." Angel laughed, the sound bright and sweet against the backdrop of Heidi's crummy day.

"I'm gonna shut up before I say something else stupid." Heidi put her head in her hands, but she was laughing too.

After they'd both calmed down, Angel said, "Are you really all right? Or should I call the medical team?"

"I'm good. I'll have a better look at things when I get home, but I feel fine." She gingerly touched her head where she'd bumped it. Painful, but nothing seemed wrong. Nothing, that was, aside from the way this scenario felt so familiar.

Angel broke into her thoughts. "People are so rude. That guy definitely didn't need to shove you to get through."

"It was kind of my fault," Heidi admitted. "I was upset about something, so I was trying to rush against the crowd."

"Still, you could've been really hurt. I'm glad you're okay."

Heidi recalled why she'd been in such a hurry and glanced around. "Hey, have you seen the bag I was carrying?"

"You mean this?" Angel reached down and held it up.

"Yes! Thank you." Heidi breathed a sigh of relief, even though she still had no idea what to do with her purchase.

"May I?" Angel pointed to the bag.

"Go for it."

Angel peered in and then looked up at Heidi with a grin. "These are awesome! Did you get them from Forbidden Charm?"

"Is that the booth on the end?"

"Yeah. I looked there earlier today, but it's not currently in the budget." Angel peered at Heidi, assessing. "You don't wear plugs."

"No." On impulse or instinct, Heidi wasn't sure which, she said, "Why don't you take these?"

"I...no way. I couldn't!"

"Yes, you can. I'm not sure why I bought them, since I don't wear them and neither does my daughter. In fact, I don't know anyone who does. I guess I just liked them. I'd rather they go to someone who will enjoy them."

Angel gently lifted them out of the bag. The plugs were black with multi-colored birds on them. She held them up to her ears. "Think they'll look good?"

Heidi wanted to tell her anything would look good on her, but she was both startled and embarrassed by that thought. Instead, she said, "Yes, very."

"Cool." Angel smiled and put them back in the bag, folding the tissue paper around them again.

Heidi sighed. "I should probably go. Maybe there's still some way to rescue this awful day."

"By listening to Leather Anvil?" Angel suggested. "You don't have to tell me, but what was so bad?"

Everything, Heidi wanted to say. "Start with remembering I drunk-dialed my ex last night and called his wife a name. Fast forward to messing up my kids' day and getting very publicly rejected by my boyfriend."

She slouched on the bench. Somehow, she'd managed to get together with Hot Tom, and at the same time, also managed to lose him. That was apparently how she rolled, although the details on it remained fuzzy.

"Aw, I'm sorry." Angel patted her back, and Heidi's weird dream-memory-deja-vu made her laugh and cry at the same time.

"I just wish," Heidi said, sitting up and wiping her eyes, "that I could—" She cut herself off. Why did she feel so much like she'd made the same wish before, and that it was a terrible idea?

"What do you wish?"

"Nothing." Heidi shook her head. "It's stupid."

"No, go on," Angel prompted.

"I wish I could do it over. Get it right."

"Would that help?"

"I...don't know. It's silly anyway. You can't go back and do things over."

"Can't you?"

Heidi stared at Angel. Of course it wasn't possible. She could get up tomorrow, which happened to be Mother's Day, and hope to make things right with her kids. Maybe they would go somewhere special for lunch or see a movie they all liked. Anything. She could call both Tom and Evan and apologize for her behavior. But no, she could not have this specific day to do over.

"It's just a saying," she told Angel. "Like saying you wish a fairy would come and refill the cinnamon sugar."

"What?" Angel laughed.

"When I was a kid, we had this bottle with cinnamon sugar in it. I never saw anyone refill it, but it was magically always full, even when I knew we'd used it. So I made up this story about a fairy coming in at night and putting it in the jar. Wishing I could do my day over is like that."

"If you say so." Angel reached down and picked up a sprig of lilacs from beside the bench. Heidi couldn't fathom how it hadn't been trampled or crushed by a grabby child. "Make your wish," Angel prompted.

Heidi laughed. "That's dandelions, not li-i-lacs." She stuttered the word, certain she'd said that before but unable to recall when.

Angel shrugged. "I think it works with lilacs too. Especially on the first day of the festival."

Heidi didn't really wish for a do-over, or not exactly. She closed her eyes and thought about what had gone wrong, wishing she could undo the pain she'd caused. She thought about the kids and how much she'd messed things up. Then she thought about Tom and hoped he was all right. She couldn't quite bring herself to wish she'd been nicer to Jen, but she did wish for a way to make it right with Evan.

"Did you do it?" Angel asked. When Heidi nodded, she said, "Now, blow on it, or it won't come true."

Heidi did so, and then she put the sprig to her nose and inhaled. She loved the fragrance of lilacs.

Angel stood. "I should go back to the booth. Come on. I'll give you a CD." She winked. "In exchange for the plugs, of course."

***

VII

By the time Heidi arrived at home, all of her children were there. Kate had reheated the previous night's chicken enchiladas and generously shared them with the younger two. Heidi was worn out, disappointed, and irritated by the weird feeling of familiarity chasing her all day. She wanted to curl up in bed and sleep, possibly not waking up until all her children were adults.

She shuffled through the mail, making note of the bills and tossing the rest. She couldn't process anything at the moment, so she hoped she'd managed to save the correct pile. There were too many chores to finish before bed, so she began emptying the dishwasher and refilling it. She heard a soft sound behind her, and she turned. Kate was sitting at the kitchen table. Heidi left the dishes to go sit with her.

"Did you find a dress today?" At least Heidi remembered that was on Kate's agenda, even if she could barely keep track of her own responsibility.

"Yeah." She didn't sound happy, though.

"And the game?" Heidi didn't want to ask directly about what was on Kate's mind. She would need time to warm up to it.

Something nagged, a vague sense she should know what Kate wanted to tell her. Kate had said it before, Heidi was sure, and she wasn't remembering an important conversation. Had she not really been listening to the kids lately? That was possible, with the end of the school year–and Kate's official childhood–looming.

"It was great. We won, and I hit a home run. But you missed it, as usual."

As usual. Those words clicked. Heidi tried desperately to hang onto whatever it was she was missing, but it kept pulling away just out of reach.

"I'm so sorry. I know today was busy..."

"So? I'm just sick of feeling like I'm the least important thing in your life."

Anger and guilt warred in Heidi for pole position. "I'm doing my best," she said. "There's one of me and three of you. I can't be everywhere at once." She'd told Kate that before too, and now it felt as if they were doing a well-rehearsed tango.

"Exactly!" Kate glowered at her. "Our activities are more important than we are."

"I'm trying to help you plan for your futures."

"That's just it," Kate said. "You're really good at 'planning for our futures,'" she made air quotes, "but you suck at doing things that matter right now. You schedule us so hard you can't even show up. And I'm not even sure I want to *go* to college."

There it was. The thing Heidi had been trying to grasp. She knew that. But how? Had Kate told her before, and she wasn't listening?

"I...know," Heidi said, deflating.

"But–wait. What?" Kate leaned away, clearly perplexed.

"Somehow, I had a feeling you were going to say that," Heidi corrected herself, even though that didn't feel quite true.

"You're mad. I knew you would be mad." Kate looked down.

"I'm not–okay, yes. I'm mad. You have a full scholarship."

"I knew it. This is my decision, Mom. Not yours. You can't make me go just because you wish you had."

This wasn't how Heidi wanted the conversation to go. "I don't want you to regret it, that's all."

"You're always telling us that. All you ever do is push us to plan ahead, never make decisions because it feels right. And then you miss things because you were thinking six months ahead and not a week from now. Just because you were stupid at my age doesn't mean that I am!"

"It's not just at your age!" Heidi snapped. "Tom and I broke up."

Kate stared at her. "You regret breaking up with him? Or being with him?"

"I don't know," Heidi said. "I feel that way about a lot of things."

"Well, maybe think about it before you try giving me life advice next time."

Kate got up from the table and headed to her room, closing the door quietly behind her. A moment later, Jilly crept out to the living room with her sketchbook. When Heidi went to check on Max, he was fast asleep with his tablet on his chest, headphones still on. Heidi gently took them off and set them on his bedside table with the tablet then tucked him in. He briefly stirred but didn't wake.

She would have to tell Max and Jilly about Tom, but it could wait until morning. She hadn't planned to tell Kate either, but it had popped out. Heidi returned to the kitchen and finished the dishes.

By ten o'clock, all three kids were finally settled for the night. Heidi heated some milk, added a tea bag, and plunked herself down on the sofa with the cup. She turned on the television and flipped through channels, but she wasn't interested in anything that was on. Every now and again, she would think something looked familiar and would try to pause and watch, but she couldn't concentrate. Her head hurt again.

She let her mind wander back to her conversation with Angel. It had been so easy to pour out her bad day on a complete stranger. Yet Angel hadn't complained or offered advice or done anything other than give Heidi water and a listening ear.

Heidi remembered giving Angel the plugs, and her cheeks heated. It had been silly, and she shouldn't have done it. But it had gotten her a free CD, at least. Heidi went to the kitchen and picked up the bag. Leather Anvil's *Sonic Pixie Dream Girls*. She opened the CD to play it and saw a lilac-colored business card tucked into it. Angel Flores, Lilac City Social Media Management. The font for her name was a delicate script, a deeper purple than the card, and the logo was a sprig of lilacs with angel wings. Beneath the phone number, Angel had written, "Call me sometime."

Heidi's legs felt like jelly even tucked up underneath her. She was glad she was sitting. As tempting as it was to call Angel right away, she decided to enter the number in her phone and call in the morning. She opened her contacts and stared.

Angel's number was already there.

When had that happened? Maybe Angel had gotten hold of her phone and put it in while Heidi was distracted. But that made no sense; her phone had a code lock. Had she put it in herself and forgotten?

It made Heidi feel weird, so she put her phone away and headed for bed. Maybe this whole day would be gone from her memory come morning.

DAY THREE

I

The smell of coffee from the automatic pot woke Heidi from a deep sleep. She stirred restlessly, vaguely recalling that she'd been dreaming—something about a woman with light brown hair and hazel eyes. Cass, Jilly's viola teacher. That was odd, and she had the feeling she'd dreamed the same thing before. She squinted and peered around. Gray light filtered in around the curtains. She blinked, trying to clear the sleep from her eyes, then opened them fully.

The light sent piercing pain through her eyeballs, and her head throbbed. She had a fuzzy recollection of celebrating with some friends from work last night, but she blanked on why. She squeezed her eyes shut then rubbed them. After several attempts, she was able to keep them open. She switched on the radio on her bedside table, hoping that listening to her favorite radio station might both wake her up and jog her memory.

"Goooooood morning, Rochester! We're live here at the Lilac Festival, where the parade begins in less than a half hour!"

At least fifty percent of her memory began functioning again before Angel Flores finished speaking.

Swearing, Heidi threw off the covers and dashed around, yanking clothes off hangers and out of drawers. Why hadn't her alarm gone off? She was going to be late. There was only enough time to throw on clothes, leave a note for her kids, and grab her coffee to go. She had to be at Highland Park by ten-thirty, and it was five past now. Not even enough time for a shower.

After she tugged a pair of jeans loose from the mess in her drawer, she paused with it in her hand. Something about today was maddeningly familiar, but she couldn't place the niggle in her mind. Running behind wasn't unusual lately, so it couldn't be that. She dragged on the jeans, threw on a white T-shirt, and added a deep violet flannel button-up.

At her dresser, she stared at her reflection. Her outfit felt all wrong, but maybe it was because she didn't have time to look her best. At least she could bring some lip gloss with her to freshen up. Taking a deep, cleansing breath, she fished around in the top drawer among her lacy underwear to find it. The ring. If she couldn't be dressed up, then she'd at least have the best piece of jewelry she could afford when she proposed to Benji underneath the huge magnolia tree right at the top of the hill. If she wanted this relationship to last, she was going to have to make it happen herself.

Heidi carefully put the velvet box into her shirt pocket and patted it. No sense losing it or all her plans would go awry. With her hand still on the pocket, she had the strangest feeling they already had. That couldn't be right. To distract herself, she glanced at the bed but knew she didn't have time. She left it unmade and went into the kitchen to get that much-deserved—and needed—cup of coffee.

Kate was already at the table. She had cards and envelopes laid out and was filling them in with her careful, neat handwriting. She looked up when Heidi entered.

"What's all this?" Heidi asked. As soon as the words were out, a switch clicked, and she remembered.

Kate's mouth hung open for a full five seconds. She closed it and glowered. "Mom. Graduation? You know, that thing I'm doing in six weeks? These have to go out as soon as possible."

"Oh, damn. I'm sorry, sweetie. I totally forgot. I'll be home to take them to the post office as soon as I do this one thing." Heidi frowned. Hadn't they had this discussion? Maybe that's why she remembered it.

A sly grin blossomed on Kate's face. "You mean Benji? Today's the big day. I can't wait to hear all about it."

Benji. Right. Heidi had a strange thirty seconds of racking her brain. If she was supposed to marry someone named Benji, shouldn't she at least recall who that was? She must've had more alcohol at dinner than she'd thought. Since when did she ever get drunk? She was going to have words with her coworkers on Monday. A brief pause later, and she remembered Max's friend Kayla was Benji's daughter.

"Right, yes. Proposing to Benji. I should get going, then. You're taking Max to and from play rehearsal, right? Jilly's viola recital is this afternoon."

Another open-mouthed stare. "Again, Mom. You know I can't. I have a game, and then I'm going dress shopping with Bre and Amber for the prom. It's in two weeks, remember? You were supposed to ask Dad."

Heidi didn't hold back on her swears this time. She also knew without a doubt they'd exchanged the same words, but she couldn't for the life of her recall when. "I was? Guess I forgot. I'll call him on my way to the park."

"Thanks, Mom. And don't worry about the invitations. I'll drop them off on the way to the game. See you there?"

"I wouldn't miss it." Heidi bent and kissed the top of Kate's head, trying in vain to figure out why saying that felt so wrong. "I'll catch up later, with good news, I hope."

Kate wished her luck, and Heidi dashed out the door. On the way, she phoned Evan. She wasn't looking forward to talking to him, especially after the heated argument the previous night. Like everything else this morning, the post-fight hangover felt frustratingly familiar. She cringed, reminding herself that if she'd actually had too much to drink, she shouldn't have called him in the first place, definitely not to accuse him of failing his kids. Evan and Wifey Number Two never seemed to have time or interest in anything outside their own lives. She probably shouldn't have said that out loud to him, but he should absolutely not have called her a bitter wench. On the other hand, now here she was, asking him for more favors, this time due to her own poor planning. Kettle, meet pot.

She shook her head at the creeping feeling of déjà vu. She knew she and Evan did this dance a lot, but now she remembered thinking that exact phrase about herself. Which made no sense, so she ignored the memory itch and hit speaker phone while waiting for Evan to pick up.

"Morning, sunshine," Evan said when he answered.

The combination of Evan's sarcasm and the gloomy skies made Heidi even more irritated. "Hey. I need a really huge fav—"

"No," Evan said. "Our niece's baptism is today, and we're getting ready for it. We talked about this. You can't depend on me for every last thing when you're not organized enough. Whatever you need, get Kate's help or do without."

"Evan. They're your kids too, and you hardly see the-e-em..." She trailed off, knowing for sure this time she'd said those words. And not just in the context of arguing with Evan but literally in this specific moment. She tried to remember, but it wouldn't come to her.

"I have them every weekend that you're working, and I do the best I can the rest of the time. But you—"

Heidi cut him off. "I know I only call you when I'm a mess, but please, Evan. Today is important to me."

"Wait, what did you say?"

"I said today is important."

"No," Evan said. "Before that. About only calling me when you're a mess." His voice softened.

"Isn't that what you were going to tell me? Something about my asking you for stuff because I can't get my shit together."

"I—yeah. How'd you know?"

Heidi smiled in spite of herself. "You're a bit predictable."

"The answer's still no, but...Heidi, call sooner next time, okay? I can't always say yes, but I'll try to do it more often."

He ended the call, and Heidi threw her phone onto the passenger seat. She sighed. He was right. Nothing said she couldn't get to the park, pop the question, and be done in time to watch Kate's game, pick Max up from rehearsal, and have Jilly at her recital. Then she'd be free and clear to get back to the park for the rest of her date with Benji to see the opening concert at the festival. She'd prove she had everything under control.

***

<h1 style="text-align:center">II</h1>

Traffic by the park was going to be horrible. Heidi had gotten almost all the way to the park before she remembered Angel Flores announcing the parade. On any other day, she would've loved to stay home and listen to Angel and her co-host talking about the floats from the comfort of her own bed. This was not any other day, and Heidi had to get to Benji as soon as possible. She rerouted herself and headed for the community college shuttle parking instead.

By the time the shuttle arrived and everyone was uncomfortably tucked into school bus seats, the sky looked threatening. Heidi crossed and uncrossed her fingers several times that it wouldn't ruin Kate's game—or her proposal to Benji. That magnolia tree at the top of the hill was not going to give them shelter in a downpour.

The shuttle stop was in a completely different part of the park, so for a few minutes, Heidi was turned around. She finally figured out what direction to head just as her phone buzzed in her pocket.

"Hey, Benji," she said. "I'm almost there. Just give me another five minutes to..." She trailed off, trying to recall when she'd said that exact thing to Benji before. Something was very wrong.

There was a long silence on Benji's end. Then, "Heidi, is everything okay?"

That was one thing Heidi loved about Benji. She was always concerned and in tune with Heidi's moods. Maybe a little too concerned sometimes, but it was nice to have someone worry for her.

"I woke up late. I'm still a little out of it." Hopefully that was convincing because *I feel like I've done this before* probably wouldn't go over so well.

"No problem. I have a little time. But don't you have to get to Kate's game?"

"Not for a little bit. I want to see you first."

"Okay, well, if you're sure this is a good idea. You said you had something for me."

Heidi smiled. It was going to work out, just like she'd planned. "I definitely do."

"Cool. I'll see you in a couple."

Heidi was almost to the spot now. She could see down to the street where the parade was, more or less, even if she couldn't tell what was going on. She breathed a sigh of relief, and the most bizarre thought popped into her head: *Made it this time.*

This time?

She stopped and stood still, taking some cleansing breaths. There was a powerful scent of lilacs, as if the whole park had blossomed while she was paused. Heidi opened her eyes. It didn't make any sense. The lilacs were definitely not yet at their peak. The scent faded, and all that remained was the same disquiet that had plagued Heidi all morning.

She set off again, and that was when she realized the flaw in her plans. Roughly two and a half seconds later, she was drenched in the downpour.

Why couldn't her massive case of did-this-before have warned her what was coming? Cursing every last living thing, Heidi ran for shelter. All around her, people were calmly opening their umbrellas. If any of them were experiencing déjà vu, they'd been properly warned. Or they'd done the sensible thing and checked the weather forecast before leaving home.

Heidi huddled under one of the few trees with enough leaves to provide shelter. It wasn't, as she'd thought, pouring. Just a steady, cold rain. She pulled her phone out again.

"Benji?" Heidi's teeth chattered.

"You got caught in it, huh?"

"Yeah. This is the worst. I'm sorry."

"It's fine. Go, get warm and dry. We'll see each other later, okay?"

"But—"

"Nope. Warm and dry. You need anything?"

"Thank you, but no. I'll catch you later at rehearsal."

"You got it."

Mercifully, Heidi's phone had a waterproof case. She looked at the time before putting it away and groaned. Late, of course, and her shoes were already squelchy. She set off toward the shuttle stop, grumbling about wasting the money loud enough that several people turned to either glare or laugh. Heidi didn't care, as long as she didn't screw up the next part of her day as badly as this part.

***

III

Heidi pulled into the parking lot at the ball field. It didn't look as though the heavier rain had come through here. It was drizzling, though, so she grabbed the umbrella out of the map holder. For a moment, she stood with the car door still open, contemplating the item in her hand. She had a feeling it was going to prove useless, but she couldn't say how she knew that. With a full-body sigh she backed up and went to close the door. At the last second, she pulled her flannel out of the way.

How had she known it was about to get caught? It was more than her keen observation skills. Heidi had seen it in her mind as if replaying a memory or peering into the future. She couldn't decide which. When this day was over and she had five minutes to think, she was going to sort out whatever malfunction she'd caused by overindulging with her coworkers.

Unfortunately, that reminded her of the mess she'd made with Evan. That would have to be addressed too, but not until she'd made it through everything else. She closed off that part of her brain and headed for the team tent. As she ran toward the bleachers, the wind picked up and tugged on her umbrella. She braved the misty rain and closed it before it could flip inside out.

Under the tent, she shook the droplets off herself. All the other parents were huddled at the edge of the tent, watching the action on the field. It hadn't rained as hard here as it had in the city. She joined the group, cheering along with them for the girl on the pitcher's mound.

She shivered and backed up a little to pull her damp flannel tighter. It didn't help. A moment later, someone behind her said, "Hey."

Heidi turned around and had to hold in a sigh. It was Hot Tom, the gorgeous single dad who took care of a lot of general organizing for the team. Heidi concentrated, trying to remember which kid was his. Nevaeh— that was it. Not one of Kate's closest friends, but Heidi thought she remembered the two of them spending some time together. Unless that was another one of her distorted mind-pictures.

He turned that mega-watt smile on Heidi now. "How's it going?"

"G-good," Heidi said through chattering teeth.

Tom frowned. "Are you cold? Do you need a jacket?"

"Freezing," she admitted.

"Here." Tom reached into a bag and pulled out a sweatshirt with the team's logo on it. "These came in, and there were a few extras."

"I'll give it back next time." Heidi frowned. There went the feeling again that she'd said the same thing before.

"No need. Keep it." Tom had a lot of very white teeth.

"How much do I owe you?"

"On the house. Like I said, there were extras."

Heidi pulled on the sweatshirt and put up the hood to hide her messy, rain-soaked hair. One of the other parents turned around and scowled at her, as if Heidi had planned her natural shower in order to entice Hot Tom into some web of her womanly wiles. Heidi laughed, only realizing she'd done so out loud when Tom glanced at her in confusion.

"Sorry," Heidi said, but she giggled again.

"What?"

"Thank you for the sweatshirt." She moved closer and leaned in. "I think one or two of the others believe the sweatshirt isn't the only warming up going on between us."

Now Tom laughed, and Heidi relaxed. He leaned closer as well. "I do know what you all call me, of course."

"Ha! I figured as much." She grinned. "I'm wrecking their fantasy right now by talking to you."

"Good. That is, if you mean the idea that I'm an unapproachable object of their dreams."

"That's exactly it." Heidi peered back out to the field. "Nevaeh's your daughter, right?"

"That's her. Oh, she's at bat."

"Let's go watch her."

They watched the game in silence for a few minutes. By then, the misty rain had stopped, and the clouds were parting to reveal pale sunshine. Heidi inhaled; she loved the scent of damp earth after a rain, especially in the spring. She was startled when the scent of lilacs hit her. They were at the ball park, and she hadn't seen any bushes. Maybe she'd missed them.

As suddenly as it came, the lilac fragrance dissipated. Heidi turned her attention back to the game just in time to see Kate crack the ball with her bat. It sailed away, well beyond the reach of the outfielders. There was some yelling, and then Kate was rounding the bases. Heidi cheered along with everyone else. For once, she felt as if she'd been able to fully be present for Kate's big moment.

She watched the rest of the half-inning and then checked the time. If she didn't leave right away, she'd be late getting Jilly to her recital. Heidi thanked Tom again for the sweatshirt and then excused herself. She ran back to her car.

Inside, she tossed the umbrella in the back and pulled off the sweatshirt. Jilly was supposed to get herself ready to go, and she was responsible enough to do so. But now Heidi needed to change after getting caught in the rain like that. Hopefully she'd have enough time. She focused all her attention on getting to Jilly and having her downtown to warm up.

***

IV

Back at the apartment, Jilly was waiting by the door with her viola. "Mom! Let's go!"

Heidi didn't have a moment to think or to change her clothes. She pulled a sweater out of the coat closet as Jilly ran past her out the door. Heidi fiddled with the lock on the door and followed Jilly to the car.

"Don't worry," she said. "We'll be there. I'll text Cass…" She trailed off.

While she'd definitely texted Jilly's teacher a time or two about the lesson schedule or payment, she wasn't in the habit of sending her random messages. "Never mind. She's probably busy setting up. We might be five minutes late or so, but I'll have you there in plenty of time."

"Okay." Jilly seemed to relax.

Heidi peered at her in the rearview mirror, but Jilly wasn't looking at her anymore. She had her sketch book out and was doodling in it. Once they were on the highway, Heidi pulled out her phone and turned it all the way off. No sense in being rude during the recital, and with how her day had gone so far, she was apt to forget once they got there.

It was a relief when Heidi pulled into the driveway of Cass's Park Avenue studio. Traffic was a little thick, leaving Heidi wondering why the recital was this weekend and not separated from the Lilac Festival and Mother's Day. She supposed there was never going to be a perfect date for it, so it might as well be now rather than later.

Inside the studio, an older student greeted Jilly and led her away to the warm-up room. Heidi entered the performance space, set up with a piano and music stands. She slipped into a row toward the back. Around her, parents and other various family members were talking quietly. Heidi spotted Evan and Jen with their toddler toward the front. She tried to shrink herself so they wouldn't see her, but they never turned around.

The recital was about what Heidi expected. Some younger children, one stumbling through a painful rendition of *Minuet in* G, and a few older ones sprinkled in between. The pieces generally became more complex as the recital went on. Jilly performed beautifully, of course. Heidi was proud of the work she'd put into practicing and polishing her piece, Isaac Albeinz's *Tango*. Heidi wished she'd recorded it, but she was glad to see Evan had. If they could manage to be on speaking terms, maybe she'd ask him to send it to her.

When the last student, a high school senior, finished, Cass stood. "Thank you all for coming and for sharing your children with me. Why don't we go in the other room and enjoy the refreshments you all brought?"

Heidi groaned inwardly. She'd forgotten. Everyone was supposed to bring something to share, and she'd been so wrapped up in the rest of her day that she hadn't done it. She scowled at Jen's back, knowing she'd probably brought some perfect dessert to share. As before, Jen didn't turn around at all.

In her embarrassment, Heidi hid in the recital hall until everyone else had filed out. She used the excuse of checking her messages. That was when she discovered the glaring error in her day.

She'd forgotten about Max.

When she turned her phone back on, a dozen messages popped up: from Max, from Benji, and even from Kayla. Heidi's face burned as she hit

Benji's number.

"Oh, my god. I'm so sorry!" she exclaimed the minute Benji answered.

"Where the hell are you?"

"Jilly's recital. I forgot the dessert for it too."

"You didn't even call! Max was really worried when we couldn't get hold of you. And you're worried about dessert?" Benji sounded somewhere between panicked and angry.

"I'm really, really sorry."

Benji sighed heavily. "I know this day was busy for you, but you could've asked. You know I'd have taken Max home or even out shopping with us like we originally planned."

"Shopping?"

"For the extra stuff the kids need for their costumes. It's just tights and stuff. Remember? I said if you gave me the money, I'd get Max's when I took Kayla."

Heidi honestly didn't remember, but she didn't want to keep going in circles. "I can get Max on the way home from the recital."

"I already took him home."

"Are you with him?"

"Yeah, we're still here."

"I'll be home with Jilly soon, and we can go together for dinner. The kids are fine. I told Kate there's leftovers in the fridge."

"I'll wait for you, then."

Benji ended the call, and Heidi sat for a couple minutes taking deep breaths. She could handle this. A quick hello to Cass to thank her for the day, then back home with Jilly. Since Benji was already there, Heidi had a little wiggle room to change clothes and fix her hair. This was definitely a workable plan.

She left the recital hall and found Jilly talking to the girl who had greeted her when they arrived. She was the one who performed last on the program.

"Mom, this is—"

Much as Heidi wanted introductions, she was also in a hurry now that she knew what she'd been forgetting. "Jilly, we need to get going."

"But, Mom! This is Megan, the girl I told you about."

Heidi didn't remember anything about Megan. She was about to say something when a rumpled-looking man came up behind Megan and extended his hand.

"Dominic," he said. "Megan talks all the time about what a great kid Jilly is."

Heidi's insides were a wobbly, anxious mess, but she smiled anyway. "Good to meet you." She wished she could say she recalled Jilly talking about Megan, but she didn't.

"Jilly? You ready?" Heidi asked. "We have to get to Max. He's with Benji."

"Okay."

Heidi hadn't even managed to greet Cass, but she didn't want to keep the others waiting. Jilly skipped toward the door with her viola and music in hand, and Heidi followed her out of the building. Good thing she had time on the drive home to figure out how to make it up to both Benji and Max for her mistake.

***

V

Heidi and Benji carried their food outside. Red Osier this time, of course. Heidi was oddly relieved, as if something fit into place in a way the rest of the day had not. She'd moved like she was inside her own personal cloud, and this lifted the fog slightly. She clung to having something in common with Benji, but she wasn't sure why.

They sat at a table where a family with small children was already unpacking their food. Heidi remembered the days when she and Evan were committed to perfect parenting. It was one of the things about being so young when they'd had Kate. Everyone had been waiting for them to fail right from the start, so they'd always gone the extra mile. Heidi wondered where they'd derailed. Somehow, she'd become the overachieving, give-them-every-advantage parent, and Evan had become wrapped up in his own life. They never seemed to meet in the middle.

Thinking about Evan and his lack of interest in his children these days made Heidi annoyed, so she turned to Benji. "How was the rest of your day?"

"Good." Benji seemed much more interested in her sandwich than in conversation.

"And..." Heidi prompted.

Benji looked up. "Now you want to talk?"

Heidi was taken aback. "Well, yes. We're on a date."

Benji put her food down. "Okay, so let's talk. Maybe about the fact that you left Max with me without asking, and you didn't give me the money for the costume pieces. Or we could discuss how Max and Kayla both want to go to theater camp, and Max says he's been trying to tell you for weeks, but you weren't listening."

"Jeez," Heidi muttered. "So, we're not talking. We're arguing."

"If you want to think of it that way."

"I thought this was going to be our chance to catch up," Heidi said. She pursed her lips at the way her voice sounded so whiny.

Benji sighed. People around Heidi did that a lot, and it left her feeling as if she were exasperating every last person in her life. Heidi tried to keep the lid tight on the anger building in her. Wasn't anyone able to see the kind of pressure she was under all the time?

"Heidi." Benji put a hand on top of hers. "I'm angry, but I want to work this out. You almost ditched me this morning, calling at the last possible second to tell me you were late. It wasn't a big deal, since I was running behind. But almost an hour? And then you gave me five minutes before you ran off to Kate's game."

"It was important to her. Evan couldn't go."

"I know. But...I always feel as if I come last. We could make this work, if we pooled our resources. Isn't that what you always say you want?"

Heidi thought about it. Yes, that's what she wanted, but from Evan. She wanted her kids' father to seem more committed to their family. Her shoulders slumped when she realized Benji wanted the same thing for Kayla.

"This isn't going to work, is it?" Heidi asked, her eyes stinging with tears. "It's never going to work."

"I don't know," Benji said. She sat up straighter. "That isn't what I said, though."

"Is it what you meant?" Heidi felt as if she'd heard that sentiment before, but it couldn't be right. Benji was the first person she'd dated seriously since Evan, unless she was having a massive memory block. Which, given the rest of her day, could be true.

"No, it isn't." Benji squeezed her hand. "I think it can work fine. But only if we both understand what the other person needs. You never seem to think you can ask for my help with anything, which makes me think you believe I shouldn't ask you either."

Heidi withdrew her hand and covered her face. She peered out through her fingers. "Oh, god. I'm sorry."

"For what?"

"I was going to try to fix this. Like, I wanted to..." Heidi cleared her throat. "...propose. If we were married, wouldn't that solve some of this?" She shook her head and continued before Benji could interrupt. "Except I know better. It won't make any of our problems go away." Just like it hadn't when she married Evan.

"I don't think I'd have said no, if that helps," Benji replied. "But you're right. We have to work on what's gone wrong, not add new dynamics."

"So...is that what we're doing?" Heidi's hope was an odd mix of wanting Benji to say yes and wanting her to say no.

"Let's take it one day at a time for now."

They finished dinner in silence, and Heidi wasn't sure how to interpret this. She had another flash of déjà vu, sitting at this particular picnic table and having other, similar conversations. She knew that wasn't possible, but her brain wouldn't let it go. In the same way, she understood things were over with Benji. Even if they kept trying, they weren't going to be able to make it work. After two years, they were heading in different directions even if the way forward wasn't clear yet.

Benji stood and collected her trash, and Heidi followed. Benji put out a hand. "I'll get that."

Heidi nodded and leaned over to kiss Benji's cheek. "Did you still want to go to the concert?"

"Why not?"

The woman at the other end of the table gave Heidi a disappointingly familiar sympathetic look. Heidi shrugged and turned away. She and Benji set off for the grassy hill by the stage.

Leather Anvil had just started. They were one thing Heidi and Benji had in common, although Heidi had been a fan longer. She knew all the words to most of their older songs, while Benji was familiar with their newer music.

For a little while, they simply enjoyed themselves. Benji wasn't much of a dancer, but she didn't object when Heidi stood up with half the crowd and moved to the music. Heidi focused on the melody, not on her miserable failure of a day.

After Leather Anvil finished, the sky was darkening. Heidi pulled Benji to her feet, and they said their goodbyes. There was no way to tell what sort of future they had, but Heidi assumed they were on their way to being over. It hadn't been an official breakup, but it had definitely sounded a lot more like a finale than an entr'acte.

She wandered over toward the vendors, hoping there might be a tent with Leather Anvil merch. Maybe she'd buy a shirt or a CD. The crowd had thinned, and the breeze was picking up. Heidi wished she had more than her flannel to keep warm. She ducked her head, pulled it tighter, and pressed on.

At the end of the line of vendors was a jewelry booth. There was a lot of variety in the handprinted pieces. When Heidi looked at the earrings, a pair of black plugs painted with rainbow birds stood out. They were so strangely familiar she felt faint from grasping for the memory. The only thing her mind located was Angel Flores, the morning show host. Except Heidi had no idea if she wore plugs or what size they'd be if she did.

She had to get out of there. In a rush, she whirled around and dashed away from the tent. Not looking where she was going, she smacked into a tent pole with the full force of her body. Her head bounced off it, and this time, she was sure she was going to pass out. She crumpled to the ground.

A moment later, several faces peered down at her. Someone reached out a hand, and Heidi took it. And then she almost fainted again when she saw the hand belonged to Angel Flores.

"Hey," Angel said. "Are you okay?"

Heidi gingerly touched the bump on her head. "Yeah," she said. "I think so." The words sounded far away even as they came out of her mouth.

"Can you stand?"

Heidi let Angel help her up and lead her to a bench. As they sat, Heidi took in Angel's appearance: matte purple lipstick, knitted rainbow beanie, a lot of piercings—including plugs—and a Leather Anvil shirt partially covering a winding tattoo on her arm. Heidi's stomach turned to jelly, and it had nothing to do with her injuries or the other general weirdness of her day.

Angel smiled, and Heidi flushed with the realization she'd been staring. "Sorry," she said.

"No worries. So, are you okay? Want me to get some water?"

Heidi closed her eyes against another dizzying wave of déjà vu. No, she wasn't okay, but it wasn't because of the bruise on her head.

"I'm all right, but water does sound good."

Angel left her on the bench and returned a moment later. "Here."

Heidi drank about half the bottle in one go. Then she sat fiddling with it while she watched the concert on the children's stage. She had no idea who those people were.

"Better?" Angel asked. Heidi nodded. "I'm Angel," she said. "But I take it you knew that."

"From the radio." Heidi giggled nervously. "I listen to you every day on my way to..." Heidi trailed off, fighting the urge to repeat something she was sure she'd said before. But when?

"On your way to..." Angel motioned for Heidi to finish.

"Work."

"Yeah? Where do you work?"

"I'm a nurse's aide at RGH." Heidi drank some more water. "I'm Heidi, by the way. You like Leather Anvil?" Now she frowned because it didn't seem right, as if something had changed in the direction of the conversation that, to Heidi's knowledge, she'd never had before.

"I do some work managing the band's social media and marketing stuff. Martina's an old friend."

"You know the lead singer?"

"Yep. Are you a fan?"

"Yeah." Heidi sighed. "My ex and I used to love them."

"Ex...oh. I'm sorry."

"No, it's fine. I still like the music, even if I don't like my ex all that much." Heidi groaned. "Both exes. I think my girlfriend broke up with me, and then we watched the concert together. That was weird. And sorry for the overshare."

"It's okay." Angel giggled. "You'd be surprised how often that happens to me."

No, for some reason, Heidi would not. But all she said was, "Oh, yeah?"

"Perks of being a radio host, maybe. We do that segment where people can win stuff for calling in with personal stories."

"Right! Well, and you do have a nice face." Heidi's cheeks instantly burned. "I mean–" Crap on a cracker, she had definitely not meant to say that.

Angel's laughter warmed Heidi. "Thank you, I think."

"I'm gonna shut up before I say something else stupid." Heidi put her head in her hands, but she was laughing too.

When they'd calmed down, Angel said, "That bump looked pretty bad. Should I radio the medical team?"

"No, I'm good. I think I'm going to take a walk and clear my head."

"Are you alone?" Angel's brow crinkled with a worried frown.

"Yes, but I'm sure I'll be fine. I have my phone."

"Hang on, I'll come with you."

She stood and held out her hand to pull Heidi up. Then she bent to pick up a sprig of lilacs someone had dropped. Probably a kid whose parents made them put it "back in nature," even though the damage was already done when they plucked it.

Angel stopped at the booth and picked up a CD, and then she and Heidi walked along the outside of the booths rather than on the path. The scent of lilacs was thick, which surprised Heidi. Hardly anything was blooming yet, but she could smell the flowers as if they were at their peak.

Somehow, it didn't feel strange to walk beside Angel in silence. Heidi didn't remember feeling this much at ease in a long time. Too many worries, too much stress, too busy. That was her life. But here, she had no pressure to do or be or prove anything.

Heidi stopped to finish her water. Then she turned to Angel. She hated to go, but the kids were waiting. They had things to discuss, including Heidi having to tell Max that she and Kayla's mom weren't getting married after all.

"Thank you," Heidi said to Angel.

"No problem. Here, I grabbed this for you. If you need anything, my business card is inside."

"Are you sure?" Heidi looked at the CD. Leather Anvil's new one, *Sonic Pixie Dream Girls*.

"Yes. Perks of my connections." Angel grinned.

"A definite improvement on the rest of my day," Heidi said.

"Glad I could help."

Heidi blew out a long, shaking breath. "I just wish..." She clamped her lips shut, getting the strangest feeling it would be a bad idea to finish that sentence.

"What do you wish?"

Heidi shook her head. "It's stupid."

"No, go on," Angel prompted.

"I wish I could do my day over." Heidi clapped a hand over her mouth, wanting to stuff the words back in.

"Are you gonna hurl? Do I need to move?" Angel stepped back.

Heidi lowered her hand. "No. I shouldn't have said that out loud."

Angel shrugged. "It's your wish."

"Wishing is stupid. Magic isn't real."

"It's not?"

Heidi laughed. "So you believe in Santa or the Tooth Fairy or the Great Pumpkin? I mean, sure, I can wish. But that doesn't make things happen. I'm not a little kid who can be convinced by a parent."

"If you say so." Angel smiled, something that looked secretive and knowing. She handed Heidi the sprig of lilacs. "Make your wish," Angel prompted.

Heidi laughed. "That's dandelions, not..." Now Heidi knew she'd said that before, but she didn't have the time to put together when.

Angel shrugged. "I think it works with lilacs too. Especially on the first day of the festival."

Heidi closed her eyes. She almost didn't make a wish, but at the last second, she wished to erase her painful day.

"Did you do it?" Angel asked. When Heidi nodded, she said, "Now, blow on it, or it won't come true."

Heidi did so, startled when she once again caught the sweet scent of lilacs as if the whole park were in bloom.

Angel put a hand on Heidi's shoulder. "Have a good night. And..." Angel blushed. "Call me sometime."

She walked away, and Heidi stared after her, unable to move or call out even though she wanted to.

***

VI

Heidi couldn't remember exactly how she'd gotten home. Everything after Angel was a blur, and her head still hurt. The kids had reheated the previous night's chicken enchiladas and left all the dishes in the sink. After the day she'd had, the last thing Heidi wanted was more chores, especially ones the kids should've known to do themselves. But none of them were around, and she was too tired to go get them.

She shuffled through the mail, barely noticing what was in it before setting it aside and getting to work on the kitchen. She heard a soft sound behind her, and she turned. Kate was sitting at the kitchen table. Heidi left the dishes to go sit with her.

"Did you find a dress today?" That was probably the topic least likely to start a war.

"Yeah." Kate didn't sound happy.

"The game was good. I saw your home run."

"You did?" Kate stared at her.

"Yes, of course. I said I'd be there."

"Well, yeah, but I didn't see you." Kate smiled, but then she turned sullen again. "You left me to deal with Max being mad all night that you forgot him."

Heidi rubbed her temples. "I'm sorry. I should've just come home anyway. It wasn't all that great for me either."

"For you?" Kate's mouth hung open. "How about for us?"

Heidi had a feeling they'd been down this road before, and not only from past arguments. Like everything else today, this felt familiar and strange. "I'm doing my best," she said. "There's one of me and three of you. I can't be everywhere at once." She'd definitely said that to Kate before. Probably the last time they'd had this same fight.

"Exactly!" Kate glowered at her. "Our activities are more important than we are."

"I'm trying to help you plan for your futures."

"That's just it," Kate said. "You're really good at 'planning for our futures,'" she made air quotes, "but you suck at doing things that matter right now. You schedule us so hard you can't even show up. And I'm not even sure I want to *go* to college."

Heidi knew that. But how did she know? Had Kate mentioned it? Heidi closed her eyes, trying to recall, but her brain was mush.

"Say something," Kate demanded.

"I...know," Heidi said. "I think you told me. Maybe?"

"No, I didn't. Have you been going through my texts or something?" Kate crossed her arms.

"No!" Heidi shook her head vigorously. "You know I wouldn't do that. Are you sure you never told me? I could swear I remember having this same conversation."

"You're mad. I knew you would be mad." Kate looked down.

"A little, yes. You have a scholarship. But mostly I'm upset that you..." Heidi paused. "I was going to say didn't tell me, but you did. Or something. I'm sorry, I'm really confused right now."

"That makes two of us," Kate said. "I didn't want to tell you because I know you want me to make different choices than you. But you can't make me go just because you wish you had."

"I realize that. I don't want you to regret it later."

"You're always telling us that. All you ever do is push us to plan ahead, never make decisions because it feels right. And then you miss things because you were thinking six months ahead and not a week from now. Just because you were stupid at my age doesn't mean that I am!"

Heidi gaped at Kate. That speech...she'd said it before. She'd yelled the exact same thing at Heidi, whether a week ago or in a dream or...

"Mom!" Kate snapped.

Heidi felt faint. A rush of disjointed memories hit her hard, crashing together. She had no idea which ones were real. Shaking, she tried to cover for the out-of-body experience she was having.

"Sorry. It's been a really terrible day, and Benji and I broke up. I think."

"You...think." Kate sat back, arms crossed.

"We said we were taking some time, but I'd say it's over."

"Max doesn't know?"

"Not yet."

Kate nodded. "I'm sorry, Mom." She bit her lip. "Is that why you're always on us about regretting things?"

"Because of Benji?"

"Not really. Relationships in general, I guess."

Heidi took Kate's hand. "It's a lot of things. Not making snap decisions. Not planning ahead. I wish I'd known at your age how to do that."

Kate looked at their joined hands and then up at Heidi. "I'm not making a snap decision, you know."

She pulled her hand away and stood to go to her room, closing the door quietly behind her. A moment later, Jilly crept out to the living room with her sketchbook. When Heidi went to check on Max, he was fast asleep with his tablet on his chest, headphones still on. Heidi gently took them off and set them on his bedside table with the tablet then tucked him in. He briefly stirred but didn't wake.

She would tell him about Benji in the morning, if anything made sense by then. Kayla had probably already texted him anyway. Meanwhile, she would sleep off the weirdness of feeling like she'd lived multiple lifetimes in a single day. Definitely no alcohol for her tonight.

Jilly went to bed a little before ten. Heidi heated some milk, added a tea bag, and plunked herself down on the sofa with the cup. She turned on the television and flipped through channels, annoyed that it all appeared to be repeats. Eventually, she turned it off again.

Heidi remembered the Leather Anvil CD Angel had given her. She set down her mug and went to the kitchen to find the bag. *Sonic Pixie Dream Girls.* She opened the CD to play it and saw a lilac-colored business card tucked into it. Angel Flores, Lilac City Social Media Management. The font for her name was a delicate script, a deeper purple than the card, and the logo was a sprig of lilacs with angel wings. Beneath the phone number, Angel had written, "Call me sometime."

Heidi caught a whiff of lilac briefly, but it faded. Her legs felt like jelly, and she had to sit. When she pictured Angel, Heidi smiled. Talking to her had been the one truly nice thing about the day. Heidi would call her in the morning; it was far too late now. She opened her contacts to enter the number and stared.

It was already there.

Heidi shook. Something was definitely wrong. All day, she'd had the sense of living in a double reality, but this was beyond the feeling of déjà vu and into seriously weird territory. Heidi put her phone away and headed for bed. A good night's sleep—that's what she needed. In the morning, all of this would be behind her and she could start over.

DAY FOUR

I

The smell of coffee from the automatic pot woke Heidi from a deep sleep. She stirred restlessly, vaguely recalling that she'd been dreaming—something about a woman with brown hair and eyes. She looked a bit like Cass, Jilly's viola teacher, but not exactly. With a gasp, Heidi sat bolt upright in bed. Instantly, she regretted her poor life choices. The light filtering in around the curtains made her head pound. She lay back down, fighting the dizziness.

Had she really gotten drunk last night with her coworkers? She didn't remember, but her headache told a different story. It had given her weird dreams, too. She leaned down and switched on the radio on her bedside table, hoping that listening to her favorite radio station would soothe her and help her wake up a bit.

"Goooooood morning, Rochester! We're live here at the Lilac Festival, where the parade begins in less than a half hour!"

More weird, overlapping memories, some including Angel Flores, the morning show host on WNDR now announcing the parade. Had Heidi met her once? Maybe she'd dreamed that too, right along with Cass.

Heidi threw off the covers and dashed around, dragging clothes off hangers and out of drawers. There was something she was supposed to do today, but her brain wasn't functioning. All she knew was she would be late. There was only enough time to throw on an outfit, leave a note for her kids, and grab her coffee to go. She had to be at Highland Park by ten-thirty, and it was five past now. Not even enough time for—

She paused with her hand in her drawer, attempting to pull a pair of jeans loose. How had she known she wouldn't have time to shower if she didn't even know what she was late for? She yanked out the jeans, dragged them on, and pulled a white T-shirt over her head. She took a deep violet button-up out of her closet and stood at her dresser, staring at her reflection with the shirt in her hand.

She'd worn this before. Not before-before, as in, this was her standard outfit. Before as in literally this exact moment on this exact day. That was not possible, and she reminded herself that she and too much alcohol definitely did not mix well. She tucked her favorite lip gloss into her jeans pocket, hoping its presence would make her feel better. Something told her she needed an item out of her top drawer, but hell if she knew what it was. She fished around until her fingers closed on a small, velvet box. She withdrew her hand and opened it. A ring.

Now her memory rushed back, disjointed and confusing though it was. She had planned to propose today, at the top of the hill in Highland Park. Among the lilacs and right beneath the big magnolia. It was the most romantic spot she could think of. She also had the strangest feeling she'd tried that idea another time, and it hadn't worked, which made no sense. She hadn't been married or engaged or planning to be engaged to anyone in her life besides Evan.

Until today. Heidi carefully put the velvet box into her shirt pocket and patted it. Whatever else happened, she needed to keep the ring safe until she figured out what in the world was going on. She glanced at the bed but knew she didn't have time. She left it unmade and went into the kitchen to find the cup of coffee she now desperately needed.

Kate was already at the table. She had cards and envelopes laid out and was filling them in with her careful, neat handwriting. She looked up when Heidi entered.

"What—never mind." Heidi definitely remembered asking Kate about this before, and she recalled Kate saying these were graduation invitations. "Sending these out today?"

Kate nodded. "It's in six weeks. They have to go out as soon as possible."

"Of course. I'm not sure I'll have time to mail them today." Heidi frowned. She thought she'd offered to do it, but now she was telling Kate she couldn't.

A sly grin blossomed on Kate's face, and Heidi couldn't shake the feeling she knew what Kate was going to say. However, what came out of Kate's mouth wasn't what Heidi expected. "You mean Dominic? Today's the big day. I can't wait to hear all about it."

Who the hell was Dominic? Heidi hid her reaction from Kate. Why had she been anticipating a different name? Not that she could recall specifically who, but she definitely wasn't expecting it to be the polite parent of another viola student. For some reason, Heidi was beginning to feel like she was two steps behind everything today.

"Dominic. Of course. I have to go." She forgot about the coffee for the moment and stepped toward the door. Then she turned around. "I feel like I'm supposed to ask you something about Max's play rehearsal, but I can't remember what. I know Jilly's viola recital is this afternoon. Were you going to pick him up?"

Kate stared at her. "No? My game won't be done in time, plus I'm going dress shopping with Bre and Amber for the prom. I thought you asked Dad. You called him yesterday."

Heidi groaned. That was the one thing she did remember, and she knew exactly why she hadn't gotten around to asking. "I'll just call now. Or in the car. Whatever."

"Cool. And don't worry about the invitations. I'll drop them off on the way to the game. See you there?"

"I wouldn't miss it." Heidi bent and kissed the top of Kate's head, knowing something was wrong there too. "I'll catch up later, with good news, I hope."

Kate wished her luck, and Heidi dashed out the door. While sitting in her car, she phoned Evan then put it on speaker and left it on the seat next to her as she pulled out. This all felt familiar, and she wasn't looking forward to talking to him. She cringed, remembering she'd called him under the influence to berate him about how he and Jen—wife-the-second—were lacking in parenting skills. She probably shouldn't have said that directly, but he shouldn't have called Heidi a bitter wench. On the other hand, now here she was, asking him to help her out, this time due to whatever it was today she had planned and couldn't quite bring into focus. Kettle, meet pot.

She gasped, remembering she'd thought that phrase about herself, more than once. It brought back the crawly déjà vu feeling. None of this day made sense so far. Hopefully talking to Evan would clear her head, even if he was the last person she wanted to speak to.

"Morning, sunshine," Evan said when he answered.

"Oh, my god, why do you always say that?" Heidi snapped. She sucked in a breath. "Shit. I'm sorry."

"Okay. Well, screw you too, babe. I don't have time to get yelled at a second time in less than twelve hours."

"I know I wasn't at my best last night. I think I had too much to drink, and I honestly don't know what happened. Hell, I don't know what's happening now, except Kate told me I was supposed to ask you to get Max from play rehearsal or something."

"No," Evan said. "Our niece's baptism is today, and we're getting ready for it. We're barely going to make it to Jilly's recital as it is. We talked about this. You can't depend on me for every last thing when you're not organized enough. If Kate can't help with the driving, then ask one of the other parents."

"Evan. They're your kids too, and you hardly..." Another fit of déjà vu. She'd said that already. Not before-before, but before-on-this-day. "Never mind. I'll just...do whatever."

"You will?" Evan's incredulity made Heidi wince.

"I guess I should've called sooner, but I think today was spur of the moment. It's important, but I'll try to make it work. Somehow."

"What did you say?"

"I said today is important."

"No," Evan said. "After that." His voice softened.

The conversation was definitely going slightly differently than Heidi remembered. She and Evan did this dance a lot, but she felt like there was a script, and she'd just gone off it. "I said I'll try to make it work."

"I really think you can. You're good at this, Heidi, even if you get a bit intense."

Heidi smiled in spite of how off-kilter she felt. "That's the nicest thing you've said to me in a while. You sure you can't pitch in?"

"I really can't. But I'll work on doing it more often."

He ended the call, and Heidi threw her phone onto the passenger seat. She sighed. Was he right? Could she do all this if she put her mind to it? She made a mental list: get to the park, pop the question, watch Kate's game, pick Max up from rehearsal, and have Jilly at her recital. If she made it through all that, her reward was...a concert? She strained to remember. Yes, that was it. She had a date. With Dominic, at least if he was the one she was proposing to. She had to get moving or everything would go south, if it hadn't already.

***

II

Traffic by the park was going to be horrible. Heidi remembered just in time about the parade and decided to take the shuttle instead. It would probably be delayed, but what difference did another few minutes make?

On the bus, Dominic called her. "Heidi? Where are you? It looks like it's about to rain."

"I know," she replied. "I'm on the shuttle now."

"Should I meet you at the stop?"

Heidi didn't want to ruin her big, romantic moment by finding a different location. On the other hand, getting caught in the downpour would probably ruin it equally. "Okay."

The bus let everyone off, and Heidi smelled the change in the air. All around her, people were opening umbrellas. No one wanted to let a little rain prevent them from enjoying the festival. Heidi wished she'd brought hers, but she'd left it in the car.

Dominic was off to the side, waiting. Heidi smiled when she saw his umbrella. Even if she couldn't remember most details about their relationship, she saw he was the type to be prepared and to make sure he took care of her. She stepped off the bus just as big, fat drops began to fall.

Heidi dashed over to Dominic and huddled under his umbrella. He put an arm around her and led her away from the crowd. The parade had probably finished recently, from the way the crowd moved almost as one in the same direction. Heidi tried to steer Dominic in the correct direction, toward the big hill.

"What's the rush?" he asked.

"I have to get to Kate's game, and there's something I want to show you." Heidi peered up at him, trying to give him a winning smile.

Dominic shrugged. "Okay. I don't have a lot of time. Megan and I have plans before the recital."

Heidi stopped walking and closed her eyes. She tried to picture Megan. It took a while before her sliding memories produced a picture of an older teenage girl. Jilly talked about her sometimes. Heidi had assumed at first that Megan was the same age as Jilly, but she was graduating, like Kate.

Dominic prompted the conversation again. "It's Megan's last one."

"Right," Heidi said. "I sometimes forget our daughters are about to finish high school."

They walked all the way to the hill and up the path. Heidi had one slightly damp sleeve by the time they arrived, but the umbrella had protected the rest of her. She frowned at the odd feeling she should be soaked through. It wasn't as if she wanted to be wet; if she did, she could easily tell Dominic to move the umbrella. It was more like she felt as if not being wet was changing the course of history.

They stood under the big tree, and Heidi faced Dominic. This was it, the moment she'd rushed through her morning for. She took a deep breath and held Dominic's free hand.

"I, uh..." She cleared her throat. "I wanted to ask you something."

Dominic's warm, soft smile melted Heidi's heart. "Yes?"

Now or never. "We've been together a while, and...will you marry me?" She asked the question in a rush, then looked down. She wasn't sure she wanted to meet Dominic's gaze.

"Yes," he said then leaned in to kiss her forehead.

Heidi fumbled in her pocket and pulled out the ring. "Here."

As he helped her slip it on his finger, she thought about how at least she'd made this one thing perfect. A few people around them clapped, and the rain slowed as Dominic kissed her. Heidi smiled against his lips, but something felt...off. Wrong. Like a crack in a phone screen. She pulled away but tried to make it seem like a natural end to the kiss.

Her day was already strange, but she couldn't shake the feeling she was missing something vital. All Heidi could hope was that Dominic hadn't noticed anything. She slipped her arm through his and started walking along the path.

"Would you like to come to lunch with Megan and me?" Dominic asked. "I'm sure she'd love to know, and I can't think of anyone else I want to tell first."

Without processing what it meant, Heidi said, "That sounds really nice. Is it okay if I get Jilly too? Then we can pick up Max and head for the recital. I'm sure he could come along with us after his rehearsal."

"Perfect!" Dominic grinned. "I parked in the shuttle lot too, so we can take the bus and meet up. I'll let Megan know we're on our way."

Caught up in the moment, Heidi didn't even take her phone out of her pocket to check the time as she and Dominic walked back to the bus stop with linked arms.

***

III

Heidi still hadn't checked her messages when she and Jilly arrived home after lunch. There was just enough time for Jilly to change and get her viola before they were out the door again to pick up Max. It wouldn't kill him to watch his sister one time.

As predicted, Jilly was as excited as Megan that their parents were getting married. She talked Heidi's ear off the whole way to the school. Heidi tuned out most of it. She couldn't quite muster the same level of enthusiasm, but she was sure it was a result of her hangover, the morning rush, and her busy afternoon ahead. At least she had a date with Dominic back at the Festival later, where they could spend time at the concert and just relax.

Heidi sat in the car outside, waiting. The rehearsal ran over time, and Heidi drummed her fingers on the steering wheel while Jilly continued talking about her plans for adding another sister. At last Max came out. He ran over to the car, but he didn't get in. Heidi put the window down.

"What's up? We have to go," she said.

Max pointed to a girl halfway across the parking lot. "Kayla's mom said I could go with them to get costume stuff we need for next week."

Heidi peered around him. "And she'll bring you home after? Does she know where you live?"

He rolled his eyes. "Yes. I have my key, before you ask. So can I?"

Heidi looked in the rearview mirror at Jilly. "Do you care?"

She shrugged. "Nope."

"Okay." Heidi pulled out her wallet. "Is this enough?" She handed Max some cash, but not before briefly wondering how she'd known to have it with her.

He counted it. "I think so. I'll tell Kayla's mom I'll pay her back if it's not. Thanks, Mom!" He called the last bit over his shoulder as he jogged to the other side of the lot.

Heidi headed for the city to Cass's Park Avenue studio. She loved watching Jilly play, but for some reason, she felt as if she'd sat through several recitals already. She wondered why Cass had planned it for the day before Mother's Day, and then she frowned. She'd definitely had that same thought before, and not only when they were given the recital information. She wanted to scream in frustration at the barely-there memories.

Inside the studio, an older student greeted Jilly and led her away to the warm-up room. Heidi entered the performance space, set up with a piano and music stands. She slipped into a row toward the back. Around her, parents and other various family members were talking quietly. Heidi spotted Evan and Jen with their toddler toward the front. She tried to shrink herself so they wouldn't see her, but they never turned around.

Megan was last on the program. After she played, Cass stood. "Thank you all for coming and for sharing your children with me. Why don't we go in the other room and enjoy the refreshments you all brought?"

Heidi could've kicked herself. She'd forgotten about bringing cookies. Hopefully, Jilly wouldn't be too upset with her. After all, the rest of the day had been relatively drama-free, aside from whatever happened on stage at Max's rehearsal. Heidi still had a feeling something wasn't quite right, but now wasn't the time to dwell on it. She decided to hide in the recital hall and check her messages before joining the others. That way, she wouldn't have to explain anything.

That was when she discovered the problem her memory gaps had caused. She'd forgotten entirely about Kate's game.

Kate had sent her half a dozen texts. They started out asking where Heidi was, and they ended with angry emoticons about Heidi missing her important, game-saving home run. Heidi called her instead of texting back.

"I am so sorry," she said the minute Kate answered.

Kate huffed. "Not now, Mom. I'm about to shower and go shopping. You at least could've texted me or something."

"I was out with Dominic, Megan, and Jilly." Heidi paused. "Celebrating."

"Yay," Kate deadpanned. "I'm happy for you. But you missed my game, even though you said you'd be there."

"I can't always be with every single one of you," Heidi snapped.

"I know! But how about you at least tell us that instead of acting like you have it one hundred percent under control?" She huffed again. "I have to go. I'll see you later." She ended the call.

Heidi sat there for a few minutes and then stood to head for the reception area. Maybe a cookie would make her feel better about messing up with Kate. She stepped inside and looked around for Jilly. In the corner, Megan was talking her ear off about something. Heidi smiled. Those two were quite a pair. Maybe they wouldn't get along so well once their households were combined. But both Kate and Megan were heading for college in the fall, so Heidi hoped there wouldn't be too much to worry about.

She didn't see Dominic, so she approached Cass instead to thank her. "What a great recital," she said.

"Thank you!" Cass smiled. "Jilly is a wonderful student. I'm excited to see how she does when she reaches middle school next year."

"Don't remind me," Heidi said with a laugh. "I can't believe she's already finishing fifth grade."

"It goes by so fast, even for us teachers." Cass nodded to Megan. "I remember when she was tiny and just starting out." She smiled. "I heard from Jilly that your families are combining. Congratulations!"

"Thank you. I should probably go find Dominic now. It looks like Jilly's ready to go."

Cass patted her shoulder, and Heidi went to see where Dominic had ended up. She assumed he was using the restroom, as he wasn't back in the recital hall nor in the warm-up room. Heidi had never been anywhere else in the house/studio, and she felt awkward looking around the rooms not being used for the recital.

She heard quiet voices, so she followed them around a corner. Old houses like this one were a maze, and she was already turned around. Hopefully whoever was in the room could redirect her. Heidi approached and made to open the door when she froze.

Through the narrow window in the door, she caught a glimpse of two people: Dominic and one of the other parents. Heidi didn't know the woman very well, only in passing when there was an event like this. At first, she thought they were only talking. But then she saw the woman push Dominic up against a wall with a giant music staff on it. She kissed him as if her life depended on it.

Heidi would've gone in under the assumption the woman was assaulting him, but Dominic looked every bit as if he was consenting. He tangled his hand in her hair, and pulled her close by the waist.

Fuming and with her cheeks red, Heidi turned away. What sort of people used a kids' recital to hook up? Right—she and Dominic did, once. Her faulty memory chose that moment to provide a clear reminder of how the two of them met, back when he was still *technically* not yet divorced.

She would deal with her no-good, cheating, soon-to-be-ex-fiancé later. For now, she had to get Jilly out of there without alerting anyone to the problem. Easier said than done, but Heidi was determined. She rounded the corner back the way she'd come and saw she was on the other side of the reception room. She entered from the back, put on a smile, and took a chocolate chip cookie from the table. She could definitely do this.

***

IV

Heidi dropped Jilly off at home with Max. Kate would be there as soon as she finished dress shopping, and angry or not, she would figure out dinner for the three of them. It wasn't her style to use her siblings to punish Heidi for her flaws. Meanwhile, Heidi made her excuses to Dominic and Megan, saying she wanted to freshen up before the concert. The most she did was change her T-shirt and add some makeup. Usually, she didn't wear much. But she was still furious, and she wanted to look good while telling Dominic exactly where he could shove the ring she'd given him that morning.

At the Festival, she maintained her calm, cool exterior. She and Dominic carried their food outside. He'd gotten them both Zweigel's red hots and curly fries, probably the last thing Heidi would've eaten if she'd been the one ordering. It didn't matter. She wasn't hungry anyway.

The whole day felt like a mess, and this was like having a nightmare but being able to shout at the monsters to go away. With any luck, she'd get rid of Mr. Kissy-Face and still have time to enjoy Leather Anvil. Even with the weird holes poked in her memory, she knew Dominic hated them. He'd only come to make her happy.

They sat at a table where a family with small children was already unpacking their food. Heidi watched them for a few minutes, and it was odd that she could predict what the young mother was about to take out of their bag before she did it. When she got home, she was definitely going to take a hot bath and analyze why her day felt like she'd already lived it. Not now. First, she had to ditch the jerk across from her.

Speaking of His Royal Cheatingness, Dominic interrupted her rage with, "The recital was fantastic, wasn't it?"

Oh, he did not just go there. It was all the opening Heidi needed. "I guess it was, for *some* people." She placed her hands flat on the table and stared him down.

"Uh...okay?" Dominic squeaked. "Heidi, what's gotten into you?"

"I think a better question is who you've gotten into," she hissed.

"Heidi?" His voice was small and weak. Not unlike his personality.

"I saw you. In the practice room. I don't even know who she is, other than having a kid in the recital."

Now it dawned on him, and his face went white. The young adults with the kids both looked over, their eyes big as saucers and their mouths open in shocked Os. Heidi snorted and looked away from them.

Dominic looked down at his food. His fingers twitched. There was a long silence, during which the family next to them didn't move an inch.

Heidi caught them out of the corner of her eye, but she forced herself to focus on Dominic, waiting for his reply.

At long last he said, "I was never a priority for you. Tonight, I was going to tell you it was over. But you proposed, and stupid me, I thought that meant maybe we'd finally have time for each other. Then I saw Helen, and I remembered why this was never going to work."

"Oh, that is good," Heidi said, her nostrils flaring. "Blame me for cheating instead of having a grown-up conversation about what was wrong and how you felt. Why the hell does no one ever tell me what you all want or expect from me? I did that once, and my marriage ended in a steaming pile of dung. I'm not doing it again. Feel free to go bang Helen or whoever she is." Heidi leaned forward. "And I want my goddamn ring back, you asshole."

The young father gasped and covered his kid's ears. Heidi held out her hand for the ring, which Dominic pulled off and dropped there. He stood, leaving her with his uneaten food. Heidi huffed and began picking up. The young mother gave Heidi a sympathetic look, to which Heidi only nodded. She had a weird feeling they'd met somewhere before and that for some reason, this woman consistently felt sorry for Heidi. It annoyed her, so she hurried to throw out the trash and escape the picnic tables.

Leather Anvil was on stage, beginning their first song. Good riddance, having Dominic gone. Heidi didn't relish having to explain the breakup to Jilly, especially after they'd had lunch with Megan. But telling her now would be infinitely better than finding out years down the road about Dominic's inability to keep it zipped. She'd been down that road once, finding clues that Evan was involved with someone else. It had been the final straw.

Heidi listened for a while, but she was too upset to enjoy it. Instead, she wandered over toward the vendors. She definitely needed something to make it up to Kate for missing the game and to Jilly for the train wreck of breaking up with Dominic.

At the end of the line of vendors was a jewelry booth. There was a lot of variety in the handprinted pieces. When Heidi looked at the earrings, a pair of black plugs painted with rainbow birds stood out. She knew those plugs. Two different memories warred in her brain: one of buying them and giving them to Angel Flores, and one of fleeing from them. She was frozen to the spot, staring.

"Pretty, aren't they?" said a voice behind her.

Heidi jumped about a mile. She turned around, and there was Angel, in a Leather Anvil shirt and a rainbow beanie. All the blood rushed from Heidi's head, and black spots swam before her eyes. There was nothing she could do to stop it. As if in a dream, she slithered to the ground. Something hit her in the head, and she heard muffled shouts before everything went dark.

She had no idea how long she was passed out. Not long, she assumed, but something had bumped her head, and it hurt. She opened her eyes when the scent of lilacs hit her nostrils. It wasn't lilac perfume; it was real, as if the entire park had bloomed while she was unconscious. It faded almost as soon as it arrived.

Several faces were peering down at her. Someone reached out a hand, and Heidi took it. And then she almost fainted again when she saw the hand belonged to Angel Flores.

"Hey," Angel said. "Are you okay?"

Heidi gingerly touched her head. "Yeah," she said. "I think so." The words sounded far away even as they came out of her mouth.

"Can you stand?"

Heidi let Angel help her up and lead her to a bench. Gratefully, she accepted the water bottle Angel held out. The crowd had thinned, and people were no longer staring at her. She took a long drink while she watched the performers on the children's stage. It wasn't so long ago that she'd been in this same area, sitting on the grass and laughing with Evan as their kids ran around and danced to the music. Now, Heidi didn't even recognize the band.

"Better?" Angel asked, breaking into her thoughts. Heidi nodded. "I'm Angel," she said. "But I take it you knew that."

"From the radio. I listen to you every day on my way to..." Heidi trailed off. She'd had this conversation with Angel before. "...work. I'm a nurse's aide at RGH." Heidi drank some more water. "I'm Heidi, by the way."

"Nice to meet you," Angel said. "Sorry it was under such weird circumstances."

It was, Heidi reflected, but for some reason, she suspected even weirder than Angel knew. She'd been here before, in this spot. Her whole day had felt like being nagged by a persistent fly. Sitting here on the bench everything felt strange and familiar and...right, somehow.

Angel's hesitant voice interrupted again. "Are you sure you're okay? Should I go get the medical team?"

Heidi vaguely wondered why she hadn't already. "No, I'm good. Missing the concert, though."

"That one?" Angel pointed to the kids' stage with an incredulous look.

"No." Heidi laughed when Angel relaxed, looking relieved. "Leather Anvil." Heidi indicated Angel's shirt. "You're a fan too?"

"I do some work managing the band's social media and marketing stuff. Martina's an old friend."

"You know the lead singer?" Heidi couldn't stop the words, not even knowing she'd said them before.

"Yep. We went to the same high school. She was a couple years older, but we were in the same crowd."

Heidi sighed. "My ex and I used to love them."

"Ex...oh. I'm sorry."

"We haven't been together in years. Guess I was feeling nostalgic." Heidi groaned. "Because now I can add another ex to my growing list." She flushed, but then she frowned. What growing list? She hadn't dated much since Evan; Dominic was the first long-term relationship she'd had since they split.

Angel giggled nervously. "You have a lot of exes who like Leather Anvil?"

That broke the tension Heidi had created. "No, just the one. Tonight, I dumped a guy who was cheating on me *and* hated Leather Anvil."

"No loss there, then." Angel smiled.

Heidi thought about it for a moment. "You're right. I was mad, but how could I think someone who doesn't love them belongs in my life?" She laughed.

"Right, the cheating is totally fine. But not loving Leather Anvil? Deal breaker for sure."

They were both giggling madly, enough that a few people passing by eyed them. Heidi didn't care. She'd had a horrible day, and sitting here with Angel and laughing about it felt good.

"Don't know what I was thinking, going out with him."

Angel stood. "They're still playing. Want to go listen?"

"Definitely!"

Heidi accepted Angel's hand to pull herself off the bench. As they straightened, Angel picked up a small sprig of lilacs someone had dropped by the bench. Surprisingly, it was unharmed, not trampled or wilting. Angel tucked it behind Heidi's ear.

Heidi expected Angel would let go of her hand once she was up, but she kept hold of Heidi and led her through the crowd and back toward the main stage. The sky was dusky now, all the hues of the beautiful blooms in the park. Leather Anvil had the crowd on their feet, dancing.

"You wanna dance?" Angel asked.

"Okay."

They moved to the music under the darkening sky, a light breeze ruffling their hair and cooling them even as their bodies warmed from the dancing. Angel spun Heidi and dipped her, startling a squeak out of Heidi and making them both laugh.

When the music slowed, Angel pulled Heidi close. Heidi didn't stop to think why it felt right or why being in Angel's arms made her belly and limbs quiver like gelatin. Her heart raced, and she knew she had to let go before she did something foolish. With a sigh, she released Angel and stepped back.

"Everything okay?" Angel asked.

"My head hurts a bit," Heidi said.

"We can sit down."

So they sat in the grass for the rest of the concert, and Angel leaned against Heidi as the last cords sounded. She smiled up at Heidi then shifted and stood.

"I need to get back to the booth," Angel said. "They were probably expecting me sooner."

"No problem." Heidi followed suit and stood. "I'm sorry about dumping my problems on you and then stealing you away from your job."

"Oh, I don't get paid for this, so don't worry. They have other people working there."

"Still, you didn't need to deal with my crummy day."

Angel shrugged. "I'm used to it."

Heidi's stomach dropped. So this wasn't anything other than Angel being a nice person. Why did that hit so hard? Heidi swallowed her disappointment and said, "Oh?"

"Perks of being a radio host, maybe. We do that segment where people can win stuff for calling in with personal stories."

"Right," Heidi said. "Well, and you do have a nice..." She trailed off. When had she told Angel that before? Too late, she realized she'd failed to finish her sentence at exactly the wrong point.

Angel laughed. "So I've been told." She winked.

"Face! I was going to say face," Heidi said.

"Gotcha," Angel replied with a wink.

"I'm gonna shut up before I say something else stupid." Heidi covered her eyes with her hands, but she was laughing too.

When they'd calmed down, Heidi saw they were back outside the jewelry tent. She couldn't say why, but she had an overwhelming need to purchase those plugs with the rainbow birds. Indicating to Angel to wait, she ducked inside. There they were, the very last pair in their row. The woman selling them was already beginning to pack up for the night, but Heidi stopped her.

"Can I buy those, please?" She pointed to the plugs.

The woman rang her out and wrapped them in tissue paper before carefully setting them in the box. Heidi carried them back outside. Angel waved to her, and Heidi dashed over.

"Before you go, these are for you." Heidi thrust the box at her. "For taking care of me after I fainted." She wished she could add that it was much more than that, but it sounded foolish, and Heidi had no idea where those feelings came from.

Angel opened the box and grinned. "I love these! They're the ones I saw earlier and planned to come back for, but they weren't in my budget."

She grabbed Heidi's hand. "C'mon."

Heidi let Angel pull her along to the Leather Anvil booth. It felt natural, right somehow to be with Angel. It was more than being able to lay aside her disappointing day for a while. She felt entirely at ease, like a giant weight had been lifted. She paused, thinking she'd had the exact same idea before. Heidi knew she had, but she shook it off and waited outside the booth while Angel plucked something out of a box.

She came out and handed Heidi a CD. "A trade, this for the plugs."

"Thank you," Heidi said. Their new one, *Sonic Pixie Dream Girls*.

"Perks of my connections." Angel grinned.

"A definite improvement on the rest of my day," Heidi said.

"Glad I could help."

Heidi didn't want the evening to end, but she had to go home to the kids. Had to explain to Jilly that she wasn't marrying Megan's dad. It all rushed back in at once.

"Are you okay?" Angel tilted her head.

"Not really. Time to go home and deal with the consequences of my day."

"Oh." Angel reached up and plucked the sprig of lilacs from behind Heidi's ear. It still looked as fresh as when she'd put it there.

"I just wish..." Heidi clamped her lips shut, refusing to finish that sentence.

"What do you wish?"

Heidi shook her head. "Nothing."

"No, go on," Angel prompted.

"I wish I could do my day over." The words came out despite Heidi trying to hold them in, as if she had no choice. "I shouldn't have said that out loud."

Angel took her hand and placed the lilacs in it. "Make your wish again."

Heidi laughed. "That's dandelions, not..." Heidi had said that before; she had a feeling it was more than once. "...lilacs."

Angel shrugged. "I think it works with lilacs too. Especially on the first day of the Festival."

Heidi closed her eyes. She almost didn't make a wish, but at the last second, she wished to erase her painful day.

"Did you do it?" Angel asked. When Heidi nodded, she said, "Now, blow on it, or it won't come true."

Heidi did so, startled when she once again caught the sweet scent of lilacs as if the whole park were in bloom.

Angel put a hand on Heidi's shoulder. "Have a good night. And..." Angel blushed. "Call me sometime."

She re-entered the booth, and Heidi turned away, feeling like she'd missed something important.

***

V

Heidi was still floating from her encounter with Angel when she arrived home. The kids had reheated the previous night's chicken enchiladas and left all the dishes in the sink. Kate was still angry, then.

Heidi rifled through the mail, set it aside in one big pile, and rolled up her sleeves to work on the dishes. Behind her, someone sighed, and she turned around to see Kate at the kitchen table. Heidi slid into a chair across from her.

"Did you find a dress today?" A hole in Heidi's memory filled in as she recalled asking Kate that before.

"Yeah."

"I'm sorry again about the game."

"Whatever."

"I know I said I'd be there, but Dominic asked me to lunch after I proposed, and...well. I'm sure you'll be happy to know we're not getting married after all."

Kate's eyebrows shot up. "You're not?"

"Nope."

"Why would I be happy about that?"

Heidi shrugged one shoulder. "I suppose because I deserved what happened, sort of a just reward for missing your game."

"Mom, what?" Kate frowned. "What happened?"

"Dom was cheating on me with someone named Helen. And I probably should've seen it coming, given that he was willing to date me before he was even divorced."

"I'm pissed about the game, but no one deserves that. He's a jerk."

"Maybe. According to him, missing your game was...a symptom. He was feeling neglected, kind of like you."

Kate stared at her lap, her lower lip drawn in. There was more on her mind, and Heidi was determined to listen. She had a feeling they'd already discussed whatever it was on Kate's mind. Yet another strangely familiar interaction.

"Sometimes it feels like our activities are more important than we are." Kate peered up at Heidi.

"I'm trying to help you plan for your futures." Heidi sighed, knowing that wasn't the right response. "I always figured you'd each find something you loved, and trying many different things was the way to discover your passion."

"That's just it," Kate said. "You're really good at 'planning for our futures,'" she made air quotes, "but you suck at doing things that matter right now. You schedule us so hard you can't even show up. And I'm not even sure I want to *go* to college."

Heidi sucked in a breath even though she'd somehow known that was coming. She opened and closed her mouth, unable to form words through the sludge in her brain.

"Say something," Kate demanded.

"Did you...wait." Heidi took a deep breath. "Did we talk about this already, and I've forgotten?"

"What?" Kate scowled. "I've never said anything. You probably wouldn't have listened anyway. Were you going through my phone?"

The accusation was as familiar as the rest of their discussion. "No! Of course not."

"You're mad. I knew you would be mad." Kate looked down.

"A little, yes. You have a scholarship. But mostly I'm upset that you..." Heidi paused. "I was going to say didn't tell me, but you did. Or something. I'm sorry, I'm really confused right now." To add insult to injury, Heidi's memories fractured again, and she was sure she'd said the same thing before.

"That makes two of us," Kate said. "I didn't want to tell you because I know you want me to make different choices than you. But you can't make me go just because you wish you had."

"You're right."

"You're always—wait, what?"

"You're right. And we need to talk about this more, but not now."

At the look on Kate's face, Heidi wished she could shove the words back in her mouth. She couldn't think straight, though, and she knew she had to be clear-headed to have a conversation that didn't end in yelling.

"Fine," Kate snapped. "I'm going to bed." She stood and began walking away, but she turned around before she reached the hallway. "Good luck telling the others about Dominic."

She entered her room and shut the door with a little less force than a slam. A moment later, Jilly crept out to the living room with her sketchbook. She kept her back to the kitchen, and Heidi wondered if she'd heard any of their conversation. It was possible she already knew about Dominic. Heidi wasn't sure whether that would make the next day's recap of events easier or harder.

Jilly went to bed a little before ten, and Heidi checked on Max. He was asleep with his headphones on, so she gently extracted them before returning to the kitchen. She heated some milk, added a tea bag, and curled up on the sofa. For some reason, she decided not to bother with the television. She had a nagging sense she already knew there wasn't anything on she wanted to watch.

Still antsy from the day's events, Heidi remembered the Leather Anvil CD Angel had given her. She brought her tea to the kitchen and sat down with the CD. *Sonic Pixie Dream Girls*. She opened the case and saw a lilac-colored business card tucked into it: Angel Flores, Lilac City Social Media Management. Under the phone number, Angel had written, "Call me sometime."

The fragrance of lilacs wafted to her nostrils, and Heidi wondered if the card was scented. She pressed her nose to it, but the smell faded. A nervous thrill ran up Heidi's spine, and she pictured Angel. Her rainbow beanie, her hand reaching down to help Heidi up, the way she moved to the music, the sprig of lilacs she'd tucked behind Heidi's ear. Heidi had half a mind to call her right away, but she knew it was too late. Instead, she would put the number in her phone and...

It was already there.

The awful déjà vu was back. Heidi's legs shook as she stood and dumped her tea in the sink. She needed sleep. A good night's rest and this would all be behind her. And Angel's phone number wouldn't mysteriously be in her phone after all.

Day Five

I

The smell of coffee from the automatic pot woke Heidi from a deep sleep. She stirred restlessly, vaguely recalling that she'd been dreaming— something about a woman with brown hair and eyes. She resembled Cass, Jilly's viola teacher, and yet somehow was different. Heidi squeezed her eyes shut. Maybe if she didn't open them, she wouldn't have to deal with the headache she knew was coming.

The dream was fading from memory, but a lot of other things were not. For example, she could either fight the urge or give into it to lean down and switch on the radio on her bedside table. She gave in.

"Goooooood morning, Rochester! We're live here at the Lilac Festival, where the parade begins in less than a half hour!"

That was it, she was absolutely never, ever, ever going drinking with her coworkers again. Not even to celebrate proposing to her...whatever. Girlfriend? Boyfriend? As predicted, her head throbbed.

Heidi shoved the covers down and rolled out of bed. Even if she'd had so much booze she couldn't remember details of her relationship, she knew damn well where she was supposed to be in twenty minutes. She had enough time to drag random clothes out of her drawers and throw them on. She would leave a note for everyone about where she was and when she'd be back.

She paused, staring at her reflection with her violet button-up in her hand. Conflicting memories raced through her head. She'd screwed this day up before. Sitting on the end of her bed, she tried to piece it together. The only thing she recalled clearly was meeting Angel Flores at the Lilac Festival and coming home to three angry and disappointed kids. Was that part of her dream? Some other life, in which she'd made a mess. A warning to her to get it right.

Heidi needed time to think, to figure out what she'd done wrong the previous time. Or times, something told her. She had a nagging suspicion she'd been having a recurring nightmare, sort of like dreaming about being naked on stage in Kodak Hall or mixing up her schedule on the first day of school. That had to be it. How else would she have so clearly remembered having done all of this before?

Except there was Angel. The thought of her, of sitting with her on that bench near the kids' stage at the park, wouldn't leave Heidi alone. If Heidi could make it through the day intact, she could find Angel.

Midway through reaching for her lip gloss, she stopped again. Why would she need to find Angel if her day went as planned?

She tucked the lip gloss in her jeans pocket and the ring box in her shirt. Brushing away all thoughts about Angel, she left her bed unmade and went into the kitchen to find the cup of coffee she was definitely going to need to face the day.

Before Heidi entered the kitchen, she knew Kate would be at the table with her graduation invitations and envelopes laid out. Sure enough, there she was, was filling them in with her careful, neat handwriting. She looked up when Heidi entered.

"Sending these out today?" Heidi asked, trying to mask how creepy it felt to know what was going to happen before it did.

Kate nodded. "It's in six weeks. These have to go out as soon as possible."

"Of course. I'm not sure I'll have time to mail them today." Heidi felt faint. She wasn't sure she could do anything today, let alone add more errands.

A sly grin blossomed on Kate's face, and once again, Heidi knew what Kate was going to say, even if she had no idea what name would be attached. "You mean proposing? Today's the big day. I can't wait to hear all about it."

"Yes. Um…Dominic?" she tried.

"Who?" Kate shot her a puzzled frown. "You mean Malcolm?"

Right. Heidi would find his contact info in her phone later, which would probably jog her memory of how they'd met. Why was she having this much trouble remembering who she was in a relationship with?

"Malcolm. Yes. Which means I should be leaving instead of talking to you." She forgot about the coffee for the moment and stepped toward the door. Then she turned around. "Were you supposed to get Max from rehearsal?"

Kate stared at her. "No? My game won't be done in time, plus I'm going dress shopping with Bre and Amber for the prom. I thought you asked Dad. You called him yesterday."

Heidi groaned. She didn't want to think about drunk-dialing her ex-husband and the fight they'd had. How was it she remembered that part and nothing else about what was going on? "I sort of had a fight with him yesterday after I got home."

"Mom! You and Dad need to get it together. I want you both at graduation, but not if you're going to act like two-year-olds with a toy. Seriously!"

"Don't worry. I'll call and apologize, then beg him to take care of stuff with Max."

"Cool. Thank you. And don't worry about the invitations. I'll drop them off on the way to the game. See you there?"

"I wouldn't miss it." Heidi bent and kissed the top of Kate's head, wondering why it felt wrong to tell her that. "I'll catch up later, with good news, I hope."

Kate wished her luck, and Heidi dashed out the door. While sitting in her car, she phoned Evan then put it on speaker and left it on the seat next to her as she pulled out. She had to make it right with him and maybe with Jen, his wife. The previous night, she'd accused him of bad parenting and Jen of keeping him from his kids. Not that his response, calling her a bitter wench, was a whole lot better. Evan had been sober, as far as she knew. But being drunk and rude was probably a step below being sober and rude, so she had to at least try to make it right. Her vague, dream-like memories suggested she'd done the opposite before.

"Morning, sunshine," Evan said when he answered.

Evan's sarcasm annoyed her, but she pressed on. "Hey. I'm really sorry about last night."

"Last night?" Evan paused. "Ah, right. When you said we stopped caring about the kids the minute we had a mini-Jen. Although I don't think you actually used her name. Didn't you call her—"

Heidi cut him off, knowing exactly what she'd called Jen. It wasn't repeatable. "I know I wasn't at my best. I had too much to drink, and that wasn't why I'd intended to call you. I'd really wanted to ask if you would be able to get Max from rehearsal."

"No," Evan said. "I told you last night, but I guess you weren't with it enough to remember. Our niece's baptism is today, and we're getting ready for it. We're barely going to make it to Jilly's recital as it is. We talked about this. You can't depend on me for every last thing when you're not organized enough. If Kate can't help with the driving, then ask one of the other parents."

"Evan..." Heidi stopped. She'd been on the verge of throwing the same accusations at him again. But he was going to Jilly's recital, right? He wasn't missing out on anything of Max's, and Kate just wanted one of them at her game. "Never mind. I'll work it out. I think I have an idea."

"Uh...okay? Then why did you call me?"

"I only just thought of it," Heidi said. Or actually hadn't come up with anything yet, but she was sure she could.

"That makes sense."

"I really am sorry about yesterday. I'll try to call you sooner next time. This was..." Heidi tried to remember. Why was it she hadn't called Evan with more than a day's warning? "...somewhat unplanned."

"Wait," Evan said. "What?"

Heidi knew for sure this wasn't how the conversation went in whatever weird dream she'd had. Or was having. She pinched herself to make sure she was wide awake.

"I said this was unplanned."

"Yeah, I heard that, and it sounds like you. But before. About calling me."

"I'll try to call sooner. I've been leaving things until the last minute, and not only when I make a spur of the moment decision."

"What decision was that?"

Heid was taken aback. She hadn't meant to say anything, and now she wasn't sure what she meant by it anyway. She needed some time to work it out in her own head before telling Evan.

"Never mind. For some reason, I don't think today is going to go the way I wanted anyway. I'll figure it all out." At least she hoped she would.

"I really think you can. You're good at this, Heidi, even if you get a bit intense."

Heidi smiled in spite of how off-kilter she felt. "That's the nicest thing you've said to me in a while." She sucked in a breath. She'd said that to dream-Evan; she was sure of it.

"I'll work on helping out more often," Evan said. "As long as I know when I'm needed."

He ended the call, and Heidi threw her phone onto the passenger seat. She sighed. Same old Evan, then. He wanted her to track everything, plan everything, organize everything. He could pop in when a window of opportunity appeared. It was no wonder she hadn't asked him sooner.

There was nothing to do but give today her best shot. She made a mental list: get to the park, pop the question, watch Kate's game, pick Max up from rehearsal, and have Jilly at her recital. If she made it through all that, her reward was the Leather Anvil concert at the Festival. And maybe, a tiny voice said, seeing Angel. She cut that thought off at the knees. Whoever Malcolm was, Heidi intended to give him her attention, not a radio DJ she had notions of having met in the park. Nothing, not even a cute radio DJ, was going to stand in the way of making this all work.

***

II

As it turned out, Heidi did not have a plan. Not in the slightest.

Whether it was because she was late or for some other reason, Malcolm never showed up at the park. He didn't text her either, not that Heidi would've noticed or cared. She was focused on getting to Kate's game, for which she was also late—and wet. Somehow, she'd known she needed her umbrella, and yet she'd still left it in the car.

Heidi stood at the edge of the tent, shivering and avoiding the other parents. For some reason, she especially didn't want to talk to Hot Tom, the man now surrounded by a gaggle of flirty parents of various genders. She barely registered Kate's home run before taking off to pick up Max.

Inside the school, Heidi continued her plan to distance herself from other humans. She paced while she waited for the rehearsal to end. Giving in, she texted Evan instead, begging him to pick up Jilly. She was lucky he said yes with only a few choice words in response. Jilly would still be late, but not as late as if she'd had to wait for Heidi.

She didn't give Max a choice and dragged him away from his friend Kayla. Her relationship with her would-be fiancé wasn't the only thing she'd forgotten that day. Max reminded her about buying a couple of costume pieces and then spent the drive to Park Ave whining about how he was going to be in trouble and how he'd rather have gone shopping with Kayla and her mom. By the time they pulled into the parking lot, Heidi wished she'd sent him with them.

She slid into her seat with a scowling Max at her side. Several rows up, she spotted Evan. He turned around, and Heidi tried to shrink into herself. Too late. Evan spotted her and a frown creased his brow briefly before he saw Max and his features relaxed. Heidi sighed, and the woman in front of her turned around to glare.

Only two more students played. Heidi was horrified to realize she'd missed Jilly. There was a small chance Jilly had been too focused on performing to notice, and Heidi clung to that hope as people began moving into the reception room.

No such luck. Jilly spotted her and in a flash was at her side. "Mom! You missed it."

"I—" Heidi's tongue stuck.

Jilly rolled her eyes. "You could've just said you weren't coming. Dad said you'd be here when he picked me up."

"I really did mean to be, but Max's rehearsal went over."

Turning to Max, Jilly said, "Why are you here?"

"Mom made me." Max shrugged. "I'm gonna get a cookie."

"Me too."

Cookies. Another thing Heidi had forgotten. Every family was supposed to supply some for the reception. Maybe Evan and Jen had brought something. Knowing Jen, probably pretentious, homemade cookies, not the store-bought ones Heidi would've supplied if she'd remembered.

Well, nothing for it except to eat a cookie, say something nice to Jilly's teacher, and drag the kids home. For some reason, she was no longer looking forward to seeing Malcolm or watching the Leather Anvil concert.

***

III

Heidi was supposed to meet Malcolm at the food tent, but he was nowhere to be found. No texts or voicemails, either. She scowled at her phone, willing it to ring. Or maybe not. Did she want to meet Malcolm at all? According to her short-circuiting memories, she didn't know anything about him.

She perused her options inside the tent and finally settled on grabbing something from Tahou's. The greasy mess of potatoes, mac salad, and meat wasn't something she would ordinarily eat, but nothing else looked any more appealing. She dumped some Frank's Red Hot on top, closed the container, and carried it to a picnic table.

A family with a baby and a toddler were already seated at the other end. They looked familiar, but Heidi couldn't place where she knew them from. Maybe they were family members of one of the kids' friends.

The tag-team tactics of the parents as they fed the children reminded Heidi of when she and Evan did the same with their little ones. It brought on a surge of memories, good and bad. Their relationship hadn't always been as bitter and distant as it was now.

Heidi stared down at her food and took a halfhearted bite. It was already starting to go cold, the grease congealing. Tahou's really was much better with a lot of alcohol first. She'd gotten a Genesee Cream Ale, but it wasn't quite the same as being half-drunk and giggling through a plate with...Malcolm. Right. That must've been why she'd ordered from there in the first place. Her brain helpfully supplied that Malcolm loved a red hots plate, mac salad and home fries, smothered in hot sauce.

Heidi distinctly did not and regretted everything except the Genny. She managed a few more bites before giving in and tossing the rest. She paused a little way from the table, still watching the young family. The mother looked up at her and smiled before popping another bite into the baby's mouth. Whatever she was feeding the infant looked much more appetizing than what Heidi'd attempted to eat.

Malcolm still hadn't called or texted, and Heidi didn't care. She was worn out from a day of driving around, and all she wanted was to watch Leather Anvil and collect her thoughts. They were on stage, playing their first song. Heidi swayed to the music, her plastic cup of Genny still in her hand. She and Evan both liked Leather Anvil, and listening to them made her miss him in a way she hadn't done in years. She wondered if he and Jen ever danced to them in the moonlight, enjoying a rare child-free evening.

Heidi swallowed around the lump in her throat. She didn't know whether the rush of emotions was from the long day, her fight with Evan, being stood up, or something else entirely. In any case, she couldn't stay and allow the music to bring up infinite painful memories.

She wandered over toward the vendor tents even though she didn't have much money and no idea what she would purchase if she did. In the first one, a woman was selling handmade jewelry. Heidi admired her skill as she browsed. When she came across a pair of black plugs with rainbow birds, she had a sudden urge to buy them.

Once she had them in the bag and was outside the tent, she stood on the pavement and tried to figure out what had come over her. She didn't wear plugs, and no one she knew did either. Or did they? A vision of Angel Flores came to mind, but Heidi didn't know whether she wore anything like that or not. She'd only ever seen Angel's professional photos on the side of the city bus. At least, she thought that's the only time she'd seen her. So why did a new image appear in her mind's eye of a Leather Anvil T-shirt and a rainbow beanie?

Heidi was sure she was losing it because not only did she recall Angel in that beanie, she also had a flash of memory of the two of them dancing to Leather Anvil as the evening darkened. That couldn't be right. It must've been something Heidi dreamed, though she couldn't fathom why.

She wasn't paying attention to the fact that she was in the middle of foot traffic until someone yelled, "Watch it, lady!" and shoved into her from behind. Heidi went sprawling, bashing her knee and elbow and striking her head as she rolled away from the main path. She curled in on herself to avoid being hit a second time.

Strong hands gripped her, and Heidi pushed up from the ground to assist her rescuer. She flopped onto the grass and tried to clear her head so she could thank the person. When the dizziness faded enough to look around, she saw Angel Flores sitting toe-to-toe with her. Heidi almost passed out for real.

"Hey," Angel said. "Are you okay?"

Heidi put a hand to hear head. Everything felt normal, and there was no blood when she pulled her fingers away. "Yeah," she said. "I think so."

"Can you stand?" Angel rose to her feet and held out a hand.

Heidi hesitated, wondering if the déjà vu was from the bump on her head or her dream. When she finally let Angel pull her up, she almost passed out again. Angel wore a knitted rainbow beanie over her dark hair, and she had a full row of earrings down each ear, ending in tunnels in her lobes. Her black T-shirt bore Leather Anvil's logo, and the sleeve hid the top of her branching tattoo.

"Whoa, there." Angel caught her as she swooned. "Sure you're all right?"

"F-fine. Yep." Heidi nodded, closing her eyes and trying to clear the fog from her brain.

"Maybe a little walk?" Angel suggested.

"Good idea." Anything to avoid having to think about what was going on.

"I need to tell the others where I'm going." Angel smiled with her matte purple lips. "Come with me for a sec."

They stopped at the Leather Anvil booth, and Angel pulled two bottles of water out of a cooler at the back. She handed one to Heidi and unscrewed the top on the other. Heidi took a long drink, and the cool liquid soothed her.

"I'm Angel, by the way."

Heidi stared at Angel's outstretched hand for a moment before accepting it. "Heidi. And I do know who you are. From the radio."

"Right." Another bright smile.

"You look different, though." Heidi clamped her mouth shut. That wasn't the most tactful thing she could've said. Maybe either the Genny or the whack to her head had loosened her tongue.

Angel only laughed. "Those head shots for the bus are awful. I look like a Rachel Maddow wannabe. It's so not my style or even how I dress for work." She looked down at herself. "Neither is this, but I definitely don't look like I'm going to the office."

"Whose idea was that?" Heidi wrinkled her nose.

"The station's. Who even knows why? We play alt-rock. It's not like it's somehow going to gain more listeners if they think we groove to Badflower or The Things We Were in power suits."

Heidi giggled. "I'd think maybe the opposite."

Angel shrugged. "It doesn't seem to matter either way."

"True. I listen every morning on my way to work."

"Oh?" Angel's eyebrows rose slowly. "Well, that's at least one, then."

Heidi frowned. "Not a popular station?"

"We used to be. Announcing the Lilac Parade was a way to put us back on people's radar, I guess." Angel shook her head. "Listen to me, going on about it to a total stranger." She reached out as though she wanted to touch Heidi's head. "And you with this bump. Ignore me. My job is usually great."

You're great, Heidi wanted to say.

Angel burst out laughing. "Glad you think so."

Oops. "Did I say that out loud?"

"You did. Don't worry—I'll chalk it up to that goose egg you've got growing there."

The two of them walked in the opposite direction of the main stage, toward the hill where the children's concert was going on. They sat on a bench, and Heidi sighed. What a way to end a perfectly miserable day.

"Hurts?" Angel asked, breaking into Heidi's melancholy.

"Not really. Or...not my head, at least."

"I saw you bashed your leg, too. Need some ice?"

"No, it's not that." Heidi fiddled with her water bottle. "It fits, hitting my head. One more thing to add to my list of why today sucks."

"Want to talk about it?"

Did she? Angel was a stranger, despite Heidi's familiarity with her voice. She supposed it couldn't hurt. Certainly wouldn't make things worse than they already were. And if Heidi was right, this was probably all a long, strange dream anyway. Telling Dream-Angel about what had gone wrong might make it all go away.

"I messed everything up. Some of it was definitely my fault, like calling my ex-husband to yell at him last night and then arguing again today. And barely getting my kids where they needed to be and missing my youngest's viola recital. But who even knows where my date ended up?" Heidi didn't add not exactly knowing who her date was.

"Sounds like you need a break."

"A...break. Yeah." Heidi huffed. "I'd love one, but someone seems to need me every minute of every day."

"Do they?" Angel tilted her head.

This was an argument Heidi remembered having, although the face attached to the other side was hazy. She'd certainly fought with Evan about it, mostly yelling at him to do his part. It had definitely come up while dating, and her commitment to her kids was a deal-breaker for some. It seemed that's what had happened tonight with...Malcolm. Right.

"My kids have always come first, but it feels lately like I'm failing even them."

Angel nodded. "I don't have kids, but my brother and sister-in-law do. I see this with them, and there's two of them to manage it. Must be harder when you're on your own."

"It is, but..." Heidi pursed her lips, considering how to phrase it. "There's so much judgment and competition. I'm supposed to give my kids all the advantages I never had and also prove I can manage it all."

"Wow. That's a lot to take on."

Heidi nodded, not trusting herself to speak without crying. She blinked, trying to clear the sting in her eyes.

"Can I offer you some advice?" Angel held up a hand. "You don't have to take it. This is from seeing what my brother and his wife go through."

"Uh." Heidi cleared her throat. "Sure."

"Say no sometimes. To anyone, not only your kids."

"I've tried!" Heidi threw her hands up in frustration. "It doesn't work."

"Because you always go back on your no the minute anyone complains?"

Heidi was about to disagree, but Angel was right. Heidi was in her current mess because she hadn't said no. She'd taken on everything she thought she should, and everyone had lost—including herself.

"I don't know how to stop," Heidi whispered.

Angel laid a hand on her arm. "It took my brother a long time before he figured out he didn't have to be someone else's idea of a perfect father."

Heidi wanted to ask how he did it, how he found balance and changed his perspective, but she didn't get a chance. Angel stood and held out her hand again. Heidi accepted it and got to her feet slowly in case she felt dizzy. Everything seemed okay, so she nodded at the unasked question she saw in Angel's expression.

"I'm good," she said. "Nothing I can't cure by going home and resting."

"I'm glad. I need to get back to the booth," Angel said and began walking, Heidi at her side. "They were probably expecting me sooner, but...well, I was enjoying sitting here with you, to be honest."

"Even though I, a total stranger, dumped all my problems on you? I hope they don't dock your pay."

"Oh, I don't get paid for this, so don't worry."

"No? I figured managing the band was a side job or something."

"Not at all. Martina's a friend, so I help her out with this. And I'm not her manager."

Heidi's mouth dropped open. "I should've figured you knew Leather Anvil. That's so cool."

"Maybe someday I'll get the chance to introduce you." They'd arrived back at the Leather Anvil booth, and Angel slid behind the table. "Here. For now, take this, on the house." She handed Heidi a CD—*Sonic Pixie Dream Girls*.

Heidi stared at it for several seconds. She looked down at the bag she still had clutched in her hand then thrust it at Angel. "For taking care of me after I fainted and for the CD." Heat flooded Heidi's cheeks, and her whole body tingled pleasantly with nerves. She had no idea what she was doing, only that it felt right.

Angel opened the bag, pulled out the jewelry box, and popped the lid. "I love these! They're the ones I saw earlier and planned to come back for, but they weren't in my budget."

Heidi didn't want the evening to end, but she had to go home to the kids. Had to explain everything and make it up to them somehow.

"Are you okay?" Angel tilted her head.

"I will be, as soon as I face the consequences of my screw-ups today."

"Don't forget what I said."

Angel glanced at the ground and bent over. She came back up with a sprig of lilacs. Heidi marveled at how it hadn't been trampled by passing traffic. Angel handed it to Heidi with a smile.

"I just wish…" Heidi clammed up, having another flash of memory. Not this time. She wasn't going to say it.

"What do you wish?"

Heidi shook her head. "Nothing."

"No, go on," Angel prompted.

It was almost like Heidi's mouth worked of its own accord, without her permission. She couldn't stop the words that tumbled out. "I wish I could do my day over."

Angel wrapped her fingers around Heidi's hand with the lilacs in it. "Make your wish again."

Heidi laughed, the sound high and hysterical. "That's dandelions, not…" She'd said it before, maybe multiple times. In her bizarre dream, of course. Even so, the word popped out. "…lilacs."

Angel shrugged. "I think it works with lilacs too. Especially on the first day of the Festival."

Heidi closed her eyes. She could at least pretend to wish. That's what she intended, anyway, but the words floated around in her skull, like trying not to think of an elephant.

"Did you do it?" Angel asked. When Heidi nodded, she said, "Now, blow on it, or it won't come true."

Heidi did so, startled when she once again caught the sweet scent of lilacs as if the whole park were in bloom.

Angel put a hand on Heidi's shoulder, her cheeks pink. "Maybe call me when you find your balance."

She turned away to help someone who had come to look at the merch, and Heidi watched her for another moment or two before heading for her car.

***

<h2 style="text-align:center">IV</h2>

When Heidi arrived home, she closed the door and leaned against it with her eyes shut. She had to process the evening before speaking with anyone else. If she couldn't see them, she could pretend they weren't there for five minutes until she gathered her wits. She smelled the reheated enchiladas from the previous night. Good; that meant Kate had fed everyone.

Heidi pushed off the door and stepped into the kitchen. She rifled through the mail Kate had left on the table, set it back down without making any sense of it, and checked to see if the kids had cleaned up after themselves. They had not. With a deep sigh, Heidi rolled up her sleeves and turned on the tap. When she finished, she turned around and was startled to see Kate sitting at the table.

Hoping to stay casual, Heidi said, "Did you find a dress today?" She cringed at the familiar crawling sensation of having asked that before, probably more than once.

"Yeah."

"Nice game today."

"Whatever."

"No, really. I did see your home run. I had to leave before I could tell you."

Kate's eyebrows shot up. "You did?"

"Yep."

Kate eyed her suspiciously. "Okay. But both Max and Jilly are mad at you, so obviously something happened."

"I dragged Max to the recital, but we missed Jilly and forgot to bring cookies. Don't worry. Karma got me later."

"Uh...what?"

Heidi pinched the bridge of her nose. "Malcolm stood me up. I'm not even sure I care, to be honest."

"I gotta say, Mom, I was surprised you were getting married. You never seemed that into him."

"Clearly he felt the same."

"Sorry."

Kate stared at her lap, her lower lip drawn in. Like everything else, this was familiar-but-not. Heidi reached into her flawed memory, hoping to find a clue, but she came up empty. While she was thinking, Kate started speaking again, still not making eye contact.

"Sometimes it feels like our activities are more important than we are." Kate finally peered up at Heidi. "It's like...like you think we need to be perfect so you look better."

That sounded remarkably similar to what Angel had said. Heidi sighed. She was going to protest, but both Angel and Kate were at least partly right. "I suppose that's true, in a sense. Not the way you mean it but because I wanted to show everyone I was good enough at parenting. That I could plan for your futures and set you up for better than what I had."

"That's just it," Kate said. "You're really good at 'planning for our futures,'" she made air quotes, "but you suck at doing things that matter right now. You schedule us so hard you can't even show up. And I'm not even sure I want to *go* to college."

Heidi waited for the shock to hit her, but she only felt calm, as if she'd known Kate would say that. "I suspected." She frowned. "Did you already tell me that and I forgot?"

"N-no," Kate said. Her face had gone pale. "Were you snooping in my phone?"

"No! Of course not."

"I only told a couple of my friends." Kate looked down. "I hope you're not too mad."

"Maybe? I don't know. I need time to absorb this. You have a scholarship. Mostly I'm upset that you…" Heidi paused. She'd been about to say Kate hadn't told her, but now she wasn't sure which end was up anymore. "I'm sorry, I'm really confused right now." To add insult to injury, Heidi's memories fractured again, and she was sure she'd said the same thing before. "It's been a weird day. Do you think we could talk about it tomorrow?"

"We're not going to get anywhere different by waiting. You can't make me go just because you wish you had."

"You're right, I can't. And we need to talk about this more, but *not now*. Please."

"And you won't save up all the yelling for later?"

"Cross my heart. I want to wait to talk so I can listen better."

Kate nodded and stood. After one last puzzled glance at Heidi, she headed for her room. Heidi made herself tea and took it to the sofa. She picked up the TV remote but put it back down again. Instead, she set down her mug and retrieved the *Sonic Pixie Dream Girls* CD from where she'd left it in the kitchen. She opened it and saw a lilac-colored business card tucked into it: Angel Flores, Lilac City Social Media Management. Under the phone number, Angel had written, "Call me sometime."

Heidi smelled lilacs again, maybe from the card, but the scent faded quickly. She wanted to call Angel right away, maybe ask her advice on what to do about Kate, but it was already after ten. She settled for adding the number to her contacts and took out her phone. As she hit the "plus" sign for a new contact, the crawling sensation was back. As soon as Heidi began entering Angel's name, it popped up. The number was already in her phone.

Heidi almost screamed, dropping her phone and clapping a hand over her mouth so she wouldn't wake the kids. This was one thing too many to be a coincidence, but Heidi had no ability to piece it together. She picked her phone off the carpet, set it on the coffee table next to her mug, and went to bed. She could deal with it in the morning, unless she got lucky and it all disappeared by then.

DAY SIX

I

The smell of coffee from the automatic pot woke Heidi from a deep sleep. She stirred restlessly, vaguely recalling that she'd been dreaming—something about a woman with brown hair and eyes. There was something compelling and familiar about her. Heidi threw an arm over her eyes to protect them while she opened them slowly. She already had a headache.

She tried to hang onto the dream, but was already gone. Even so, she knew for sure she'd had the same one before, just as surely as she knew she needed to turn on the radio on her bedside table. She had to hear Angel Flores's voice.

"Goooooood morning, Rochester! We're live here at the Lilac Festival, where the parade begins in less than a half hour!"

Heidi didn't have to wonder what it was she was supposed to be doing or whether she'd make it on time. Like with the dream, she was one hundred percent certain she was about to be late to propose. Given that, she decided to stay in bed a few extra minutes and collect her thoughts. At least, collect them to the degree her throbbing head allowed.

Maybe she didn't have to do this. She'd been in the same position before, leaving everyone—including herself—angry and disappointed. Skipping this one thing in order to make sure she did right by her kids would be fine.

Heidi sat bolt upright. Where had that thought come from? How could she have done this before? She tried to puzzle it out despite her still-sleepy, hangover-hazy brain. The only thing she found was a string of names: Cass.

Tom. Benji. Dominic. They repeated themselves over and over. Cass-Tom-Benji-Dominic. Cass-Tom-Benji-Dominic. People she knew, some better than others. People she'd met at her kids' activities.

People she'd proposed to.

That made no sense. And yet, Heidi remembered it clear as day. Or clear as a recurring dream, perhaps. None of them had worked out. So maybe that meant today was supposed to go differently, even if she had no idea what name to attach to the proposal she was about to postpone.

Heidi shoved the covers down and rolled out of bed. She carefully selected her clothes, wanting to reflect how she dressed when not in her work uniform. She somehow didn't feel the need to dress up, not if she wasn't on her way to the park to propose.

She paused with her violet button-up in her hand. Two people came to mind. The first was Cass, Jilly's viola teacher. Heidi recalled having a crush on her for a long time. She'd moved on, but dreaming about her brought the feelings back up. Guilt, too. She shouldn't be thinking about a beautiful, sweet woman if she was meant to propose to someone else. She knew instinctively it wasn't Cass she was supposed to meet.

The second person who randomly flashed through her mind was Angel Flores, the morning show DJ who was announcing the parade on WNDR. Not the Angel whose face was plastered on city buses but the one who wore a rainbow beanie and a Leather Anvil T-shirt. Heidi frowned at her reflection. How had she known that?

Right. Recurring nightmare of reliving the same day. Or was she, in actual fact, reliving the same day? A never-ending loop of trying to make things work in the wrong ways and with the wrong people. Somehow, she had to figure it out.

She tucked a lip gloss in her jeans pocket and fished the ring box out of her underwear drawer. She left her bed unmade and went into the kitchen for her cup of coffee.

Kate was at the table, filling out graduation invitations with her careful, neat handwriting. She looked up when Heidi entered.

"Sending these out today?" Heidi asked, then mentally smacked herself for not stopping the words before they left her mouth. She had to be careful not to repeat everything about the day, including what she said to people and when.

Kate nodded. "It's in six weeks. These have to go out as soon as possible."

"Of course. Want me to mail them?"

"Uh...Sure?" Kate blinked. "But...weren't you going to the park this morning?"

"No. I decided to wait until later, when I can relax. Let's get you kids through your stuff, and then I'll take care of mine."

A sly grin blossomed on Kate's face, and Heidi braced herself. It was incredibly weird, knowing what someone was about to say before they said it. "You mean proposing? Today's the big day. I can't wait to hear all about it."

"Yes. Um...?" She was blanking on a name. That was probably either the hangover or the fact that she knew she'd done this several times already. Names were hard.

"Michelle?" Kate prompted.

Ah, that was it. Eventually, she knew the memories would hit. Distorted, far away as if in a tunnel, or belonging to some other life, but they'd be there. Michelle clearly meant something to everyone else. Heidi would pull up her contact information as soon as she had her coffee. She would text and explain why she couldn't meet her, and everything would be fine.

"You're taking Max with you, right? And I'm getting him later."

"Yes, he can ride with me to school in a bit. But I thought you were supposed to ask Dad to get him because you need to take Jilly to the recital."

Heidi groaned. The one thing she recalled perfectly was her stupid drunk-dial to Evan. Instead of asking him to pick up Max, she'd yelled at him. "I forgot."

"You...forgot." Kate stared at her.

"I was kind of busy telling him everything I hate about him." And his wife, but Heidi didn't want to cause any more problems than she already had.

"Can you two figure this out before graduation? I'd like you both there, but not like this."

"Don't worry. I'll call and apologize at some point. But I can handle it with Max."

"Cool. Are you coming to the game?"

"I wouldn't miss it." Heidi bent and kissed the top of Kate's head, glad that was one thing she'd be able to fix about all the versions of today she'd tried so far. "We'll catch up tonight. I'm going to call Michelle and suggest just dinner and the concert."

Kate wished her luck, and Heidi took her coffee into her room. She closed the door and set her mug on the bedside table. Once she was seated, she scrolled her contacts to find anyone named Michelle. Lucky for her, there was only one, and she could see right away she had the right person.

Michelle answered on the first ring. "Hey."

"Hi, sweetheart. I'm so sorry to cancel on you, but I forgot about Kate's game. How about if we meet up later at the concert?"

There was a long, long pause. "What concert?"

Now it was Heidi's turn for silence. She knew for sure that was how this went: A missed proposal, running around all day, things screwed up, and then...damn it. Every time, the person she was supposed to propose to backed out at the concert.

Heidi cleared her throat. "Leather Anvil. At the Lilac Festival. You know, greasy festival food from a truck, crowded picnic tables, and sitting in the grass like college kids to watch local musicians. Dream date."

"Oh." There was something soft and dreamy in that one syllable. "It does sound really nice."

Finally, Heidi was with someone else who shared her taste in music. "So are we on? For some reason, I thought we'd already planned this."

"We hadn't, but I'd love to."

"Great! Five-thirty, then?"

"Perfect. Heidi, this is amazing. I've been wanting to see Leather Anvil, and this is going to be so much better than trying to meet up during the stupid parade."

Heidi laughed. "I know, right? Okay. Love you, and I'll see you later."

She ended the call, feeling relieved. She could definitely do this. Stretching out on the bed, Heidi dozed, forgetting about her coffee, until she heard the door open and close. Max and Kate, on their way to the school. Heidi roused herself and made the bed. Well, look at that: one thing that was different from before. Two, if she counted postponing the proposal.

That only left apologizing to Evan. Heidi sighed and pulled out her phone again. She hit Evan's number and put the phone to her ear.

"Morning, sunshine," Evan said when he answered.

Evan's sarcasm annoyed her, but she pressed on. "Hey. I'm really sorry about last night."

"Last night?" Evan paused. "Ah, right. When you said we stopped caring about the kids the minute we had a mini-Jen. Although I don't think you actually used her name. Didn't you call her—"

"I did, and I'm sorry." She was sorry to Evan, anyway, not necessarily to Jen. But he didn't need to know that.

Evan huffed. "Apology accepted. Now, what is it you need?"

"Nothing," Heidi said. "That's really why I called."

"Oh. Uh...okay."

"I might as well tell you the truth. I was supposed to call you last night and ask you to pick Max up from rehearsal. But...you have something today? And I skipped my morning plans. I'm going to Kate's game, but I can leave early, get Jilly, and bring Max with us. So we'll see you at the recital?"

"Wait," Evan said. "What?"

Another thing Heidi had changed. She had a plan. It would be perfect. No mistakes. "I said we'll see you at the recital."

"Yeah, I heard that, and it sounds like you. But before. About calling me."

"I was going to, but I decided it's fine and I should just apologize."

"You had plans, and you changed them? Are you okay?"

"As far as I know, other than this damn headache. I'm never drinking again."

Evan laughed, and it was nice to hear that sound instead of another angry huff. "You were never able to hold your alcohol, were you?"

"Not a bit."

"I'm glad things are okay. We should talk later. You're good at this, Heidi, even if you get a bit intense sometimes." He paused. "Maybe I should be too."

Well, look at that. She and Evan could be civil. She added another tally mark to her "fixed it" column. Could this day get any better?

"I'll make you a deal," she said.

"What's that?"

"I'll call you sooner, and you can help out a bit more."

"I like it. Have a great day, Heids. See you and the kids later."

He ended the call, and Heidi tucked her phone away. He hadn't called her by that nickname in years. She hoped that was a good indication of how the day was about to go.

Heidi made a mental list: watch Kate's game, pick up Jilly, get Max from rehearsal, and make it downtown for the recital. That was doable. She stood and looked herself over in the mirror. She really should've used her extra time to shower, but she looked all right. Perfect for a day of running and a concert in the park, anyway. She fluffed her hair and then paused.

If this was all so perfect, then why couldn't she get both Cass and Angel out of her mind?

She shook her head. Now was not the time to ask questions. It was the time for action, something Heidi was good at—Evan had said so, and Heidi knew it to be true. She left her coffee on her bedside table. Who needed it? She felt good as she walked out the door and into her day.

***

II

Heidi's plan was fail-proof. On her way to Kate's game, she recited the steps over and over in her head: *Watch the game. Get Max. Attend the recital.* She had disjointed memories of doing it all ass-backwards before in her jumbled dreams and flashes of déjà vu. Well, not this time. Something told her Kate was going to have a big moment at the game that she shouldn't miss, and she had to get Jilly *before* picking up Max. Yes, that would do the trick.

Armed with her agenda, Heidi dashed from her car to the team tent. Her focus was on Kate, not on how wet she'd gotten, her hair drying into a frizzy mess, or Hot Tom, who was currently in charge of water bottles and orange wedges. Sure enough, Heidi was right there to cheer for Kate after her big, game-saving home run.

After the game, Heidi gave Kate a big, damp hug and wished her well with prom dress hunting. She made it home with less than fifteen minutes to spare before having to get Max, although something told her she'd be fine. His rehearsal was going to go over the scheduled end, so she relaxed and dried her hair while waiting for Jilly to change.

Jilly had protested, of course. She'd wanted the last few minutes before having to be ready. Heidi convinced her this was for the best so they wouldn't be late. By carefully calculating the amount of time needed for each step, Heidi managed to have the schedule planned down to the minute. Jilly was going to have to fit herself into the agenda.

At the school, Heidi tapped her fingers on the steering wheel. She didn't have time to spare to go inside the school. Instead, she texted Max and told him to get his butt out to the car the minute rehearsal ended.

When he arrived at the car, he opened his mouth to say something, but Heidi shushed him. "Get in. We need to have Jilly to the recital in—" she looked at the car's clock "—fifteen minutes." And it was an eighteen-minute drive.

Max turned his body toward the window, scowling and with his arms crossed. Heidi didn't have time to deal with his epic pouting session. He could attend his sister's recital without complaining for once.

With a minute to spare, thanks to her lead foot, Heidi's tires squealed on the way into the parking lot at the rear of the Park Avenue studio. Max threatened to stay in the car, but Heidi ignored him and opened his door. The three of them tumbled into the building, and an older student whisked Jilly away to the warm-up room. Heidi sank into a seat, breathing a sigh of relief despite the glower Max shot her.

Jilly played beautifully, of course. When she began, Heidi caught sight of Evan and Jen, a few rows up. Evan had slid out of his seat to crouch in the aisle with a camera. Of course he would record it. Heidi had her phone, but it hadn't occurred to her to make a video. Well, whatever. Evan could have this one moment to be a perfect dad. Heidi had succeeded at everything else, so she was feeling generous.

Everything, that was, except one teeny, tiny detail.

When the recital was over, all the families were invited to join Cass and the students for a reception. The same one Heidi was supposed to supply cookies for like all the other parents. She groaned, and Max eyed her.

"What?" he asked.

"I forgot to bring cookies."

Max shrugged. "I'll bet Dad and Jen brought some. Jen makes awesome peanut butter chocolate chip cookies."

Because of course she did. Even if Heidi had remembered, she'd have picked something up from Wegmans, not made them herself. Before she could respond to Max, Jilly bounded up.

"Hi, Mom!" She was grinning, and it made Heidi happy she'd been able to finally see her play.

Wait...that wasn't right. Heidi had seen her recitals lots of times. Where had that thought come from? She shook her head. Clearly, she needed more sleep.

"You were pretty good," Max said. High praise indeed.

"Thanks! Wanna go get a cookie with me?"

"Yeah, okay."

Heidi watched them go, waiting a minute before following them into the other room. She should say something to Cass, but her mind was already three steps ahead. She had to get the kids home, change her clothes, and make it to Highland Park to meet Michelle and see Leather Anvil. She could do this. Already her day hadn't been bad, simply crowded. Taking a deep breath, Heidi made her way to Cass to congratulate her on the recital.

***

III

Heidi was running late, but she met Michelle at the food tent, and they took their curry outside. It looked and smelled amazing when she opened the styrofoam box. The day hadn't been *perfect*-perfect, but it had been nearly as good as. A little awkwardness getting every place she needed to be, and a bit of a kerfuffle over Max's costume pieces after she and the kids arrived home, but otherwise not bad. Heidi felt accomplished. Two of her three kids had experienced triumph as well, and she'd promised Max to take him shopping the next day even if it was Mother's Day. Besides, that would give her some time alone with him. All she had to do was make sure to do the same for the others.

She glanced up when Michelle sat across from her, and out of the corner of her eye, she spotted a family with a baby and a toddler. They looked vaguely familiar, but hell if Heidi could place them. The family looked happy and relaxed. It reminded Heidi of the good years with Evan, when they'd taken the kids all over in hopes of giving them a lot of good memories.

Heidi returned her attention to the present, to Michelle. To the woman who was enjoying her curry and talking excitedly about the concert. It was too bad Heidi's memory wasn't functioning; she couldn't even recall how they'd met. Heidi felt...nothing. Her heart was a blank slate when it came to Michelle. Yet here she was, supposedly about to propose to her.

She patted her pocket where she'd put the ring after changing. It felt heavy, as if it were weighing her down. Michelle smiled and tilted her head in question, but Heidi didn't have an answer. In fact, she didn't have anything at all to say to Michelle.

This wasn't how the day was supposed to end. Any minute, Heidi would think of something to say. She would propose, Michelle would say yes, and they would go dance to Leather Anvil until the sun went down. This was the exact moment Heidi's brain chose to supply her with the name of the other band: Generation Xerox, a 90s cover band. For no good reason, Heidi remembered that Cass liked them, and she wondered if Jilly's viola teacher was somewhere in the crowd.

Heidi shook her head. That wasn't an appropriate thought to have when she was seated across from her would-be fiancée, enjoying some really good curry. Once again, Heidi opened her mouth, but no words came out.

"You seem distracted," Michelle said. "Everything okay?"

She sounded hopeful, as if she knew Heidi had been planning this day to be special for the two of them. When Heidi's tongue finally loosened, the exact wrong words came out. "I think we should...break up." She cringed and clapped a hand over her mouth, wishing she could ram the sentence back in.

"Oh." Michelle stared at her. "I wasn't expecting that."

Neither was I, Heidi thought. "I'm sorry. I—"

Michelle pushed the rest of her dinner away. "I should go."

And that was it. Heidi put her head in her hands. Out of the corner of her eye, she spotted the young mother. She'd paused with the spoon halfway to her baby's lips and was peering at Heidi. It was impossible to tell if her expression was sympathetic or reproachful. Heidi shrugged, and the woman turned away.

Not much to do except clean up from the meal, which gave Heidi twenty seconds of something to focus on other than how she'd ruined a great day. What was she supposed to do, though? Pretend she had enough feelings for Michelle to marry her? That would go about as well as her marriage to Evan. They would end up resenting each other. Regardless of whether she loved Michelle, Heidi knew no one deserved to live like that. Michelle should be with someone who could give themselves fully to the relationship.

With a heavy sigh, Heidi trudged toward the vendor tents. The first one was jewelry, and Heidi browsed the selection of earrings. She spotted a beautiful pair of black plugs, hand-painted with rainbow birds. If Heidi had been with Michelle, she'd have bought them for her. As it was, they only made Heidi sad about not having anyone to give them to.

Head down, Heidi ducked out of the tent. She was so absorbed in her own thoughts that she didn't see the big man until he rammed into her with an angry, "Watch it, lady!" She flew backwards, smacking her head into a stand full of handmade hats and scarves. Her ears rang, and the sounds of the crowd became muffled. Heidi covered her head and sank down, shrinking against the hat rack.

"Hey, back off!" someone yelled.

The space around Heidi cleared, and she slowly lowered her arms.

Standing over her, face in shadow, was someone in a rainbow beanie. Heidi wasn't sure if it was due to hitting her head or because of her mangled memories, but the beanie looked familiar. She squinted, trying to place its owner.

"You okay?" Beanie extended a hand to Heidi, who accepted it and rose awkwardly to her feet.

"I'm fine. A little stunned, but nothing too bad."

Beanie pulled Heidi away from the tent, leading her around the back of the vendors. "Wait here."

She returned a moment later with two bottles of water. Heidi opened hers and took a long drink before returning her attention to Beanie. With a start, she realized it was *the* Angel Flores, from the radio—and from Heidi's dream.

"I'm Angel, by the way."

Heidi stared at Angel for a long moment before she could formulate a sentence. "I know who you are." She shook her head. "Sorry. I'm Heidi."

"Nice to meet you." Angel's smile was broad and cheerful. "Wish it could've been under better circumstances."

Heidi laughed. "No kidding. I probably deserved it, though."

"You deserved that guy shoving you?" Angel scrunched her nose; it was cute, Heidi thought.

"Maybe." Heidi shrugged one shoulder and took another sip of water. "I just broke up with someone. She wasn't exactly expecting it. We weren't even fighting or anything."

Angel began walking toward the hill where the children's stage was. "So what went wrong?" She glanced at Heidi. "I'm sorry for prying. You don't have to tell me."

"It's fine. That's the thing—there wasn't anything wrong, and that's exactly it. There wasn't anything right, either. It was...bland. This morning, I thought we were the ideal couple, but tonight, I'm not sure why we were together. Like a perfect Instagram photo, with about as much substance."

Angel nodded. "It's good you realized it, right?"

"I guess. Until a few minutes ago, I thought everything was perfect. Then we were sitting there, eating our curry, and...I don't know."

"Perfect?" Angel's eyebrows shot up. "If it exists, it's overrated."

"Maybe, but it's pretty tempting to aim for it when it feels like everyone's waiting for your next screw-up."

"That seems like a lot to carry around."

They sat on a bench a short way from the children's concert. Heidi didn't recognize the performers. It had been a long time since any of her kids had been young enough to bring them to watch. She took the opportunity to glance over at Angel, noting her black Leather Anvil T-shirt, the vine tattoo peeking out from under the sleeve, and her matte purple lips.

And the plugs in her earlobes. Heidi hadn't realized this was Angel's everyday look.

"You're dressed a bit differently from your picture on the bus," Heidi remarked. When Angel glanced over, a smile lifting one side of her mouth, Heidi flushed. "Sorry."

Angel laughed. "Those head shots for the bus are awful. I look like a Rachel Maddow wannabe. It's so not my style or even how I dress for work." She looked down at herself. "Neither is this, but I definitely don't look like I'm going to the office."

Heidi opened and closed her mouth. She distinctly remembered Angel saying that before. It must've been in an interview or something because Heidi had never met her in person before today. At least, not that she knew of.

"I like this better."

"Me too."

Heidi motioned to Angel's shirt. "You like Leather Anvil?"

It was Angel's turn to blush. "I'm friends with Martina, so I help out sometimes. I'm supposed to be working at the vendor booth right now."

"But you're here with me. I'm sorry." Heidi hung her head.

"Nah, it's fine. There's other volunteers." Angel stood and held out her hand, a gleam in her eyes. "C'mon. I think we could both use some fun."

They headed toward the main stage. For some reason, Angel kept hold of Heidi's hand, and it made her warm despite the cool air. On the hill, a substantial crowd had gathered to hear Leather Anvil—or possibly Generation Xerox and were simply waiting out the opening act. Some were seated on blankets, and others were dancing. A handful of children were running around, laughing.

Angel dragged Heidi into the middle of the dancers, and they joined in the fun. Heidi had a strange memory, like a split-screen, of having done this before. She passed it off as mixing up tonight with a memory of her early years with Evan. It was probably caused by a combination of dealing with her ex and whacking her head.

Leather Anvil began a slower song, and Angel turned Heidi to face her. Angel was shorter, and she had to reach up to put her arms around Heidi's neck. It felt good to sway with the music and not have to think about anything but the rhythm and the person in her arms.

When Angel rested her head on Heidi's shoulder, a prickle worked its way up Heidi's spine. It felt so right and so wrong all at once. Angel was gorgeous and sweet and had taken time out of her evening to tend to Heidi. Yet Heidi had only broken up with Michelle a half hour ago or so. Was she ready to jump into something else? Was Angel even asking, or was this simply her way of helping Heidi feel better?

Heidi pulled back to look at Angel. "I—"

Angel smiled and put a finger to Heidi's lips. "Let's enjoy it for now, okay?"

Heidi could do that. She settled in, wrapping her arms around Angel's waist. She felt the warmth of Angel's body against hers, and she leaned into it. The scent of lilacs rose around her, and she wondered if Angel had purchased some of the perfume from one of the vendors. It faded, though, and Heidi decided it was her imagination.

When the song ended, Heidi walked Angel back to her booth. They passed the jewelry vendor, and on impulse, Heidi said, "Wait here."

She left Angel on the path, looking mystified as Heidi ducked inside. She found the plugs with the rainbow birds and bought them. Somehow, she sensed it was important to do so, though she couldn't have explained why. She returned to the path, pleased to see Angel still there.

"Here," Heidi said. "These are for you. You know, for taking care of me after that fall."

Angel opened the box and stared, open-mouthed, at the plugs. "Oh, I love them! I was going to buy them, but..."

"Not in your budget?" Heidi guessed. She frowned. How had she known that's what Angel was about to say?

"Right," Angel agreed. "Thank you." She leaned in and kissed Heidi's cheek. Angel's face was as red as Heidi assumed her own must be.

They continued to the Leather Anvil booth. The crowd had thinned a bit, and the music coming from the stage stopped. Angel started to step behind the table in the booth but turned around.

"Can I offer you some advice?"

Heidi shrugged. "Sure."

"Maybe you don't need to try so hard to be perfect." Angel laid a hand on Heidi's arm, and the skin tingled where her fingers touched. "My brother learned the hard way how not to be a perfect father. Don't make his mistakes."

Heidi wondered what those were, but she felt it might be overstepping her boundaries to ask. "I'll try."

"Good." Angel smiled. She plucked something off the ground then slid behind the table and reached into a box. Turning back to Heidi, she said, "Here. Take this, on the house. In exchange for the plugs."

She handed two things to Heidi. The first was a CD—*Sonic Pixie Dream Girls*. The second was a sprig of lilacs. Heidi smiled and put the sprig to her nose, wondering how the flowers had stayed so fresh when they'd been lying on the ground.

"Make a wish," Angel said.

Heidi giggled. "That's dandelions, not..." She clamped her lips shut, now one hundred percent certain she'd said that before.

"Not lilacs?" Angel tilted her head. "I think it works with them too.

Especially on the first day of the Festival."

Heidi willed the words not to rise to the front of her mind, but it was useless. Without permission, *I wish I could do this day over* popped into her brain. She huffed.

"Did you do it?" Angel asked. When Heidi nodded, she said, "Now, blow on it, or it won't come true."

Heidi blew gently on the sprig, and she was surrounded by the distinct scent of lilacs. It soothed her.

Angel put a hand on Heidi's shoulder, interrupting her thoughts. "Maybe we'll meet up again sometime."

She turned away, and Heidi watched her helping a couple of people with their purchases. When it was clear Angel was going to be busy for a while, Heidi walked away, still clutching the lilacs.

***

<h3 style="text-align:center">IV</h3>

Heidi was still thinking about the events of the previous couple of hours when she arrived home. She ignored the pile of mail on the table and went straight to the sink, intending to clean up after the kids. She was surprised to find they'd already done it. Max was probably still annoyed with her for making him sit through the recital and not taking him to buy his costume pieces, but at least the kids had made things easy on her. Which was good, considering she now had to tell them she wasn't going to marry Michelle after all.

She peered into the fridge, feeling a little hungry after not having finished her dinner earlier. The kids had eaten the leftover enchiladas, but Heidi located an unopened bag of salad and some ranch dressing. That would do for now. She turned around to set it on the table and was surprised to see Kate already sitting there.

Heidi set the salad and dressing down, grabbed a bowl and fork, and sat across from Kate. She'd be the easiest to start with, but Heidi wasn't ready yet. She stalled by asking, "Did you find a dress today?" The words felt annoyingly familiar, much like many things about the day. Except they couldn't be because Kate had only gone shopping this afternoon.

"Yup! I'll show you if you want."

"I'd love to see. Great game today."

Kate grinned. "It was awesome!" She frowned. "Is everything okay? You're home kinda early."

Heidi's shoulders slumped. "I broke up with Michelle." *And met the most amazing woman, but there's no chance of that going anywhere, even if I hadn't just gotten out of a relationship.*

Kate nodded. "I don't know why, but I had a feeling."

"You did?" Heidi stared at Kate.

"I don't know. It's like..." Kate chewed her lip. "Remember when I had that massive crush on Aidan, and then we tried going out?"

"I do."

"He was...boring. To me, I mean. But he and Nevaeh are, like, the cutest. We had zero chemistry. No, like, spark, you know?"

Heidi nodded. "I remember wondering what happened because he seemed so sweet."

"He *is* sweet. But not at all my type."

"And you think Michelle is like that?"

Kate grimaced. "I hate to say it, but yeah. She was nice, but she didn't, like, fit in with us."

It was true. Michelle hadn't bonded with the kids or spent much time with them. In fact, when Heidi looked back on it, of the few people she'd casually dated, none of them seemed interested in being part of the parenting team. Heidi deflated; she and Evan hadn't exactly been great co-parents either, and now she wondered if their drama had spilled over toward Jen. If so, it was no wonder Jen tried to stay out of things.

Heidi and Kate had fallen silent, and now Heidi noticed Kate wasn't looking at her. She seemed lost in her own thoughts. Heidi reached across the table and put a hand on Kate's.

"Everything okay with you?"

Kate withdrew her hand. "Speaking of not having chemistry..." She trailed off, her shoulders tensing visibly.

"What is it?"

"I'm not sure I want to go to college. At least, not yet."

Heidi opened her mouth, but no sound came out. She closed it and sat there, looking at Kate. She'd known, but she couldn't figure out how. They'd never had this conversation before...had they?

"I know."

"Uh...what?" Kate scrunched her nose.

"I mean, I had a feeling," Heidi corrected. She thought back over the previous few weeks. "You keep ignoring things they send you, and I've had to remind you to fill out forms and such. Deep down, I guessed you weren't excited, but I thought it was nerves."

"Maybe?" Kate picked up one of the pieces of junk mail and fiddled with it. "That's probably it. Never mind." She stood.

"Wait," Heidi said. "Even if it is, we should still talk about this."

"It's fine. I'm burned out, that's all. What do you old people call it? 'Senioritis.'" Kate snorted.

"That's fair," Heidi replied. "Still, there's something behind it. I'd hate to see you waste your scholarship without us talking this through first."

Kate sat back down. "I don't know. I'm tired of all the running around we do. Sometimes it feels like our activities are more important to you than we are." Kate peered up at Heidi. "It's like...like you think we need to be perfect so you look better."

Heidi shook her head. "No, not for me. For you. I wanted to help you plan for your futures and set you up for better than what I had."

"That's just it," Kate said, her voice rising. "You're really good at 'planning for our futures,'" she made air quotes, "but you suck at doing things that matter right now." She sucked in her breath. "I'm sorry!"

"No, don't be," Heidi said. "Today was a pretty good wake-up call. I tried to make it perfect, and I still failed, at least with Michelle. Maybe we need to take some things off your plate."

"I guess that might help." Kate ran a hand through her hair. "I'll stick it out. You're right, and I don't want to waste all that money."

She left the table and headed for her room. The issue seemed to be settled, but Heidi couldn't shake the feeling there was more to it. She would worry about it another time. For now, she was going to check on the kids, make some tea, and flip channels on the TV until she found some cheesy movie to watch.

Within an hour, Jilly was reading in bed, Kate was texting her friends, and Max was asleep with his headphones on. Heidi gently removed them and tiptoed out of the room. She finally made her tea and set it on the table to go through the pile of mail she'd ignored.

She was distracted by the light reflecting off the CD case she'd left there when she went to make dinner. The lilacs had wilted, so Heidi threw them away. When she opened the *Sonic Pixie Dream Girls* case to remove the lyrics sheet, she saw a lilac-colored business card tucked into it: Angel Flores, Lilac City Social Media Management. Under the phone number, Angel had written, "Call me sometime."

Heidi smelled lilacs again and assumed it was the lingering scent of the sprig she'd thrown out. She turned the card over and over, fighting the desire to call Angel immediately. So she hadn't been wrong after all; the dance was an invitation. Heidi thought about calling one of her friends, but she recalled the previous night's celebration and thought better of it. She wasn't ready to reveal Angel to anyone else yet, not even to ask for advice.

Instead, she unlocked her phone to add Angel to the contacts. When she began entering the number, Angel's name came up. Heidi's heart galloped, and her stomach clenched. How in the world had Angel ended up there? Feeling faint, Heidi slumped into a chair. Her hands shook enough she was afraid she was going to drop her phone, so she set it and the business card on the table.

Memories blossomed in Heidi's mind like lilacs blooming in a time-lapse video. She hadn't been wrong about the déjà vu. How many times had she lived this day? Twice? Twenty? A hundred? She didn't know. The only thing she was sure of was that she'd done it more than once, failing every time.

Heidi put her head in her hands. Maybe she would be lucky, and this time she'd managed to unlock the secret. The only thing to do was sleep it off and hope a new day would start in the morning. She dumped her tea in the sink and retreated to bed, leaving her phone and the business card on the table.

Day Seven

I

The smell of coffee from the automatic pot woke Heidi from a deep sleep. She stirred restlessly, vaguely recalling that she'd been dreaming—something about a woman with short brown hair and dark eyes. Heidi had a feeling she knew this woman, but the vision slipped away from her. She kept her eyes shut as she grabbed the pillow from the other side of the bed and put it over her face.

She did not want to be awake. Not that she wanted to be back in the now-fading dream either, but at least that would've meant she didn't have to do her crappy day over again. Because now she knew without a doubt, without even turning on the radio to hear Angel Flores announcing the Lilac Parade, that she was about to do exactly that. She flipped on the radio anyway, mostly to hear Angel's voice.

"Goooooood morning, Rochester! We're live here at the Lilac Festival, where the parade begins in less than a half hour!"

Heidi wondered what she was going to need to change this time around. The pieces had finally fallen into place when she'd gone to bed last night. No, not "last night," precisely, but the last time she'd lived this day. She had vague, disjointed memories of her previous go-arounds, hazy like in a dream world. But they were mingled with her knowledge of the present, and she was having trouble picking the two apart. She sat up and hugged her knees.

A plan. That's what she needed. She had to construct her day. Maybe what hadn't worked before was that she hadn't thought it out properly. She needed a schedule, color-coded and time-stamped. That would do it. She had some paper in the living room.

Heidi slid out of bed and stuck her feet in a pair of slippers. She paused at her bedroom door and glanced back. This didn't feel right, but she couldn't pinpoint what she was forgetting. She shook herself and stepped out.

Kate was at the table, filling out graduation invitations with her careful, neat handwriting. She looked up when Heidi entered.

"Mom?" she said. "You're not dressed."

"I came to get coffee and some paper. What's..." Heidi trailed off. She'd been on the verge of asking about the invitations, even though she knew what they were.

Kate gaped at her. "Graduation? Or did you forget that too?"

"Too?"

"You're supposed to meet Vic in the park. Like, now."

"Oh, god." Heidi pulled out a chair and sat, folding her arms and dropping her head onto them. "I did forget," she mumbled.

"If you hurry, you can still get there." Kate gave Heidi a sly grin when she looked up.

"No. I'm not keeping Vic waiting. I'll call, and then I'll map my day. This has gone wrong far too many times."

"Oooookay..." Kate said, drawing out the word. "If you say so."

Heidi wasn't sure which part Kate was referring to—the phone call, the map, or Heidi's slip about the day. It didn't matter. She stood and returned to the bedroom. One mildly annoyed conversation with Vic later, and Heidi was getting dressed and shoving the ring in her shirt pocket. So much for not meeting up.

She returned to the kitchen in time to see Kate stack the invitations and set them by the door. Kate turned and gave her a once-over.

"You're wearing that?"

"It's fine. I'm in a hurry." Heidi sighed. "I may be late for your game, and I have to leave early to get Max. You gonna be okay?"

"I guess." Kate shrugged. "Wasn't Dad supposed to pick Max up?"

"No." Heidi only wished her memory of drunk-dialing Evan was as hazy as the rest. "I may have called him last night after one too many drinks. I think I called Jen something rude."

"Mom!" Kate flung her hands in the air dramatically. "Can you and Dad please cut it out? I want my graduation to be fun, not a day to babysit the two of you because you can't stop fighting like little kids."

"We'll behave. I promise. I have to go."

"Call Dad and make this right," Kate hissed before she turned and stomped off to her room.

Heidi sighed. Kate was right, but now was not the time. She eventually had to get to Highland Park, and she had to figure out what she was going to do between now and then. She went out to her car to be alone and sat in it for a full five minutes before she made up her mind. She called Evan.

"Morning, sunshine," he said when he answered.

She was not in the mood for his sarcasm, so she said everything in a rush. "Sorry about last night. I need a favor. It's quick, so don't complain. I need you to call a woman named Benji and ask her to bring Max home after rehearsal. She said she'd take him shopping for costume stuff, but you'll owe her the money after. And don't forget about Jilly's recital today."

"Last night?" Evan paused. "And what was all that other stuff? Honestly, Heidi, I can't keep up."

"Call Benji. I'll text you the number. She can get Max home. I have something important to do, and I know you do too, but I'm at capacity here. Bye!"

She ended the call and told her phone to text Evan the number. She hadn't even known it was in her contacts, but it appeared that things she did on previous versions of the day stuck. One of those, mercifully, was Benji's phone number. Now to get to the park.

Evan called her back, but she ignored all six times. Evidently, he wasn't going to keep at it. She hoped he would take care of the thing with Max because Heidi was trying very hard to figure out which step to remove in order for the day to go as planned.

She headed for the park, still feeling like there was something she'd forgotten.

***

II

In her quest to piece together what she was doing wrong, Heidi remembered one thing. In every iteration so far—that she could recall—she'd done her day on her own. The people in her life seemed to feel she wasn't involving them enough. Maybe that's what she was meant to correct.

To that end, she invited Vic to spend the day with her. Vic had been irritated at cancelling their morning meet-up at the last minute, but Heidi was certain her idea of a romantic proposal would've gone wrong no matter what. Instead, she suggested Vic meet her at Kate's game.

It was pouring buckets when Heidi left for the ball field, but by the time she arrived, it had slowed to a misty drizzle. She pulled into the parking lot, simultaneously fishing for her umbrella and parking awkwardly. Vic was waiting for her in his car and waved cheerfully. Heidi relaxed; it seemed she'd been forgiven for earlier.

On the way to Vic's car, the wind picked up, and Heidi's umbrella turned inside out. She shrieked and tried to yank it down, only succeeding in breaking it. Vic popped out of his car and immediately sheltered Heidi under his umbrella. Clearly chivalry wasn't dead.

"Hey," she said. "Thank you."

"No problem." Vic squinted toward the ball field. "Poor kids, having to play in this weather."

On the way to the team tent, Heidi pitched her crappy, cheap umbrella into the trash. She leaned a little into Vic's side, and he slid an arm around her. It was both comforting and comfortable, as if they'd been doing this for a long time. Heidi was still lost on how she knew Vic, but at least this relationship seemed stable. She could get used to this.

They ducked into the tent and stood with the other parents at the edge. The game had been going on for a while, but Heidi didn't worry about it. She'd told Kate she wouldn't be there at the start. She'd made it in time to see Kate at bat, though, and Heidi crossed her fingers. She had a flash of memory, Kate hitting a home run, and she didn't want to miss it.

Out of the corner of her eye, she saw Vic scrolling on his phone. She elbowed him, and he looked up.

"Huh?"

"Kate's at bat."

"Cool." He returned to his phone.

Heidi rolled her eyes but then chastised herself. Kate wasn't Vic's kid, and maybe he didn't even like softball. Heidi peered at him sideways. Vic was still buried in his phone, oblivious to anything around him. Heidi wondered if this was how all their dates went. She reminded herself he was a good person—based on the umbrella—and that's probably what attracted her to him.

She was drawn out of her musings by the crack of the bat and the excited cheering of the other parents. Heidi joined them as Kate rounded the bases. Once Kate's foot connected with home plate, Heidi turned to Vic.

"You see that?"

"See what?" He didn't even look at her.

"Kate just hit a home run!"

"Cool."

"What are you doing?"

Vic finally gave Heidi his attention. "Work. I need to deal with a couple of demanding clients."

"We should get going."

"For...?"

Heidi swallowed a sigh. "Jilly's recital."

"Right, yeah." Vic shoved his phone into his pocket. "Where is it again?"

"Park Ave. I'll text you the address. I need to get home and pick her up."

Heidi waved to Kate, gave her a thumbs up to let her know she'd seen the home run, and then took off with Vic. So far, this wasn't exactly the bonding experience she'd expected. Maybe being out of the rain and sitting quietly in the recital hall would be more cozy.

She knew there was something else she was supposed to do. Closing her eyes, she tried to force her brain to supply it. Aha! There it was. "Hey, can you stop at Wegmans and get a package of cookies? Any kind."

"Sure." Vic kissed her cheek and left her at her car.

Hoping Evan had called about Max's ride, Heidi rushed home. She had enough time to change into something dry and fluff her frizzy hair before she was shuffling Jilly out the door with her viola. They made it to the studio with ten minutes to spare, and Heidi congratulated herself on her accomplishments so far.

She slid into a seat and set two programs on the chair next to her to reserve it. Several rows up, she spotted Evan. He turned around, and Heidi gave him a tiny wave. His answering smile was terse, but at least he acknowledged her.

Three students played before Vic showed up, breezing in between performers. Heidi pursed her lips to keep from saying something she—and all the people around them—would regret.

Halfway through the program, Vic's phone buzzed. Heidi felt it against her hip. At least he'd put it in silent mode. Whispering to Heidi that he had to take the call, he slipped out the back. Heidi slid down in her seat, avoiding looking at anyone except the boy playing the cello.

Jilly was up next, and she played beautifully. Heidi's heart swelled with pride in the hard work Jilly had put into practicing. She was impressed with Cass, too. Not that Heidi had never been to one of Cass's recitals before, but this one was particularly good. It was no wonder Heidi had nursed a crush on her back in the beginning.

Or in another timeline, maybe.

Heidi shook that thought off. She was with Vic, and with any luck, this was the version of today she was meant to live forward. She simply had to remind herself it was part of Vic's nature to deal with work constantly.

Speaking of the man, he popped back in right before the next student played. Heidi eyed him but said nothing.

"What'd I miss?" he whispered.

"Jilly," Heidi muttered.

"Sorry." He didn't sound sincere.

The program ended with a teenage girl around Kate's age who was fantastic. Afterward, Cass stood at the podium to thank everyone for coming and invite them to the reception. People began filing out, and Jilly bounded toward them.

"Hi, Mom! Hi, Vic!"

Heidi hugged her. "You were wonderful, sweetheart. I think Dad recorded it, too." Maybe Heidi would ask him to send it to her.

"Cool! I'm gonna go get a cookie. Can I introduce you to Megan?"

"Megan?" Heidi blinked. "Oh, was she the one who played last?"

"Yeah! Isn't she awesome?"

"She sure is. I'll meet you in there in a sec, okay?"

Waving over her shoulder, Jilly bounced into the other room. Heidi was glad she'd been able to watch. Something told her she'd missed Jilly on a previous version of her day.

Vic began to walk away, but Heidi stopped him. "Can I talk to you for a sec?"

"Didn't Jilly say she wanted to get a cookie and have you meet someone?"

Cookies. Right. Heidi looked, but she didn't see a bag in Vic's hand or one on the seat. "Did you bring them?"

"Bring what?"

"The...cookies...?"

"What cookies?"

"The ones I asked you to pick up on your way here. I thought that's why you were late."

Vic frowned. "When did you ask me for them?"

Heidi sighed. "Never mind. Look, what's with you today?"

"Nothing. You asked me to come along, so I'm here."

"Yes, and you've done nothing but work the entire time."

Vic peered at his phone again then looked up at Heidi. "I thought we had an agreement. One of the reasons things worked so well between us is that we weren't up in each other's business all the time. You're busy with kid shit, and I'm working with clients practically twenty-four-seven. We see each other when we have time. I was surprised you wanted me here today, but I went along with it."

So that was it. Instead of Heidi keeping him at arm's length, they'd agreed not to try meshing their lives. Heidi wasn't convinced it worked as well as Vic thought, but it confirmed one thing for her.

"I think maybe we should...take a break. Clear our heads."

Vic shrugged one shoulder. "If that's what you want."

Was that it? Heidi wasn't sure if she'd broken up with him or simply ended the "benefits" part of a friends-with-benefits relationship.

"It is," Heidi told him. "Now, excuse me. I'm going to get someone else's cookie and meet Megan."

She stepped around Vic, who was back on his phone. She didn't turn around to watch him walk away.

***

III

Heidi dropped Jilly off at home and headed straight for the park without changing. She didn't tell the kids she wouldn't be meeting Vic at

Highland Park after all, but that's where she was headed anyway. She needed to do what she'd told Vic and clear her head. Nothing better for that than fried food and a Leather Anvil concert.

She didn't feel like eating dinner, so she bought spiral fried potatoes and sat at one of the outdoor tables. At the other end of the table, a family with a baby and a toddler were having a picnic. While Heidi was trying to place where she knew them, the woman glanced up and gave her a puzzled smile. The family's happy, relaxed demeanor reminded Heidi of the times she and Evan had brought the kids to the Lilac Festival years ago, and she smiled.

Her mood fell again thinking about Vic. She supposed she'd chosen someone so emotionally unavailable in order to avoid the painful mistakes she'd made. Blurry memories drifted in and out of her conscious thoughts, of previous versions of this day. Heidi supposed that's where she knew the young family from.

Maybe she was meant to be alone. Kate was almost grown, but she still had Max and Jilly to think of. Perhaps it was better for her to have broken things off with Vic so she could focus on them. A relationship would only complicate matters. That was it; she could manage everything in her life if she didn't have anyone else to think about. So why did that leave her feeling so cold?

Heidi ate her potatoes slowly, even as they cooled to air temperature. She propped her head on her hand, and the woman with the baby gave her a sympathetic look. Heidi figured her unhappiness must be showing to have earned it. She wasn't hungry anymore.

There wasn't much to do except clean up and hope Leather Anvil could distract her from her mood. They hadn't started playing yet, so she wandered toward the vendor tents. The first one she came to was jewelry, and Heidi browsed the selection of earrings. There was a beautiful pair of black plugs, hand-painted with rainbow birds. When visions of a rainbow beanie filled her mind, she knew she had to have the plugs. Without questioning herself, she bought them and tucked the bag into her pocket.

She knew exactly where she had to head next. On a mission, she paid little attention to the crowd around her, mostly moving in the opposite direction from Heidi. She was so focused on getting to her destination that she walked straight into a big man. He yelped and hollered at her to watch where she was going.

The force of impact sent Heidi flying into the nearest booth. She hit the table, first with her back and then with her head as she fell. A pile of CDs slid on top of her. Heidi's vision blurred for a moment, and she rubbed her head.

"You okay?" a voice asked in her left ear.

Heidi blinked and looked over. There was exactly the person she'd come to see. Angel Flores's brown eyes were full of concern. Heidi's gaze flicked from Angel's face to her rainbow beanie and then down to her Leather Anvil shirt. Just like the hazy image from Heidi's dream.

"I'm fine."

She accepted Angel's help standing. Her head ached a little, but the pain was already receding. Or Heidi was properly distracted by Angel's presence. Either way, she was all right.

Angel began picking up the fallen CDs, and after brushing herself off, Heidi helped her. The crowd thinned, people having grown bored when it was obvious nothing exciting had happened.

When they were through, Angel said, "Thank you. Are you sure you're okay?"

"I'm good. Sorry about the mess."

Angel waved her hand dismissively. "It's all good."

That was exactly when Heidi burst into tears.

She wasn't prone to fits of crying, but that was the moment everything from the rest of the day hit her. She swallowed several times and tried to rein in her emotions. A few people passing the booth gave her curious looks, but no one paid attention to her otherwise.

Heidi wiped her eyes so she could see and began walking away from the booth. She wasn't sure what she'd come there expecting. Angel was a stranger, and Heidi could hardly expect her to develop feelings in the two minutes since Heidi had crashed into her space.

"Excuse me."

The gentle tap on Heidi's arm caused her to turn around. "Oh. Um..." She blinked at Angel.

"I know you said you're fine, but you don't seem like it to me. Let me get you some water, and we'll go sit for a few minutes." When Heidi started to protest, Angel put her hands up. "Long enough to see if you need medical attention. That's all."

She grabbed two bottles of water from a cooler in the booth and led Heidi toward the children's stage. There were some nearby benches, and Angel tugged Heidi down as she sat. She handed Heidi one of the waters.

"I'm Angel, by the way."

Heidi collected herself before she could say something stupid. "Heidi."

"Nice to meet you." Angel's smile was sympathetic and concerned. "Wish it could've been under better circumstances."

Heidi's laugh was dry and bordered on hysterical. She remembered Angel saying exactly the same thing before. "I should've been paying more attention."

"That guy shouldn't have shoved you, though." Angel scrunched her nose, and Heidi's heart sped up.

"I did run into him first." Heidi sipped her water before continuing.

"My day's been so weird already. What's one more thing?"

"Want to talk about it?"

Heidi snorted. "You want to hear the personal drama of a complete stranger?"

"Sure, why not?" Angel grinned. "It's not like I was having an exciting time before."

"All right." Heidi took a deep breath. "It wasn't bad, really, but my kids all had things to do today. I've been sort of seeing someone—I guess more like friends with benefits or something like that—and I figured maybe we could...step things up in our relationship. I don't know. It didn't work out, and I had to end things. Maybe I'm better off not trying."

"Is that what you want?"

Heidi thought about it. No, it wasn't, but she also had to think about what might be best for her kids. Judging by how many times she'd been through this exact day, she wasn't cut out for long-term relationships. She also didn't appear to be cut out for having something casual. There wasn't a way to explain her strange do-overs to Angel, though, so she only shrugged.

"I don't know what I want," she admitted.

She looked over at the children's stage. The performers were unfamiliar. It had been far too long since Heidi's kids were an age to appreciate the music. She turned her attention back to Angel, studying her. Angel had on the familiar rainbow beanie and black Leather Anvil T-shirt, the vines of her tattoo peeking out from under the sleeve. Heidi wondered what it was.

"What?" Angel asked, her cheeks turning pink.

Heidi realized she'd been staring. "You look different from your picture."

Angel laughed. "Those head shots for the bus are awful. I look like a Rachel Maddow wannabe. It's so not my style or even how I dress for work." She looked down at herself. "Neither is this, but I definitely don't look like I'm going to the office."

Heidi opened and closed her mouth a couple of times, fighting the dizziness of the déjà vu. "I like this better."

"Me too." She stood. "You want to go listen to the music?"

"Don't you have to get back to the booth?"

"Nah, it's fine. I only do this because Martina's a friend." She held out her hand to Heidi.

They headed toward the main stage. Angel kept hold of Heidi's hand. Instead of dancing with the crowd, Angel stayed on the side, maybe out of respect for Heidi's injury. They swayed to the music, and Heidi allowed herself to forget all the heartache of the day. Leather Anvil played a combination of old favorites and songs from their new release.

They began a slower song, and Angel turned Heidi to face her. Heidi's breath caught, and her heart rate increased. She couldn't believe she was about to hold Angel—again. It felt as right as it had the last time she'd lived this day. Heidi wrapped her arms around Angel's waist, and Angel settled in with her head resting against Heidi's shoulder. Perfect.

Heidi sighed in contentment as the song ended, and Angel peered up at her. Angel grinned, and Heidi couldn't help smiling back as her joy bubbled over. She didn't want this to end, even though she knew it had to.

Pulling back, she said, "I—"

Angel smiled and put a finger to Heidi's lips. "Let's enjoy this. Want to go grab a coffee?"

As the sky darkened, the breeze had picked up, and now Heidi noticed the chill in the air. It was only early May in Rochester, after all. A hot coffee sounded fantastic.

"Are you sure you don't need to get back?"

"I'll check in at the booth, but I'd already told Martina I was only staying for the show. She knows I need to rest up."

"Then are you sure you want to go anywhere?"

Angel laughed. "I don't work on Sundays. It's more like I usually don't have anywhere better to be, so I like to go home and have a quiet night off."

"Oh. Well, then, I'd love some coffee. We can take my car. It's back at the college lot, though."

Angel shook her head. "I have somewhere in mind, and we can walk there. It's less than a mile."

She looped her pinky with Heidi's, and they began walking toward South Avenue, the opposite direction from the shuttle stop. As they moved farther away from the Festival, the crowd thinned to a few pedestrians heading home or to cars parked on side streets. The cloud cover made it darker than it otherwise would've been an hour before sunset.

Angel stopped at a large, brick building on the corner. At first, it appeared to Heidi like one of many older-style storefronts and apartments in that part of the city. When she looked up, she saw the sign on the front reading Equal=Grounds.

"I can't believe I've lived in Rochester my whole life and have never been here," Heidi said.

"Well, now you have." Angel squeezed her hand before entering.

Inside, Heidi closed her eyes briefly to appreciate the aroma. They ordered and brought their drinks to a table beside a tall shelf of games. On the way past, Heidi spotted a rack of Pride flags.

Once they were seated, Heidi relaxed with her chilly hands wrapped around her mug. She wanted to know everything about Angel, but she settled for asking, "How do you know Martina? Is it from playing their music on the radio?"

Angel shook her head. "I went to school with Martina's sister." She blushed. "I may have dated her for a while."

Heidi laughed. "And you stayed friends with her sister?" She couldn't imagine doing that. When she and Evan had split, Heidi didn't keep in touch with any of his family. She left the kids' visits with them to him.

Giving Heidi a puzzled expression, Angel said, "Of course. I'm still friends with Maya, too. She would've been at the booth, but she has her own. She sells the cutest handmade baby stuff. If you know anyone who's expecting or has an infant, you should check it out. Like, onesies and hats and booties and stuff. She's done some with a Lilac Festival theme for this, but she's got other ones too—geeky stuff like Star Trek and Doctor Who."

"Aw, that sounds so sweet. Wish I still had one that little to put them on." Heidi giggled. "Who am I kidding? No, I don't. I'm perfectly happy to have my youngest be ten."

"You have kids?"

"Yep." Heidi groaned. "And an ex who isn't the most reliable, but that's a story for another day."

"Did...did I read you wrong?" Angel drew her lower lip between her teeth.

"Not at all. I'm not too picky about gender, to be honest."

Angel blew out a noisy breath. "Good. Me neither, but I'd usually rather date women."

"Is this a date?" Heidi's eyebrows rose.

"Um...should it be?" Angel's grin was adorably nervous and hopeful.

"Sure, why not?"

"Because you broke up with someone today."

"Someone who I wasn't in much of a relationship with, as it turns out." Angel relaxed visibly. "Okay, then."

Their conversation veered away from the subject of relationships, and they talked and laughed together through two more rounds of hot drinks. Heidi couldn't recall a better first date since Evan. It only made her a little sad to remember how much fun she'd had with him back then. This was now, and she wanted to enjoy every moment with Angel—especially not knowing if she would get another chance.

She didn't want the evening to end yet. "Would you like to go somewhere with me?"

Angel glanced down the side street. "I live in an apartment right here."

"I'll drive you home afterward."

With a shrug, Angel agreed. They walked back to the park, past the Festival to the shuttle stop. Heidi located her car, and they climbed in. She headed back toward the city, knowing the perfect spot. Heidi parked, and the two of them walked the short distance to the bridge over the Genesee River.

High Falls was gorgeous even on the cusp of spring, with trees only beginning to turn green again. It was dark now, and the lights from the buildings behind the Falls twinkled. The two of them leaned on the railing, listening to the splash of the water and watching the mist and foam. Maybe not as spectacular as on a summer night, but still beautiful.

And romantic. Heidi and Angel turned toward each other, and Heidi's whole body tingled with nerves as she raised a hand to rest it on Angel's cheek.

"May I?" she asked, and Angel nodded.

The kiss was everything it was meant to be. Heidi was swept up in it, the misery of the day—and all the previous versions of the day—erased by the feel of Angel's lips on hers.

All too soon, Angel ended it, but she remained close. Heidi pulled her in and wrapped her arms around Angel, resting her chin on Angel's head. She closed her eyes, wishing she could stay this way forever.

"I should get home," Angel said.

"Me too. My kids are fine, but they're probably wondering why the concert took so long."

"I'd love to do this again."

"Yes," Heidi agreed. "I wish—" She cut herself off, knowing anything that came out of her mouth was a very, very bad idea.

Angel smiled. She glanced down then reached to pick something up. "Huh," she said. "Here."

She handed a sprig of lilacs to Heidi, who wondered how they'd gotten all the way to High Falls and how they'd been so well-preserved, given the constant foot traffic.

"Thanks?" Heidi put them to her nose and inhaled the lovely fragrance.

"Make that wish again."

"Oh, no, I couldn't." Heidi chuckled. "Besides, isn't that dandelions?"

"Angel tilted her head. "I think it works with lilacs too. Especially on the first day of the Festival."

For once, Heidi didn't want to do her day over, except maybe for the part where she and Angel had spent the entire evening together. Did wanting it turn it into a wish? Heidi closed her eyes, pretending to do as Angel said but giving herself time to think. At last she opened her eyes and sniffed the lilacs again. Their scent was fading already.

"Did you do it?" Angel asked. When Heidi only shrugged, she said, "Now, blow on it, or it won't come true."

Heidi blew gently on the sprig, and she was surrounded once again by the distinctive smell. She went to tuck the sprig into her shirt pocket and felt the plugs she'd bought earlier. She pulled out the bag.

"Here," she said. "These are for you. I bought them earlier, and it seems fitting to give them to you."

Angel opened the box and stared, open-mouthed, at the plugs. "Oh, I love them! I was going to buy them, but..."

"Not in your budget?" Heidi said. She cringed internally, knowing Angel had said it before.

"Right," Angel agreed. "Thank you." She leaned in and kissed Heidi's cheek. She reached into her bag. "Here. In exchange for the plugs."

She handed a CD to Heidi—*Sonic Pixie Dream Girls*. Heidi smiled and held her arms out to hug Angel again. They kissed briefly, and Angel put her hand in Heidi's as they walked back to the car.

Heidi left Angel at her doorstep, watching Heidi back out of the driveway. Heidi glanced over her shoulder for oncoming traffic, and when she looked back, Angel had already gone inside. With a sigh, Heidi headed for home.

***

IV

Heidi's feet hurt from all the walking she'd done. When she arrived home, she was grateful to see Kate had reheated the previous night's chicken enchiladas for herself and the others. There were still some leftovers, which Kate had put back in the fridge. For a moment, Heidi contemplated eating them, but all she wanted was to sit and not move for a long time.

Her mind was still on Angel as she sorted the mail. The kids had cleaned up after themselves, which surprised her. None of them were around now. Heidi took it as a good sign that no one had been waiting to pounce on her about what happened with Vic, why she was late, or any other drama about the day.

She stretched and stood to make herself a cup of tea. While she was filling the kettle, Kate came out of her room and stood in the kitchen doorway, arms folded. She was chewing on her lip.

It wouldn't do any good for Heidi to jump right into asking what was on Kate's mind. Instead, she began with, "Did you find a dress today?" The same way she'd started the conversation for...how many days now?

"Yeah."

"You don't sound too happy about it."

Kate shrugged. "Did it go okay with Vic?"

Heidi sighed. "Not exactly."

"What's that mean?"

"It means we're not getting married. Or even dating."

"Ah." Kate's posture relaxed. "So does that mean I can tell you something?"

"Sure." Heidi flipped on the tea kettle and sat, motioning for Kate to join her.

Kate perched on the edge of the chair, her knees bouncing. "I didn't think it was going to work out. He was too much like Dad."

"I discovered as much today. No, scratch that. I already knew, but dragging him around everywhere with me confirmed it."

"Do you think you'll ever get married again?"

Heidi studied Kate, wondering where this was coming from—and where it was going. "I'm not sure. Maybe not. Maybe I'm better off taking care of you guys for right now."

Kate bit her nail, making Heidi cringe. After a moment, she said, "How do you know when giving up on a thing is right?"

Heidi contemplated her question. With Evan, it had been a long, slow process of disconnecting. There had been countless arguments over both important things and petty ones. Ultimately, Evan had turned to Jen for comfort, and Heidi had tried to become Mother of the Year.

She rubbed her temples, trying to recall any details from previous iterations of her day. She'd dated a number of people, mostly ones she'd met through her children. Somehow, every single one had been the wrong person, the wrong timing, or both. With each one, she'd grown more savvy to what wasn't working until today. She'd known almost instantly with Vic.

Looking Kate in the eyes, Heidi said, "I believe sometimes you simply know. It feels right." Her gut clenched when a vision of Angel came to mind. Their evening together had felt every bit as right as ending things with Vic had.

Heidi laid a hand on top of Kate's. "Everything okay with you?"

Kate shook her head. "I've been thinking about something, but I don't want you to get mad."

"You know I can't promise that, but I'll try to keep an open mind." Heidi was fairly sure she remembered what was coming.

"I'm not sure I want to go to college. At least, not yet."

Heidi opened her mouth, thinking she would have some wise words stored up by now, but nothing occurred to her. She wanted Kate to be happy, but she still hadn't made peace with this.

"Mom, say something."

"I'm...not exactly mad, but I'm not sure it's a good idea to make a hasty decision." That was the best Heidi was going to do.

"It's not hasty! I don't think I'm ready for more school, and I really don't want to keep playing softball. I love it, but that feels like part of my life I was doing to look good on a resumé, not because it's what I want to keep doing."

"So you were only playing so you could get into college? And now you don't want to go?"

"Ugh, Mom. No. I played because I wanted to. It's fun. But it stopped being fun when it became a thing that was going to get me into a good school."

"I wanted to help you plan for your futures and set you up for better than what I had."

"That's just it," Kate said, her voice rising. "You're really good at 'planning for our futures,'" she made air quotes, "but you suck at doing things that matter right now." She sucked in her breath. "I'm sorry!"

"No, don't be," Heidi said. "It's what I was trying to do today, too. I thought if I made things work with Vic, we'd all be set up for a better future. Not money." She held up a hand to silence Kate's objection. "A family."

"So what do I do?" Kate asked.

"Think it over. We'll talk more. I'm not ready to tell you to follow your dreams like a Disney movie, but I'm willing to hear you out."

Kate nodded and left the table for her room. Heidi breathed a sigh of relief. She hadn't needed to give Kate a firm response yet, leaving her time to think about what she should say. She made her cup of herbal tea and while it brewed, she checked on the kids. Jilly was reading, Kate was on her phone, and Max was asleep. Heidi tiptoed out and settled on the couch with her mug and the CD Angel had given her.

There wasn't any real need to open the *Sonic Pixie Dream Girls* case; Heidi already knew what was in it. She remembered the lilac-colored business card: Angel Flores, Lilac City Social Media Management, with her message to Heidi underneath. "Call me sometime."

The scent of lilacs surrounded Heidi, and she had to resist the desire to call Angel that very minute. Her lips tingled with the memory of their kiss on the bridge by High Falls. Heidi closed her eyes and smiled to herself.

She wouldn't need to put Angel's number in her phone. Even with the holes in her recollections of previous versions of the day, she knew that much. She forced herself off the couch to put the CD in, grabbing a blanket on her way back. Wrapping herself in it, she curled up on the couch and fell asleep listening to Leather Anvil.

DAY EIGHT

I

The smell of coffee from the automatic pot woke Heidi from a deep sleep. She stirred restlessly, vaguely recalling that she'd been dreaming—something about an androgynous, nameless face with undefined features that slowly melted into short, dark hair and sparkling brown eyes. Heidi blinked, expecting the sunlight to make her head hurt, but she felt nothing amiss.

It surprised her to wake in her bed; she was sure she'd fallen asleep on the couch the previous night. Maybe she'd wandered into the bedroom, still half asleep, in the middle of the night. She didn't know what day it was or what time. Memories blurred with her dreams, and she wasn't sure which were real. She turned on the radio, hoping for some clues.

"Goooooood morning, Rochester! We're live here at the Lilac Festival, where the parade begins in less than a half hour!"

Heidi moaned. This could not be happening. What had she done wrong? She tried to remember, but nothing fit right. Slowly, she sat up and rubbed her temples. The only thing she knew was that she'd managed to disappoint either everyone or half of everyone no matter what she tried.

But there was also Angel.

Heidi drew her knees up and rested her chin on them, eyes closed. Yes, that part felt the most real. She'd kissed Angel under the stars. They'd walked to Equal Grounds for coffee and then taken Heidi's car to High Falls, beautiful even when the weather was still chilly at night and the trees still without greenery. The lights in the background reflected off the churning water of the Genesee River, making the atmosphere romantic.

But here Heidi sat, very likely about to propose to someone else, someone who wasn't wearing a rainbow beanie and a Leather Anvil T-shirt. Someone who hadn't spent an evening listening and talking and feeling a spark of connection with her.

Maybe Heidi didn't have to do this. She could meet whoever it was at the park, break up with them, and get on with her day. Afterward, she'd find Angel, and whatever magic they'd had, she could re-create it somehow. What if it was Angel she was meant to find? What if her day had to be perfect so her night with Angel would be too?

Heidi swung her feet over the side of the bed and stood. She stretched and began pulling out clothes. No changes there. Angel seemed to like her casual-sloppy look just fine. She did pocket her lip gloss, though. With her hand in her underwear drawer, she paused. For a few minutes, she felt around, wriggling her fingers under the cotton and lace. Nothing. No box, no ring.

Heidi frowned and tried to shake off the confusion. Well, that was one thing she must have changed, then. No ring meant she wasn't going to have to deal with proposing to someone she barely knew. She left her bed rumpled and went to make herself coffee.

Kate was at the table, filling out her graduation invitations. She looked up when Heidi entered.

"Looks like you're almost done, but do you need any help?" Maybe switching the conversation would break this endless, painful loop.

Kate shook her head. "I've got it." She tapped her pen on the table. "Everything okay?"

"Overslept." Heidi waited for the coffee to brew, relieved when it finally finished and she could take that first, miraculous sip.

"Did you call?"

"Call who?" Heidi cringed. She realized half a second too late that Kate must've meant her partner of the moment, whoever it was.

"Dad, about picking Max up after rehearsal?"

"Why—" Heidi groaned. "Jilly's recital."

As predicted, Kate gave her an incredulous look. "Mom, are you okay? You really don't look good. Maybe you should rest."

"No, I'm fine. Still waking up. I'm gonna take this to go." She held up the travel mug as if it weren't obvious.

"Go where?"

"To the Lilac Festival?"

"What for?"

Heidi blinked. "I'm not sure."

"Wasn't that tonight? You said there was some band you wanted to see. Leather Brick or something?"

"Leather Anvil."

Heidi sat at the table, relaxing once she realized she had no immediate plans. She thought about how to structure her day. Her brain supplied the helpful memory of drunk-dialing Evan, but now she wasn't sure if that was real—or real in this version of her life, anyway.

When she was done and the caffeine began to lift her fog, Heidi retreated to her bedroom. She made the bed and sat on the edge, phone in hand. After a few cleansing breaths, she hit Evan's number.

"Morning, sunshine," he said when he answered.

Same old Evan, or at least the same Evan as the previous week's worth of this conversation. Heidi replied, "Hey. I'm really sorry about last night."

"Last night?" Evan paused. "What happened last night?"

"I think I might've called you after having too much to drink."

"No?" Evan's voice rose as if in a question. "I'm a little confused here."

"Oh. Uh, me too. I had a weird dream." Heidi giggled, feeling awkward. "So I didn't call you yesterday to yell at you?"

Now Evan laughed. "Is this your idea of a joke? Haha. Good one, Heids."

"I'm serious."

"Okay..." There was a pause. "No, you didn't call me. Is everything okay?"

"Not-not really, no." Heidi ran a hand through her hair. "Must be lack of sleep. I do need a favor, though."

"What's that?"

"I need you to take Jilly to her recital."

"Oh." Evan paused again. "Why?"

"Because I have Kate's game, and I need to get Max from rehearsal. I've figured out I can do any two of those things, but not all three. It's easier for you to take Jilly because you can get to her sooner. I was going to ask you to get Max, but this will work better."

Evan was quiet for a moment. Then he said, "Yeah, I think we could manage. Just make sure she's ready and knows we're coming, okay?"

"She has to be there at two-thirty. Recital's at three. She'll be ready."

"Fine. But Heidi?"

"Yeah?"

Evan sighed. "Call sooner or plan better next time. I can't deal with the last minute stuff."

"I promise. I really am trying to get my shit together. Be patient with me?"

"I'll try." Another sigh. "See you later, Heidi."

He ended the call, and Heidi tucked her phone away. Her eyes filled with tears. She remembered having done this better on other days, but she didn't have it in her to make full restoration with Evan. The only things on her mind were finding Angel and how to make this endless day disappear.

She returned to the kitchen, where Kate had finished the invitations. Heidi pulled out a notepad and a pen. Even if she didn't have to come home for Jilly after Max's rehearsal, she still wouldn't be able to get there in time unless she brought Max. She would offer him a choice: attend the recital or leave rehearsal early. To that end, she wrote him a note excusing him in case he needed it.

"All set?" Kate asked, breaking into Heidi's thoughts.

"Yep. Dad's going to make sure Jilly gets to the recital on time, and I'll see your game and bring Max home."

Kate seemed amused by something. "Wow, Mom. I can't believe you managed to talk Dad into it."

"Right, well, I think he's seeing the, uh, error of his ways."

"And you are too? Because I want you both at graduation, acting like adults not little kids."

"Don't worry. We'll behave." Heidi stood, leaving the note on the table.

"Cool. You still need me to bring Max to school with me?"

"Yes, please. I'll trade. You leave the invitations for me to mail, and you get yourself and Max there."

"Sounds good." Kate grinned up at her.

Heidi bent and kissed the top of Kate's head, thinking her plan for the day seemed solid enough. It was so much easier without anyone but herself and the kids to think about.

***

II

After her third cup of coffee, Heidi began to feel more human. She had time to make her bed and even take a shower this time. An extra long, extra hot shower during which she worked hard to keep her mind from wandering to Angel and wondering if she would ever get to see the rest of her tattoo.

With time to spare, Heidi took off to mail the graduation invitations and watch Kate's game. It was raining by then, and Heidi cursed herself for forgetting both her good umbrella and her hoodie. She would need to make a dash for it at the park.

Despite her efforts, Heidi was soggy by the time she ducked under the team tent. The rain was much lighter here, though the wind had picked up. The game began moments after she arrived.

Shivering, Heidi wrapped her arms around herself and peered out of the tent with the rest of the parents. Around her, there was some light chatter. She hardly knew any of the others and didn't know what to say to them. A light tap on her shoulder made her jump and turn around.

"You look cold." Oh, god. It was Hot Tom, the single dad everyone lusted after.

Heidi's face burned, but the rest of her was freezing. Her teeth chattered as she said, "A little."

"Here." Tom handed her a team sweatshirt. "On the house. We have extras."

As Heidi pulled it over her head, she caught Wilhelm, the only other single father, draping his arm over Tom's shoulders. Ah, of course. They made a nice couple, Heidi thought. Tom caught her eye and put some distance between himself and Wilhelm. Heidi turned away, frowning. Tom clearly thought she had a problem with it, but she definitely didn't. She reasoned that since she wasn't dating Tom in this version of her life, he likely didn't know about her relationship history.

When Heidi returned to the opening in the tent, she saw several couples holding hands or with their arms around each other's waists. She sighed. How had she never noticed all the lovebirds around her?

Mercifully, she was distracted by Kate's turn at bat. There was a crack followed by the excited cheering of the crowd. Heidi joined them, yelling her ass off as Kate ran. She'd been there for Kate's exciting moment, and her heart swelled with pride.

Heidi stayed for a short while longer and then waved to Kate, who gave her a big grin and a thumbs up. None of the other parents seemed to notice when Heidi slipped away.

She pulled up the hood of the sweatshirt and jogged to her car. Max had opted to go home early instead of sitting through Jilly's recital, so Heidi texted him and headed for the school.

Max was waiting for her inside the double doors, scowling. Heidi politely didn't roll her eyes at her kid's dramatics, although she was tempted to tell him to save it for the stage.

"I'm missing out," he grouched as he buckled his seatbelt.

"You're playing a blade of grass. I don't think you need that much practice."

"Mom!" Max glowered at her. "I'm also playing a hyena. Besides, we're working on the songs."

"It's one rehearsal."

He huffed. "Whatever. Can you take me to get my costume pieces tomorrow?"

"Wh—" Heidi caught herself before asking him about it. Whether she remembered it or not, there wasn't any reason to say no. "Sure."

She dropped a still-cranky Max off at home and headed to Park Ave for Jilly's recital. She'd make it with a couple minutes to spare if she got lucky. In the nick of time, she slid into a seat and exhaled in relief. After browsing the program to see when Jilly would play, she spotted Evan and Jen a few rows up. Evan turned around, raised his eyebrows, and gave Heidi a slight smile. She wiggled her fingers in a return wave.

Heidi was impressed with how well the students played. Cass was an outstanding teacher, and Heidi was glad she'd signed Jilly on with her. She was even more glad when she heard how beautiful Jilly sounded on her viola.

The program ended with a teenage girl around Kate's age performing a Mozart concerto that wowed the audience. Afterward, Cass stood at the podium to offer a few words. Heidi flushed, remembering the crush she'd had on Cass in the beginning. She was still quite attractive, but Heidi surprised herself when none of the old feelings bubbled up.

Cass thanked everyone and invited them to the reception. Heidi groaned inwardly. The one thing she'd forgotten—cookies to share. Fortunately, that was the moment Jilly bounded up to her, viola in hand.

"Hi, Mom!" She grinned, and it made Heidi's day.

Heidi stood and hugged her. "I'm so proud of you!"

"Did you record it?"

"No, but I think Dad did. You can ask him to send it to you."

"Okay. Wanna get a cookie with me and meet Megan?"

"Megan?" Heidi blinked. "Right, the girl who played the Mozart."

"You remembered her song!"

"She was so good."

"Megan is awesome. Come on!"

Heidi followed Jilly into the reception room. She was relieved to see some parents had gone overboard with the cookie-making, so it didn't seem to matter that she hadn't brought any. Jilly dragged Heidi into the line. Megan was in front of them with...Dominic. Heidi remembered that much, at least. He had his arm around a woman, and a little boy who had played the cello was holding her hand. Heidi wanted to warn her about Dominic, but she decided it wasn't any of her business.

Jilly introduced Megan, and Heidi attempted polite chit-chat with her and the other adults. She glanced over her shoulder and saw Evan and Jen approaching. They stood in line behind Heidi, and she held her tongue.

Jen's tone was falsely bright as she congratulated Jilly. Heidi clenched and unclenched her fist, wishing she didn't have to restrain herself. Since when did Jen care at all about the kids that weren't hers?

Evan rested a hand on Heidi's shoulder. "She's trying," he murmured.

Heidi nodded. "Okay. Hey, did you record this? Jilly was asking."

"I did. I'll send it to you if you want."

"Sure."

That was the most polite conversation she'd had with Evan in what was probably years. Heidi smiled at him, and he offered a genuine return smile. By then, they'd reached the snack table, and Heidi turned away. It was as much as she could handle for one day.

Cass greeted her and congratulated Jilly on her performance. "She's going to be fantastic," she said.

"Thanks. She does work hard."

A woman stepped up next to Cass, and when she stood next to her, their hands brushed. Heidi pretended not to notice. She'd thought doing all this on her own would be so much easier than with someone else, especially all the different people with whom she'd cycled through this day. Now she was surrounded by couples, reminding her she was very much alone.

At least she had the Leather Anvil concert to look forward to. Angel's face appeared in Heidi's mind again. She was worth the wait and watching all the happy couples all day. If Heidi played her cards right, she could have her joy too.

With that in mind, Heidi forced herself to socialize with the other families, counting down the minutes until she could see Angel again.

***

III

Heidi brought Jilly home, dealt with her frizzy hair, and grabbed a sweatshirt. Kate would be home soon enough, and Max and Jilly were fine on their own until then. If memory served her right, Kate would feed them all dinner.

Speaking of which, Heidi decided dinner was a good idea, even if she was nervous enough she wasn't sure she could eat. She had to find Angel at the right time, which meant stalling for a bit. She bought herself a red hot with spicy mustard, a funnel cake, and a Genny Cream Ale and sat at a picnic table. At the other end was the family with the baby and the toddler, enjoying the dinner they'd packed. The woman glanced up and gave her a small smile.

Watching them made Heidi nostalgic, not only for the years she and Evan had done this but for the happy couplehood the parents appeared to have. It was subtle things like the occasional light touches of their hands or the way they moved around each other so easily to care for the children.

Heidi picked at her food, moody but not knowing where the feelings came from. She didn't miss being with Evan. She'd never fully made peace with whether or not they should've gotten married in the first place. On the other hand, she did sometimes wish she could have the kind of natural connection the young family did.

She wondered if being single in this timeline was the answer. It was clear she hadn't been able to make any of her other relationships work. What could she have done differently? Would it have changed anything?

The young family began cleaning up, and Heidi took that as her cue. She'd barely eaten half her food, but she didn't care. She eyed the Genny but ended up dumping it with the rest of her trash. Evan was right when he said she couldn't hold her alcohol, and she wanted to be clear-headed when she met up with Angel.

Heidi paid little attention to anyone around her as she headed for the jewelry booth. She recited the steps in her head: buy the plugs, find the Leather Anvil booth, meet Angel, go from there. She didn't have a plan beyond that, but she hoped one thing would lead to another. Hopefully, a repeat of the previous version of the day, with coffee and conversation and kisses under the stars. How to make that happen was anyone's guess, but Heidi was determined.

So determined, in fact, that she missed the big man headed in her direction until the last minute. She swerved before he crashed into her, but she tripped over her own two feet and landed heavily on the ground outside the jewelry tent. She was about to thank the universe she hadn't toppled anything over when a foot connected with her shoulder.

Heidi cried out and tried to roll away, only succeeding in smacking her head against the tent pole. She covered her face with her arms and curled up to avoid being hit again.

"Oh my god! Are you okay? I'm so sorry!"

Heidi knew that voice. She lowered her arms and peered up at Angel, crouched beside her. Heidi shook herself and sat up, feeling her head and her shoulder. A little tender, but nothing serious.

"I'm fine." She smiled at Angel, hoping to reassure her.

Angel stood and offered Heidi a hand, which she accepted. "I'm Angel."

"Yes, you are," Heidi mumbled.

Angel laughed. "What?"

"Oh! I mean, I know. From the radio, right? I'm Heidi."

"Always nice to meet my fans," Angel remarked, still giggling. "Come on over to my booth, and I'll get you some water. It's the least I can do for nearly killing you."

"Thank you, but I did that all on my own. It's totally my fault. I didn't see that guy, and when I tried to get out of his way, I ended up in oncoming traffic."

They walked the short distance to the Leather Anvil booth, and Angel pulled two bottles of water out of a cooler. She handed one to Heidi and took the other for herself.

"Do you need ice? Or maybe a medic?"

"No, I'm really fine." Heidi sipped her water, trying to come up with something to say. This had been so much easier the other times she'd done it. Now that she was in Angel's presence, her mind had gone blank. "You, uh, like Leather Anvil?" Heidi knew the answer already, but she needed an opening.

"Sure do." Angel grinned. "Martina's a friend from way back."

"Oh, the lead singer?"

"That's the one. You a fan?"

"For ages," Heidi said. "My ex and I…" She trailed off, not wanting to explain.

"Ah, I'm sorry," Angel said, putting a hand on Heidi's arm.

"No, no. It's not recent." Heidi's laugh was pained. "I have terrible taste in relationships, other than liking Leather Anvil." Heidi picked up a CD and pretended to examine the back before returning her gaze to Angel. "Is this your side gig? Selling Leather Anvil CDs?"

"Nah, I do it to help out. I'm filling in for Martina's sister. Maya's got her own booth to run."

"Is it also full of Leather Anvil merch?" Heidi laughed.

"Nope. Hey, I've got an idea. I'll show you. You know, to make up for smashing into you."

Heidi shrugged. "Okay."

She didn't care where Angel was taking her as long as they were together. She didn't even question why Angel wanted hang out with a complete stranger. Instead, she let Angel lead her in the opposite direction of the crowd, toward the children's stage.

Whoever was playing there wasn't familiar to Heidi. It had been years since she'd brought her kids, and she no longer recognized the performers. At the end of the row of booths, Angel stopped. When Heidi looked around at what was for sale, she gasped in delight.

There were all sorts of baby gifts, everything from onesies to hand-knitted caps and booties. Most of it was Lilac Festival-themed, but there was also a teeny, tiny Leather Anvil onesie with an itty bitty rainbow hat. Heidi glanced between it and Angel and laughed.

Heidi perused the gifts, examining the hand-lettered sippy cups and lilac-colored crocheted blankets. Everything was adorable enough to make Heidi wish she had a tiny one of her own.

"Know anyone with a baby?" Angel asked.

"Not personally, but some of my friends might." Heidi picked up one of the business cards by the cash register and thanked the woman—presumably Maya.

She and Angel left the booth and wandered toward the concert. Heidi's shoulder ached a little, and she rubbed it. Angel led her to a bench, and they sat.

"Stay here," Angel commanded. She took off and returned a few minutes later with a bag of ice, which she handed to Heidi.

"Thanks."

"If you don't mind my asking, what had you so distracted?"

Heidi cringed. She wasn't about to tell Angel it was because she'd wanted to buy the plugs and get to the Leather Anvil booth. Somehow, she didn't think that would go over well.

"It's been kind of a day. Tiring, and...well. I'm sure you don't want to hear me go on about my silly problems."

"I doubt they're silly at all, and I don't mind, but you don't have to tell me." Angel snorted. "I was so bored in that booth that I was browsing the other ones even though I don't currently have money to spend."

"I don't know if it's comforting or not that you think my issues are less boring than your booth." Heidi snickered.

"Interpret it however you want." Angel flashed Heidi another award-winning smile.

"I've had this feeling like...my life is stuck in a...rut." She'd almost said loop but decided against it. "Things didn't work out with my ex—any of my exes—and I thought being single would be easier. Turns out it's not. I still have to do all the same things I did before, on my own, while also watching all the happy couples around me. It kind of sucks."

Angel nodded. "I've been out of the dating game for a while now, so I hear you."

"I have to think about my kids and what they need, which is mostly me."

"Can you be there for them if you're not having your own needs met?"

They were quiet for a bit while Heidi pondered the question. In every previous version of the day, it had been clear neither she nor the other people were fulfilled. What would've made the difference? Heidi couldn't yet answer that, but she wished she could.

Angel glanced down. She plucked something off the ground and handed it to Heidi. A sprig of lilacs, still perfect and fresh as if it had been picked only moments ago. Heidi inhaled the scent and closed her eyes to appreciate it.

The words popped out before Heidi could stop them. "I wish—" She clamped her mouth shut.

"What do you wish?"

"Nope. I've been there and done that, and it always comes back to bite me."

"Making wishes on flowers?" Angel scrunched her nose.

"Making wishes at all."

Angel tilted her head. "I think it's different on the first day of the Lilac Festival."

"Maybe."

"Blow on it, or your wish won't come true."

Heidi opened her mouth to object but changed her mind. She blew on the blossoms, figuring her wish to answer what she should do differently might qualify. The scent of lilacs filled her senses.

"Come on." Angel stood. "Let's go hear the concert."

"Don't you have to get back to the booth?"

"Nah, it's fine. I told you I was bored." She held out her hand, and Heidi took it.

They headed toward the main stage, still holding hands. At first, they swayed to the beat, watching the others. Eventually, Angel dragged Heidi into the crowd of dancers, and Heidi laid her troubles aside. This was where she'd wanted to be, with Angel at the concert. There was nowhere better.

Leather Anvil began a slower song, and Angel turned Heidi to face her. Even knowing it was happening, Heidi still felt the thrill racing up her spine as Angel looped her arms around Heidi's neck. She couldn't remember anything else feeling as right and as perfect as this. She needed to find a way to keep it going, to keep holding Angel.

The song ended, and Heidi hesitated only a second before she said, "Do you want to go grab a coffee?" When Angel didn't answer immediately, Heidi backpedaled. "I mean, we don't have to—"

Angel smiled and put a finger to Heidi's lips. "I'd love to. Let me check in at the booth first, and then we can get out of here."

"Great! I know just the place."

Angel arched an eyebrow but said nothing further. While she ducked into the Leather Anvil booth, Heidi stopped at the one with the jewelry. She purchased the plugs in time to stash them in her pocket before Angel returned.

"All set. Where did you have in mind?"

"I think we can walk there from here."

"Oh!" Angel bounced on her toes. "Equal Grounds. Yeah, it's less than a mile up the road."

As they walked along South Ave, the crowd thinned. It was growing dark with the cloud cover, and Heidi was glad she'd worn her sweatshirt. Angel looped their pinkies together as they strolled.

They stopped outside the brick building. Angel turned to Heidi and said, "Have you been here before?"

"Only once, but I love the atmosphere."

"You know it—"

"Caters to LGBTQ folks? Yes."

It smelled heavenly inside, and Heidi couldn't wait to have a hot drink in her chilly hands. They brought their mugs to a table beside the shelf full of board games, and Heidi thought about picking one out. She decided against it because if she only had one night with Angel, she didn't want to spend it playing cards.

From their previous date, Heidi knew she could get Angel talking by asking about Leather Anvil. She opened with that, and they spent the rest of the evening talking about everything and nothing. If possible, this was even better than the last go-round of their date. Heidi kept her eyes on Angel, wanting to memorize every detail: Her dark hair poking out from underneath the rainbow beanie; her smooth, tan skin; her sparkling brown eyes; her matte purple lips. Angel was gorgeous, and Heidi thought her heart might burst from the joy of sitting across from her for a whole night.

Angel listened as Heidi talked about her kids and Evan and her struggle to find balance in everything. Heidi heard the stress under the surface as Angel described landing her dream job but barely being able to afford rent. The whole time, Heidi couldn't tear her gaze away. Her heart ached with the knowledge this might be her only chance.

All too soon, it was over, and Angel was grabbing her bag and slinging it over her shoulder. Reluctantly, Heidi followed her out of the coffee shop. They stood on the sidewalk for a few minutes, and then Angel began walking down the side street. Heidi remained silent at her side, trying to figure out how to convince Angel to repeat their moment at High Falls.

"Well, here's me," Angel said, stopping in front of a house that had been converted into apartments. She bit her lip and peered up at Heidi.

"Wait!" Heidi racked her brain, trying to come up with a way to stall. Then she remembered it: the plugs she'd bought earlier. "I have something for you." She handed Angel the bag.

She opened it and then oohed when she saw the plugs. "I wanted these, but I already told you, it wasn't in the budget. Are you sure?"

"Very," Heidi said.

"Then let me give you something too." Angel reached into her bag and produced Leather Anvil's latest CD, *Sonic Pixie Dream Girls*.

"I love it." Heidi reached out to hold Angel's hand. "I guess this is goodn—mph!"

Heidi's arms were suddenly full of Angel, wrapping her in a hug. Angel peered up at her, and Heidi's heart raced with anticipation more than nerves. Maybe this wasn't as romantic and magical as High Falls, but it was good enough. She leaned in.

"Can I kiss you?"

Their lips met almost the moment Angel said yes, and instead of pulling away and walking back to the festival, Heidi poured all her feelings for Angel into the kiss. She wanted to make the most of the moment. If she could only have Angel in her arms once, then tonight would have to be it. She mentally crossed her fingers, desperately wanting Angel to keep their momentum going.

Angel broke the kiss. "Did, um, you want to come in?" The hesitation, the stammer—they hid what Heidi saw in Angel's expression, the raw hunger.

"Yeah," Heidi said, kissing Angel again while Angel fumbled in her pocket for her key.

Maybe for Angel, this was only a single night. It was possible she did this often, with no thoughts to where it would go in the future. As much as

Heidi longed for companionship, she would take this too. It was what she'd wanted from the start of the day, and she was beyond glad Angel did too. If they could only have today before Heidi's life reset, she would take it.

They took the stairs two at a time in the shared house, and they paused outside Angel's room, where this time, it was Angel who pulled Heidi in and captured her lips. Heidi didn't want to stop, but she was also conscious of how public this was. She pulled back.

"Your housemates?" she asked.

"They won't notice or care," Angel replied. "But we can take this inside if you like."

She opened the door, and they stepped in. Heidi didn't have much time to take in the apartment's interior before they were back to kissing. She ran her hand up Angel's side, sliding it underneath her shirt. Angel wedged her leg between Heidi's. Everything was rushed and yet felt so right. Like Cinderella, Heidi feared she only had until midnight to make the most of her time with Angel. Come the new day, Angel would forget, and Heidi would have to begin all over again.

She cupped Angel through her jeans, and Angel unfastened them so Heidi could slide her hand inside. There was nothing else in the world except the two of them and this bright, hot moment, moving together in perfect harmony. Heidi couldn't believe how lucky she was; she poured everything she had into bringing them both to sweet resolution.

Angel had one hand on Heidi's ass, the other tangled in her hair, tugging with both. She gasped and pulled her mouth away from Heidi's. "God...god...so close..." She ground her leg more firmly.

That did it. They were both over the edge, the moment suspended like a note at the end of a piano solo. Heidi almost felt the air ripple. Then, slowly, everything around her came back into focus. The two of them slid down the wall in a heap, panting.

Angel rolled her head to the side to look at Heidi. "I'm sorry," she said.

"For what?"

"That was...fast."

Heidi chuckled. "You did say I needed to have my own needs met. That qualifies as one of them." She laced her hand with Angel's.

There was a long pause before Angel said, "Did you want to stay here?"

Did Heidi? She thought about it. The kids were all right. Heidi knew Kate was about to make an impulsive announcement about college, but she could wait until morning. So could Max ignoring Heidi because he was mad that she made him change his plans. There was no one to dump Heidi or be dumped by her, no one to eventually call to make things up. And if by some miracle, sex with Angel had broken the cycle, then Heidi couldn't come up with anywhere she'd rather be.

"Yeah," she said. "I'd like to stay. Let me text my oldest to let her know

I'm at a friend's place."

They stood, and Heidi stepped away to send Kate a message. She only said it had been a long day and she needed some time to deal with some things. Kate likely wouldn't assume Heidi was spending the night with someone she'd supposedly met only a few hours ago.

When she returned, Angel led Heidi to her bedroom. They shed their clothes, climbing into Angel's bed. This time, they made love more slowly but no less eagerly. Afterward, Angel pulled the covers over them, and they dozed to the sounds of the city outside the window.

When Heidi woke, it was fully dark, and the exterior noise had died down to only an occasional passing car. Angel was awake now too, gently stroking Heidi's hair. Her entire tattoo was visible, vines that wound up her arm and around her shoulder, ending in a large, purple flower. Heidi sighed as she laid her head on Angel's chest. She touched the soft skin of Angel's belly then moved her hand lower. Angel didn't shave anywhere, the opposite of Heidi.

They didn't speak other than what they needed to convey what they wanted. Heidi had never felt so loved and content. Not in the years she was married to Evan, and not with any of the people she'd dated since. In this version of her life, Heidi hadn't been about to marry Cass, now merely Jilly's viola teacher. But Heidi remembered the life in which she'd loved Cass, and even that hadn't been as fulfilling as the last eight days with Angel. When this was all over, Heidi wanted to find a way to meet Angel for real.

She closed her eyes and curled up with this beautiful, wonderful person. Angel indeed.

Day Nine

I

When the smell of coffee from the automatic pot woke Heidi from a deep sleep, she sat bolt upright. She had to blink several times to clear the sleep from her eyes. She was in her own bed, in her own room, in her own apartment.

She screamed and hurled her pillow across the room. It hit her dresser and fell to the floor. Heidi put her aching head in her hands. How could she be doing this again? Hadn't she learned her lesson? Don't fall for the wrong person, several times over. Check. She was clear on that front, and it obviously included Angel. Otherwise, why would Heidi still be doing this?

The only way she could reach Angel now was to listen to her through the radio. Heidi leaned down and switched it on, even though she knew what she was going to hear before it happened. Maybe this way was for the best.

"Goooooood morning, Rochester! We're live here at the Lilac Festival, where the parade begins in less than a half hour!"

Heidi didn't want to hear Angel greeting the city like nothing happened. Like Heidi hadn't been in her bed, hadn't seen her compact body naked, hadn't touched her everywhere. But Angel was talking about the weather and the flowers and ordinary, dull things.

While Heidi sat there, her door opened. She looked up to see Kate, Max, and Jilly, all wearing identical worried expressions. Heidi almost laughed at the way they looked stacked up, peering around the door.

"Mom, are you okay?" Kate asked.

Jilly crept in and slid under the covers, and Max sat on the end of the bed. Kate leaned against the door frame. Heidi put her arms around Jilly.

"Just a little nervous about today," Heidi told them. She had no clue who she was meant to be marrying or if there was anyone at all. By last night, she'd almost forgotten the long list of names and reasons. Cass. Tom. Benji. Dominic. Malcolm. Michelle. Vic. Who knew? Maybe it was someone she'd met in the grocery store once. The world was upside down, and even Angel hadn't made it right.

Kate came farther into the room and opened one of Heidi's drawers. She pulled out the velvet box, carefully hidden among Heidi's lacy undergarments. Turning around, she held it up.

"You'll need this today," she said.

Heidi wanted to cry. She wanted to tell Kate she would never, ever need that wretched thing again. Only one person made her feel like she didn't have to live up to some ideal version of herself. She didn't have to be the perfect, organized person her coworkers imagined she was. Nor did she have to erase the messy, insensitive person her kids and ex-husband saw her as. With Angel, none of it was right or wrong. Angel made everything fall into place, and yet here Heidi sat without her.

She threw off the covers and dashed around, yanking clothes off hangers and out of drawers. She knew this dance, having done it eight other times with seven other proposals. There was only enough time to throw on clothes, leave a note for her kids, and grab her coffee to go. She would never make it to Highland Park by ten-thirty. Besides, all she wanted to do was ditch whoever she was meant to meet and get on with the day until she could see Angel.

After she tugged a pair of jeans loose from the mess in her drawer, she paused. Angel. Wonderful, sweet Angel. Heidi never remembered the full details of her alternate lives other than Angel. Something told Heidi she was the key to everything, including extracting herself from this infuriating loop. But why hadn't it worked when they'd finally ended up together?

At her dresser, she stared at her reflection. Everything felt and looked wrong. Heidi didn't know how to fix it. She was wearing the same thing she'd worn every damn day of this cycle, and every day it looked...off. Like it wasn't her real self she saw in the mirror.

Heidi spotted the velvet box on her dresser where Kate had left it. She picked it up and fiddled with it, opening the lid and then closing it again. It had been different every time. There'd been the perfect princess cut diamond she'd had for Cass and the black band with the rose gold stripe for Tom. The Celtic knot for Benji. The gunmetal for Dominic. The gold braided twist and the rainbow steel and the pink sapphire. This time, it was a silver rose. Heidi sighed and tucked the ring into her pocket, even knowing she wasn't going to use it. She left the bed unmade and went into the kitchen to get that much-deserved—and needed—cup of coffee.

Kate was already at the table with her graduation invitations. She looked up when Heidi entered.

"What's—" Heidi stopped herself from repeating the previous eight days' words. "You need me to drop these off later?"

"Could you?"

"Sure." Heidi was planning to hide out from as many things as she could today, so she had plenty of time to run errands. The only thing that mattered was passing time until she could see Angel.

Kate frowned up at Heidi. "Are you okay? You seem like you're in a really weird mood."

"Yep, just fine!" Heidi attempted cheeriness, though she suspected Kate wasn't buying it. "Busy, busy! Gotta get to the park, and your game, Max's rehearsal, Jilly's recital...it's all under control." Heidi ticked off her schedule on her fingers. "No problem."

Kate stared at her, open-mouthed. "All that? Why didn't you call Dad?"

"Guess I forgot. I'll call him on my way to the park. I'm sure he'll be able to help."

"Hopefully." Kate shrugged. "And don't worry about the invitations. I'll drop them off on the way to the game. See you there?"

"I wouldn't miss it." Heidi bent and kissed the top of Kate's head, wishing she could pre-erase the hurt she was going to cause everyone today.

Kate wished her luck, and Heidi dashed out the door. She sat in the car before turning it on, looking at her phone. She wasn't going to call Evan. He and Jen could drive off a cliff in a bus for all she cared. Okay, maybe she didn't really want them to die, but she did fantasize about writing a story where she could kill them off. If only she were a writer.

She shook her head at her own anger. Had she ever really confronted it? Asked herself why she resented Jen and little Melloney so much?

Now was not the time. She had to go, to get away from everything for the day. There was only one place she wanted to be, and she was going to do her best to find the person who held the key to everything. She didn't know how much time she had, or how many chances to get this day right. Today was about answering those questions, not the big ones about her life and relationships.

Heidi threw her phone onto the passenger seat and sighed. She hadn't even asked Kate who she was supposed to propose to this time. Whoever it was, she planned to ghost them instead. She pulled out of the driveway and headed toward the city.

***

II

Heidi could not have cared less who she was supposed to meet in the park. She hadn't asked Kate, and Kate hadn't volunteered a name. What difference did it make? Heidi was standing them up, whoever they were. She had the ring, but she had vague notions of throwing it into High Falls out of spite.

Not that she was going to do anything of the kind. She wasn't even heading for the city. Instead, she turned toward the church where she knew Evan and Jen would be for their niece's baptism. Stalking her ex and his new wife seemed like as good a plan as any she'd come up with so far.

It was a long wait, during which time Heidi kept her car on the far edge of the parking lot, first watching all the relatives enter the church and then watching them leave again. She wondered if Evan had joined the church along with Jen. He and Heidi had never been religious; they weren't raised in any church. Not one of their three kids had been baptized, and Heidi wasn't even sure of all the details.

While everyone was inside the church, she had time to think. Like every other time she'd been through this day, she remembered a few fuzzy details of the previous ones and some fractured memories of what her life was like now. The lines blurred, though, and she couldn't always be sure a memory was something she'd done with her current—still unnamed—partner or one of the others.

She closed her eyes and tried to put things in order, but the only things she could make come out clearly were the last few days with Angel. Heidi wanted to cry when she thought about waking up alone, away from Angel. She clearly remembered going to sleep with Angel's head on her stomach, feeling utterly at peace for the first time in years. And then she'd opened her eyes to her own bedroom, to the smell of coffee, to the sound of Angel on the radio instead of in her ear.

Whatever it took, she was going to find Angel and figure out how to break the cycle. If that meant coming here to give Evan a piece of her mind and then skipping out on whatever date she was supposed to be having at the park, so be it. No matter that none of this was Evan's fault; Heidi was convinced it would make her feel better to take out her frustration on him anyway.

Heidi pulled herself together when she saw people exiting the church. She moved her car closer and got out, taking her crappy umbrella with her. She wasn't going to get soaked while having this conversation.

The sound of her door closing must have alerted Evan because he looked up. His expression when he saw her was darker than the overcast sky, but Heidi pressed forward. She was not letting this moment go. If Evan were available to help with the kids when she needed it, then she wouldn't be here telling him off right now.

"Heidi." Evan stuck his hands in his pockets and moved toward her. He winced and looked up, thought better of stepping off the church's stoop, and stayed where he was under the shelter by the door.

"Evan." Heidi remained in place as well.

"What are you doing here?"

"I came to tell you exactly what I think."

"Oh, god, Heidi, not now. We're going out to lunch with Jen's family. Can't this wait?"

"No, it can't. You've been a pain in the ass about helping with the kids, and I'm sick of it. You know we have days like today, when everyone is going somewhere. I had plans, but did you care about that when I called you? No, you did not."

"You drunk-dialed me!" Evan hissed, evidently not wanting to announce that fact to the people still streaming out behind him. "And you yelled at me about my wife and daughter."

"Your third daughter. You have two others who need your attention, too."

"Yeah, and they can have it. But maybe they're too busy with their schedules."

"They're too busy?" Heidi practically yelled, causing Evan to shush her. "Oh, that's rich. You're always putting me off when I call, telling me you can't or you have some commitment with Wife Part Deux and your tiny spawn. Reminds me a whole lot of when you didn't have time for us because you were playing hide-the-pickle with Suburban Mom Barbie at your office all those late nights."

Evan's face was a brilliant shade of crimson. He walked closer, thunder in his eyes, and stopped inches from Heidi's face. She leaned back, but he stared her down. Heidi's insides shook, but she was not budging.

"You listen here," Evan said. "At no point was I ever, ever cheating on you with Jen. I worked late, yes. And yes, I admit I was avoiding going home. We were already at a breaking point. You and I..." He shook his head, and for a moment, he couldn't speak. He looked away. When he met Heidi's gaze again, his eyes shone with tears. "I loved you. But there was no way we could make it work. We shouldn't have..." He sniffled. "Screw you, Heidi. I'm done with this. I'll call the kids directly next time, and don't bother asking me for favors. If they need something, they're old enough to ask me themselves. Stay away from me and from Jen."

He turned around, and by that point, Jen had come out of the church with Melloney on her hip. She looked from Evan to Heidi, and she scowled. Then she flipped her long hair over her shoulder and walked away. Evan followed her. Neither of them so much as gave Heidi a backwards glance.

She took a deep breath and let it out slowly. All this time, she'd been angry with Evan for messing around with Jen, staying at the office and lying to her. He'd protested her accusations at the time of their divorce, but Heidi hadn't believed him. Jen was younger, more fashionable, and much more interested in staying home than Heidi had been. She was everything Heidi thought Evan had wanted her to be.

Looking back, the truth had been staring her in the face. Evan hadn't even officially been with Jen until long after the divorce. Heidi simply hadn't wanted to see it. She'd wanted the two of them to be the bad guys, in all possible ways. If she ever got unstuck from this god-forsaken loop, Heidi was going to make it right. She crossed and uncrossed her fingers as a commitment on her way back to the car.

***

<h3 style="text-align:center">III</h3>

There was no plan. No big promises to anyone. Heidi's interaction with Evan had left her shaken, and she couldn't calm herself down.

Ever since she'd woken up alone, in her own bed, she'd felt hopeless. If none of the changes she made affected this endless loop, what could she do but give up? She could spend the rest of her life—or whatever this was—trying endless combinations of things. Or she could do whatever she wanted, knowing it wouldn't make a difference because she would do it all over again the next day.

There was no reason she shouldn't go to the Lilac Festival and drink too many Genesee Cream Ales and ignore all the texts from her kids and Evan and anyone else who wanted her attention. She could do whatever struck her fancy in the moment because when she woke up, it would be erased.

Heidi drove to the Lilac Festival. By then, the rain had let up, and she wasn't in much danger of ending up soaked through. She did remember how bad the parking was, however, and used the shuttle. Some decisions were prudent regardless of whether she would have to relive her day.

She turned her phone off and wandered around the vendor booths from one end of the park to the other. When she came to Maya's handmade baby clothes, she bought the tiny Leather Anvil onesie and rainbow beanie. Who knew what she would do with it, but it was hers now.

By dinnertime, her feet hurt from walking, her head hurt from the noise of the crowd, and her heart hurt from everything else. She wasn't hungry, but she ended up at the large food tent anyway. She bought a fried dough and a beer and sat at the picnic table with the young family. Again.

They probably thought she was weird. The mother eyed her but returned to feeding her baby. The father paid no attention to her at all, busy with the toddler. Heidi didn't even feel nostalgic for her life with Evan anymore. What was the point? Even if her morning rant was wiped clean tomorrow, she still had to deal with having called his wife a name and yelling at him for not spending enough time with their kids.

She didn't want that life anyway. Heidi had spent the previous eighteen years trying to prove herself. She had nothing to show for it except her kids resenting her limited availability and rejecting the help she'd given them to succeed. When she arrived home later, Max would be mad about the rehearsal, the costume pieces, or both. Jilly would be upset that Heidi had missed her recital. Kate would tell her about not wanting to go to college after all. Then Heidi would go to bed and wake up to do the whole thing over again. And again. And again.

Heidi hadn't even realized she was crying until the young mother handed her a tissue and gave her a sympathetic pat on the shoulder. The couple packed up their kids and left Heidi slumped at the table.

When she didn't have any tears left, Heidi stood. She didn't know where she was supposed to go, only where she wanted to go. It might be a bad idea. So far, Angel's presence hadn't changed a thing. At least it would be comforting to see her, however briefly.

On the way, Heidi stopped at the jewelry vendor. She only hesitated a moment before buying the plugs. In every version of her day, there were only two things that had ever felt perfect. One was buying the plugs; the other was dancing with Angel to Leather Anvil.

Fresh tears rolled down her cheeks the minute she was out of the booth. She was so wrapped up in her misery that she once again failed to see the big man. He barreled into her, sending her flying off her feet. Her head whipped back and cracked against the tent pole. She heard the man yell something at her, but her ears were ringing, and she didn't catch it.

"You okay?"

The sound of Angel's voice set Heidi off again, and she sobbed. Drawing her knees up, she rested her arms on them and ducked her head. Everything was wrong and horrible and she had no answers.

Through the fog, she heard Angel telling people to back off and asking someone for water. She knelt down and put an arm around Heidi.

"I've got you. Do you think you can stand so we can get away from the crowd?"

Heidi nodded and let Angel help her up. The back of her head ached, but she was otherwise fine. Angel handed her a water bottle, and Heidi drank gratefully. She wiped her eyes and nose with the tissue the young mother had given her.

Angel led Heidi to a bench by the children's stage. They sat on the bench for a long time while Heidi collected herself. She had no idea what to say to Angel or anyone else in her life. She hadn't merely messed up her day trying to be perfect. This time, she'd done the exact opposite.

"Are you sure you're all right?" Angel asked. "I can get you some medical attention."

"No, that's not necessary."

Angel peered at her. "Why do I get the sense this is about more than whacking your head on my tent pole?"

Heidi groaned. "Because it is. My life is one endless loop

of...of...horribleness."

"That bad, huh?" Angel rubbed Heidi's back. "I know we only met ten minutes ago, but I'm happy to listen."

Heidi took a deep breath. "I can't be perfect and I can't be in several places at once and I can't even make my relationships work. So today, I gave up on all of it."

"Gave up?"

"Hid here at the Festival, hoping it might all go away. Except now I have to go home and deal with the mess I made."

"Everyone screws up sometimes," Angel said as if delivering wisdom.

"Well, yeah. It seems like I do it more than average, though."

Angel chuckled. "Believe me, I've been there. I question my life choices every single day."

"You?" Heidi stared at her then shook her head. "I don't believe that."

"Do you know who I am?"

"Yeah. Angel Flores, from WNDR. Although you do look a little different from your picture on the bus."

Angel laughed. "Did you think I was a Rachel Maddow clone in real life? On an indie rock station?"

"Not really, no. But you were going to tell me about screwing up."

"Okay. Well, I have my dream job, right? Except that it's not always. It doesn't pay enough, even after doing it for years. My male cohost still earns more than I do, and he's been there half as long. I had to fight to be where I am. I should be grateful, right? Only I sometimes feel like I've put so much time into it that I didn't get to do the fun things I was supposed to enjoy at my age."

Heidi wiped her eyes again. "I had a baby when I was eighteen. I don't regret having her, but a lot of the choices I made were about giving her more opportunities than I had. I know what it's like to spend a lot of time on one thing at the expense of everything else." She also understood about proving herself, but she didn't add that.

Angel reached over and squeezed her hand. "Something I learned is that it's never too late to change how you do things. I decided that if I wasn't getting what I wanted out of my job, I would spend less energy spinning my wheels. I'm doing some other things now that make me happy. It's not about not messing up. It's what we do with it afterward."

"I'm not sure there's anything I can do." Heidi sniffled.

"There's always tomorrow," Angel said.

Heidi twisted in her seat to face Angel. Her gut twisted, knowing if she really did change everything, she might never see Angel again. Her children might not forgive her for what she'd done today, and Evan certainly wouldn't.

"I don't know..."

Angel put her hands on Heidi's cheeks and held her gaze. "Please don't give up, Heidi."

Heidi startled at the use of her name. Had she introduced herself? Her mind was too muddled to remember.

"I–I'll try," she said.

Angel stood. "Come on. Let's go listen to the concert. Surely letting your mind and body relax will inspire you, and you can figure out what to do from here."

When Heidi rose, she saw a sprig of lilacs on the ground beside the bench. Angel followed her gaze and bent to pick it up. She handed it to Heidi.

"Sounds like you need to make a wish and trust in it."

Heidi was about to object, but something made her pause. This had all started with a simple wish. Maybe she could end it with one too. She put her nose to the blossoms and inhaled their fragrance.

"Go on."

Heidi closed her eyes and wished.

"Did you do it?" Angel asked. When Heidi nodded, she said, "Now, blow on it, or it won't come true."

Heidi blew gently on the sprig, and she was surrounded once again by the distinctive smell. Maybe Angel was right and there was something special about the first day of the Lilac Festival.

When she went to tuck the flowers in her shirt pocket, she remembered the plugs. "Here," she said. "Why don't you take these? I don't know why, but I felt as if I should buy them even though I don't wear them."

Angel opened the box and stared, open-mouthed, at the plugs. "Oh, I love them! I was going to buy them, but..."

"Not in your budget?" Heidi said.

"Right," Angel agreed. "Thank you."

They walked back toward the booth so Angel could explain where she was going. When she came back out, she handed a CD to Heidi—*Sonic Pixie Dream Girls*. Heidi took it and slipped it into the bag that had previously held the plugs.

"Let's go listen to that concert," Angel said.

They walked hand in hand back to the main stage, and Heidi allowed herself to be swallowed up in the music.

***

IV

By the time Heidi arrived at home, all of her children were waiting for her. Kate had reheated the previous night's chicken enchiladas and generously shared them with the younger two. They were sitting at the table, the dirty dishes stacked neatly in the center. Kate's arms were crossed, and her expression was grim. Max had his chin propped on his hand, and Jilly looked like she'd been crying. Heidi was well aware it was her own fault.

"You missed, like, everything," Kate said, her words like ice.

"One of the other moms felt bad for me and brought me home. I had to sit on the stoop until Kate showed up."

"You never came to get me for the recital," Jilly accused. "I had to call Dad, and he was really mad 'cause he was already there and had to come back for me. Then I was late, and they had to change stuff so I could play."

Heidi sank into the last empty chair. "I know. I'm sorry."

"You were so busy thinking about *your* big day that you forgot all of us." Kate's voice quavered.

"No." Heidi shook her head. "I messed up, but that's not why. I—" She cut herself off before saying she'd only wanted to get through the day because she knew she would just have to relive it anyway. That was why she'd ignored everything, but she knew now that wasn't the answer. She could fix this, if given the chance.

"Mom?" Max was staring at her, bewildered. "You were gonna say something."

Taking a deep breath, Heidi tried to calm down before speaking again. "You three are the most important part of my whole life. I messed up because I didn't feel like being perfect anymore. I guess I just...gave up." She looked up at them. "I can't be everything to everyone all the time. But I can do better for all of you. Today sucked, and I'm sorry. But tomorrow is another day, and I think we should...have a re-do. Okay?"

There wasn't much else to say. The kids left the table and went to their rooms. Heidi stood and began clearing up the dishes. When she was through, she sifted through the mail—ads for takeout, bills, Max's braces—the same stuff she'd either looked at or ignored for eight previous days. She was about to go sit and try to watch television when it struck her.

There were some things she didn't regret. Like meeting Angel.

Heidi picked up the bag with the *Sonic Pixie Dream Girls* CD in it. She opened it and took out the lilac-colored business card. Every day, Angel had shown her something new. Heidi pictured her again now, her dark hair and sparkling brown eyes. Angel was smart and fun and attractive, but there was much more to her. She had herself more together than Heidi had ever been. What would she tell Heidi to do now?

Trembling with nerves, Heidi sat on her couch, staring at the numbers. Was it too late to make everything right? Could she make amends to every person she'd hurt in her need to erase her own regret? Angel would tell her it was never the wrong time, Heidi was sure of it. She reached into the drawer in the end table and pulled out paper and a pen. The list she was about to make would be gone in the morning, but with any luck, writing it down would make it stick in her brain. She had a lot of planning to do.

When she was done, she left the notepad beside the lamp. With a stretch and a sigh, Heidi forced herself off the couch and down the hallway to bed.

DAY TEN

I

The smell of coffee from the automatic pot woke Heidi from a deep sleep. She stirred restlessly, vaguely recalling that she'd been dreaming—something about Cass at Jilly's recital, and then about someone with sparkling, dark eyes. She squinted and massaged her eyeballs through her closed lids until she could open them. Angel. Heidi knew who she was in the dream this time. Slowly, bits and pieces from the previous night returned to her. Had she changed anything? She switched on the radio on her bedside table.

"Good morning, ROC! We're live here at the Lilac Festival, where the parade begins in thirty minutes!"

That was not the same thing Heidi'd heard every single morning for the past nine days—or however long it had really been. She rubbed her eyes again, wishing she could rewind the audio. Straining to catch something else that was off, she sat there in bed with the covers pooling around her waist.

Nothing else sounded different, but Heidi felt it all the same. She was back to being with Cass, and if she was right, she had one more chance. She threw off the blankets and dashed around, yanking clothes off hangers and out of drawers. She wasn't going to take the same route she had the past nine times.

After she tugged a pair of jeans loose from the mess in her drawer, she tossed it onto the bed. With her clothes laid out, she grabbed her phone and hit Cass's number.

"Morning!" Cass said, sounding cheerful.

"Hey," Heidi said then sighed. "Um. About this morning. I..." She chewed her nail nervously then rushed the words. "I can't meet you after all. I hope that's okay. I know you need to get stuff set up, and I don't want to take up your time, and—"

Cass laughed. "Slow down! So, you'd rather meet up at the recital later. Sounds fine to me."

"Oh, thank goodness." Heidi chuckled, but then she cleared her throat. "I need a massive, huge favor. As in, I'll buy you lattes for the rest of forever if you do this for me."

"What in the world do you need?" There was a pause. "It's not illegal, is it?"

"Nothing like that! I need you to bring Jilly with you. Kate's got a game, and I can't manage everything on my own. I know she'll be happy to help you set up."

"Sure!" Cass replied. "When should I pick her up?"

"Whenever you like. I'll be at Kate's game, but Jilly won't be home alone for long."

"Okay. I'll get her around one."

Heidi breathed a sigh of relief. "Thanks. You're the best."

Cass laughed again. "It's fine. I'm glad you called. I was concerned you were trying to fit too much in today."

"I was," Heidi replied. "But I think I've actually got it under control for once."

"Somehow I know you do. See you at three?"

"I'll be there. Are we still on for tonight after the recital?"

"If you help me clean up, then yes." There was definitely a smile hidden in the words, but Cass wasn't joking.

"I'll help you any way I can."

Heidi ended the call and then scrolled through her contacts again. She located the number Benji must've given her back when rehearsals started. She texted a message: *This is Max's mom. Would you be able to bring him home after rehearsal? I'll be happy to trade for next week.* She left her phone on the bed and began getting dressed.

At her dresser, she stared at her reflection. She'd put on a white shirt and a lightweight blue blazer. Knowing she didn't need to rush, she traded out her earrings for tiny sparkling studs and added a thin gold necklace. She fluffed her hair, remembering to grab a comb and a travel size hairspray. Taking a deep, cleansing breath, she fished around in the top drawer among her lacy underwear to find the ring. For a moment, she held the box in her hand. Then she closed her fingers around it. She placed the box carefully back beneath her undergarments and closed the drawer. It would be there when she needed it.

For another minute, she stared at the closed drawer, fighting with her emotions. Even if it had only been a dream, was she guilty of cheating on Cass? She couldn't be sure. The mere fact that she'd so easily fallen for someone else wasn't a good omen for the status of their relationship, and Heidi suspected Cass had seen the signs long before she had picked up on them herself.

No use dwelling on it now with so much to do ahead of her. She made her bed, smoothing out the covers, then stepped out and closed her bedroom door. In the living room, she checked the end table for the notes she'd made. The notepad wasn't there. Heidi thought she could remember everything on the list, given how much time she'd spent turning it over in her mind. Still, she thought it might be a good idea to jot them down. She opened the drawer to take out the notepad and pen. When she flipped to the first page, she gasped. It wasn't blank: all her carefully written ideas were still there in purple ink.

Grinning, she tucked the notepad into the inner pocket of her blazer and went into the kitchen to get that much-deserved—and needed—cup of coffee.

Kate was already at the table with her stacks of graduation invitations. She looked up when Heidi came in. "You look really nice. I thought you were meeting Cass this morning. Aren't you going to be late?"

"I called her to postpone. She's busy getting things ready for the recital, and I would like for this day to go better than—" Heidi caught herself before saying *better than the last nine.* "—any other."

Kate gave her the same sly grin as she had every other morning. "You mean proposing? Today's the big day, right?"

"Right. Yes. Well, I'm off to take Max to rehearsal, and then I have to go pick some things up. You need anything?"

"Nah. Wait, wasn't I supposed to drop him off when I went to catch the bus for the game? It's only bringing him home I can't do."

"That's covered. You sure you don't mind taking him?"

"It's fine. Go do the shopping."

Heidi gestured to the invitations. "I could wait a few minutes and mail those for you on my way."

"I was going to take them with me later." Kate sifted through them. "Besides, I still have too many to do for you to wait. I'll see you at the game?"

"You bet." Heidi kissed the top of Kate's head before pouring her coffee into a travel mug.

Something else clicked, and Heidi took an envelope and a pre-paid credit gift card out. She labeled it clearly with Max's name, showed Kate, and left it on the table. She paused at the coat closet then pulled out a hoodie. Much as she'd love to have one with the team logo on it, she felt better being prepared with her own.

***

II

In the car, she checked her messages. Benji had sent her a thumbs up and then asked for the address. Heidi quickly texted her back. *Max said you'd take him shopping with Kayla afterward. Something about costume pieces. I gave him the money. Is that okay?*

As soon as she got a *Sure!* with a smiley from Benji, she headed for the Lilac Festival. She only needed a few minutes at one of the vendors. Heidi even knew exactly where it was, after seeing it two of the previous nine days.

She remembered not to try parking on site. It was now a little after ten-thirty, and she had until noon. Kate's game was at twelve-thirty, Jilly's recital was at three, and her date with Cass was as soon as she could get Jilly home. This time around, she had a far sturdier umbrella just in case the rain started before she left the park.

Heidi rode the shuttle, which took some time due to the parade. Since she knew where she was headed, though, it was a quick dash to the vendor. Sure enough, the rain started as she ducked into the tent. It took her a few minutes to pick out the right thing, but when she saw it, she knew she had what she needed. Along with it, she bought a handmade gift bag and matching card from the next booth over. One shuttle ride later, she was back in the car. She hastily threw it all together and signed the card. Then she headed for Word of God Church. No time like the present to start behaving like an adult.

She didn't go in. It would've been a bit strange for her to attend, uninvited, the baptism of a child she was only peripherally associated with. Instead, she sat in her car, facing the garden. She opened her window despite the rain and played a game on her phone while she waited.

At last the church doors opened, and people began filing out. It took a while, but there was Evan. She tucked her phone away and exited her car. She jogged through the drizzle to the sheltered church entrance. Evan stopped dead in his tracks and stared at Heidi.

"What are you doing here?"

"I have something for you. Well, for Leah. That's your niece, right?"

Evan's face transformed from budding annoyance to utterly perplexed. "Okay," he said.

Jen, his wife, shifted their toddler on her hip and looked like she was about to say something. Evan waved her off and told her he'd be at the car in a couple minutes. With an emphatic eye roll, she whipped her straight hair over her shoulder and walked away.

"A peace offering." Heidi held out the bag. "I know I only call you when I'm a mess, and I think it's time I changed that."

"What did you say?"

"I said it's time for a change."

"No," Evan said. "Before that. About only calling me when you're a mess." His voice softened.

"Isn't that what you think? I ask you for stuff because I can't get my shit together, not because I'm asking you to spend time with the kids."

"I—yeah. How'd you know?"

Heidi smiled in spite of herself. "You're a bit predictable."

Evan smiled back, but then he turned serious. "I know you think I don't care about them now that Jen and I have Melloney. But I really do want more time with them. I guess I don't want it to only be in the car, driving them place to place."

Heidi laughed ruefully. "They're busy kids. Most of my time with them is spent in the car." She held Evan's gaze, trying to help him understand. "Don't underestimate the power of talking on the drive. You'd be surprised at how much you'll learn."

"I believe you. Maybe we can sit down and look at the kids' schedules to work something out that makes sense for all of us."

"I'd like that. A compromise between my panic and your need to see the kids more often." She held out the bag. "It really is a gift for your niece."

"Can I peek?"

"Sure."

Evan set the bag down and pulled out the contents. It was a teeny, tiny shirt with a watercolor of Rochester, a sprig of lilacs, and the words "The Flower City" in pastel rainbow lettering.

"Cute," he said and folded it back up. "Thank you."

"No problem." Heidi helped him tuck the shirt back into the gift bag. "I gotta go. I have barely enough time to make it to Kate's game. See you at the recital later?"

"We'll be there." Evan hesitated, then kissed her cheek. "I know I'm not much help today, but call me about stuff if you need to, as long as it's not the day of. I can't promise I'll say yes every time, but I'll try to help out more often." He sighed. "Jen's a good mom, but she doesn't always understand that my other kids are a priority too. It's not easy having two families."

"I understand." Heidi squeezed his hand before the two of them went in separate directions.

Heidi sat in her car for a few minutes to collect her thoughts. Steps one through three complete. Now off to Kate's ball game. She had everything under control, like always.

***

III

Everything under control, that was, except the weather. Heidi was glad she'd remembered her hoodie. As quick as she could, she stripped off the blazer and replaced it with the sweatshirt. She pulled the hood over her hair and made to grab her good umbrella. It wasn't on the seat where she thought she'd left it, and she didn't have time to hunt for it now. She spotted the fold-up one in the map holder and snorted. That was the umbrella that she'd broken on several previous versions of the day.

Well, she decided, perfection was a myth. Preparation she could do, but not perfection. She took the umbrella anyway and hoped for the best as she stepped out into the light drizzle. Then she set off at a jog toward the team tent. When the umbrella threatened to flip inside out, she braced it against the wind and it held until she reached her destination.

The game hadn't started yet, but it was a close shave. Heidi had squeaked in at the last minute. Most of the other parents were huddled under the tent, out of the rain. The coaches and team had set it up perfectly so the adults wouldn't get soaked sitting on the bleachers. The field was still relatively dry, meaning it hadn't rained as hard there as in the city. The team was playing West Irondequoit today. Heidi figured after multiple go-rounds, she ought to at least remember that much.

Tom was still guardian of the snacks and drinks. Heidi watched him talking and laughing with Wilhelm. In the version where she'd been about to propose to Tom, there hadn't been anything going on between them. But this was the "real" world, the one in which Heidi had been with Cass for almost two years. Maybe there was room for something to grow between Tom and Wilhelm.

The game started, and Heidi's musing about Tom came to an end. She huddled with the rest of the parents, watching the girls play. Eventually, the drizzle stopped, and the sun began to peek through the clouds. Heidi stepped out of the tent in time to watch Kate hit her home run. She hoped Kate heard her cheering above all the other spectators.

When the game ended, there was chaos. Parents and kids crowded around to congratulate the team on their victory. Kate finally turned Heidi's direction and waved. The smile she gave Heidi made everything else she'd done to rearrange her day worthwhile.

"Mom!" Kate yelled, making a beeline for her.

"Hey honey." Heidi accepted a muddy, sweaty hug. "Great game!"

"Did you see my home run?"

"I did. That was amazing." Heidi held Kate's hand and gave it a squeeze. "I'm so proud of you."

Kate pulled back and frowned. "Didn't you have to go get the others?"

"Nope. Max has a ride. All taken care of. And Jilly's already at the studio, helping Cass set up. I'm heading right there after I help pick up the tent."

"Cool. I'm glad you stayed. It's time to celebrate!" Kate bounced a little. "I'll shower and change back at school, and then we're going to find our dresses for prom."

"Good luck."

Kate bounded off to talk to the other girls and get a bottle of water. One by one, parents drifted away, with or without their daughters in tow. Heidi hung back to talk to Tom. She began by picking up the empty water bottles and orange rinds strewn around.

"Thanks," Tom said as Heidi tossed a couple bottles into the recycling bag.

"No problem." She paused. "I'm Heidi, Kate's mom. Nevaeh's dad, right?"

"Tom." He held out his hand and laughed softly. "I know perfectly well what nickname everyone has for me."

Heidi giggled. "It's not inaccurate."

"Thanks, I think." He flashed his very white grin.

They picked up trash in silence for a few minutes. When they were done, Tom thanked her again. Heidi gathered her things, including the umbrella, which had miraculously survived to shelter her—or break—another day.

"Hey," she said, tapping Tom on the shoulder.

He turned toward her. "Yes?"

"I, uh…if you ever need…anything…or someone to talk to who gets it, I'm here." She blew out a breath, fearing she was doing this all very badly. The things Tom had shared with her weren't ones she was meant to know in this life.

Tom's puzzled frown transformed into understanding. "You know, Wilhelm said the same thing."

"Well, then." Heidi smiled. "Maybe you don't need me after all."

"Having another friend who 'gets it'"—he made air quotes—"isn't a bad thing. Maybe you'd like to join us for coffee sometime."

"I know the perfect place."

Heidi was about to leave when Tom stopped her. "Here," he said, handing her a team sweatshirt. "I've got some extras."

She stared at the shirt in her hands, wondering if Tom had done this for all the parents or if he thought she needed help in some way. Did it matter?

"Thank you," she said.

"You're welcome."

She left Tom, the remaining team members, and the coaches to tear down the tent. All the way to her car, into the driver's seat, and back onto the road, Heidi's heart remained light.

***

IV

Heidi sank into a chair at the back of the room, making it with exactly forty-five seconds to spare before the recital started. The woman in front of her turned around to scowl at her, but Heidi only smiled in return.

She spotted Evan and Jen a few rows up. Evan turned around and gave her a tiny wave, and she waved back. A moment later, Cass stood at the podium to welcome everyone, and Evan turned around again.

It was a beautiful recital. Cass's skill as a teacher was evident not only in how well the students played but in how much respect and love they had for her. Heidi was proud of her for all the hard work she'd put in helping the kids learn and grow as musicians.

Jilly, of course, was marvelous. Heidi remembered to capture it on her phone, though she hoped Evan had gotten a better recording on his much higher quality one.

Megan finished out the recital, wowing the audience with her Mozart concerto. Afterward, Cass thanked everyone and invited them to the reception. Heidi patted the bag on the chair next to her, glad she'd taken the few extra minutes before Kate's game to stop at Wegmans. Maybe Jen had brought some perfect, pretentious treats, but at least Heidi had remembered. Besides, who didn't like Oreos?

Jilly bounded up to her. "Hi, Mom!" She grinned, and it made Heidi's day.

Heidi stood and hugged her. "I'm so proud of you!"

"Did you record it?"

"I did, and I can show you later. But you might want to ask Dad to send you his. It's probably better quality."

"Okay. Wanna get a cookie with me and meet Megan?"

"Ah, the famous Megan," Heidi teased. "She's the one who played Mozart, right?"

"Yeah! She was amazing."

"She sure was. Let's go meet her."

Jilly took Heidi's hand, something she hadn't done in years. The sweetness of it was mitigated somewhat by how forcefully Jilly tugged on her, but Heidi still appreciated the gesture. They stood in line at the cookie table. Megan was right in front of them with her father. Heidi peered around him and saw the mother of the little boy with the cello, but she didn't seem to be paying any attention to Megan's dad. Heidi breathed a sigh of relief.

After Jilly introduced Heidi to Megan, she made polite conversation with Dominic while the girls giggled together about something. Evan and Jen, with their toddler, joined Heidi in line.

Jen congratulated Jilly, and although Heidi cringed at the way she talked to her as if she were five years younger, she now understood Jen was at least making an effort. Heidi smiled at Evan, and he squeezed her shoulder in understanding.

Several cookies later, they reached the front of the line where Cass was greeting each family. She held out her hands to Heidi, who took them.

Cass—beautiful, wonderful Cass—gave Heidi a smile that almost broke her heart. Heidi knew what was coming, and even though it was the right thing to do, it still hurt. It would have to wait, though. This was not the moment.

Cass said, "Jilly, you were outstanding." To Heidi, she said, "She's going places. You watch."

"If that's what she wants, we'll see her through it." Heidi smiled at Jilly.

"I'm going to go mingle for a bit before we start cleaning up. Congratulations again." Cass let go of Heidi's hands.

Jilly grabbed another cookie and bounded away to talk to some of the other kids. Heidi hung back, watching her for a minute before pulling her list out of her pocket. She put a line through three more items and tucked it away again. The hardest part of her day was yet to come, but she'd made it this far. Heidi wasn't giving up.

***

V

Heidi met Cass as planned near the main stage food tent. They carried their dinner to the picnic tables outside and sat at the same table with the parents and the small children. Heidi watched them out of the corner of her eye as she and Cass ate.

"I'm sorry this isn't the romantic dinner you probably imagined," Heidi said.

"It's fine. We'll still be able to see the concert. What was the band you liked?"

"Leather Anvil. They're the opening act for Generation Xerox." Heidi felt guilty, sitting there with Cass when she'd rather be at the CD booth with Angel.

"Ah, right. You do like your punk."

"Alt-rock," Heidi corrected then immediately wished she could take it back. Music was one of the things she and Cass disagreed on, but there wasn't any need to correct her right now. "Hey," she said, putting her hand on top of Cass's.

Cass shifted her gaze from the family next to them back to Heidi. "Hm?"

"The recital was great. You're so good with those kids." Heidi smiled and rubbed Cass's hand with her thumb.

"Thank you." Cass visibly relaxed.

This was the moment Heidi had been dreading, but she knew she had to do it. "I wanted to talk to you about something." Heidi set down the fork she'd been using to eat her curry.

"Oh?" Cass withdrew her hand and did the same. "What's wrong? You seem...sad."

"I..." Heidi breathed slowly to calm her nerves and hold back tears. "I was going to make it all romantic and everything. I'd originally planned it for this morning, but then I decided it would be rushed. But…"

Cass's eyebrows shot up. "What's going on?"

"I wanted to ask you to marry me. But…" Heidi closed her eyes. When she opened them, the woman at the other end of the table was watching the two of them. "I think maybe we're better off…" She couldn't say it.

Cass was silent for a long time. At last she said quietly, "You're right." Her eyes shimmered with tears.

"I've had a feeling for a while now that we were going through the motions." Heidi kept her gaze on Cass, trying to convey how much she still loved her even if they weren't in love. "At first, I wondered if we were simply bored. I thought a fun, romantic date here and proposing to you at the top of the hill would make it right. But I know better now."

"It's not—" Cass stopped. "I was going to say 'it's not just you,' but that seems so flat. I love you, Heidi. I do. But our lives don't mesh, and it's time we both admitted it."

"I'm trying to be better about keeping track and not falling into the trap of overcommitment and perfectionism. But it's a process, and you don't need to try to fit yourself in as my lowest priority."

"Running a business takes so much time," Cass said. "I thought maybe you were avoiding me because I work so many hours. So I told myself the problem was you and your messes and dramatics, even though I know my schedule is equally to blame."

Heidi laughed. "Well, you're not wrong about the messes and dramatics. But I wasn't doing it to avoid you."

Cass gripped Heidi's hands. "What about Jilly?"

"I'll talk to her tonight. She's a smart, good-hearted girl. I don't think we need to worry too much as long as we're okay."

"We are. I don't want to lose your friendship." Cass offered a half-smile. "Through everything, we've at least managed to maintain that much."

"We have."

When they finished eating, they stood and hugged. That was it. There was nothing more to be said between them for now. Everything with Jilly and her viola lessons would work out fine in the end.

Heidi watched Cass go, and the woman at the other end of the table, now finished feeding her infant, gave Heidi a sympathetic look. Maybe she'd been there too before meeting the man who was hitching a backpack higher on his shoulders. Heidi smiled at her to reassure her, and the woman smiled back. Then Heidi gathered her trash and tossed it into the barrel by the path.

By then, Leather Anvil had started to play, but Heidi was on a mission. She didn't have time to stop and listen. She had to get to the CD booth to find Angel.

She ducked in and out of foot traffic, bypassing the jewelry booth she'd eagerly scouted in previous versions of today. She finally spotted the right one and made straight for it.

Angel wasn't there.

Heidi wanted to cry. She had to find the person she'd spent every evening with for the last ten days, the person she'd gotten to know over coffee and dancing to Leather Anvil. She wanted the scent of lilacs and the feel of Angel's soft lips and skin against hers. But the person in the booth was a bleached blond who looked barely past their teens. Heidi didn't recognize them.

Maybe she'd dreamed it. Maybe Angel only existed in some whacky version of her life where she hit her head hard enough to see stars. This time, she'd beaten the crowd here, and the man who had pushed her before wasn't there. Maybe neither of them was real.

Except Heidi knew Angel was an actual, live human, having heard her on the radio for the last year and a half. So where was she now, and who was this person in the booth?

"I'm sorry," Heidi said to no one as she burst into tears of frustration and disappointment. She turned to go, but she bumped into someone because she wasn't paying attention. "Sorry," she mumbled again.

"No problem. Are you okay?"

Heidi blinked away her tears. She knew that voice. Her heart and her stomach both did flip-flops. "Yeah," she said. "I think so." She wiped her eyes.

"You want to go sit?" When Heidi nodded, Angel grabbed two waters and called to the blond in the booth, "Be back in a couple minutes."

Heidi followed the rainbow beanie and Leather Anvil T-shirt over to a bench, and the two of them sat. Angel opened one water and handed it to Heidi. She took the other herself and sipped it, silently watching the kids' concert. After a few minutes, she turned her attention to Heidi.

"I'm Angel," she said. "But I take it you knew that."

"Heidi." She took a gulp of water. Nothing for it. She'd already broken up with Cass, and that had gone okay. Maybe Angel would be all right with a bit of weird in her day. "This is gonna sound nuts, but I don't really care if it does. You ever have one of those days that feels like you keep doing the same things over and over? Like a hellish version of déjà vu?"

"Like you're stuck in a loop, everything repeating itself?" Angel arched her pierced eyebrow, and Heidi wondered how she hadn't noticed the curved barbell on any of the previous days.

"Yeah. Wait." Heidi stared at her, trying to figure out if Angel meant what it sounded like she did. "So that doesn't seem strange to you at all?"

Angel laughed. "Define strange."

"I made this stupid wish that I could...have a do-over." Heidi cringed, but Angel didn't look as confused as Heidi felt. Maybe Angel was taking it as a metaphor. "I kept trying to get it right, to be the perfect mom who can do everything. Only I never could, except for one thing."

Angel's purple lips curved into her beautiful smile. "And now?"

"I don't think there's any such thing as perfect. And if there is, I'm not sure I want it anyway. I'd rather be ordinary." Heidi wanted to reach out to Angel, to take her hand, to kiss her. But she couldn't. Not until they'd had some time in the real world to be sure. "I'm sorry to dump all this on you."

"It's all right. Sounds like you've done a lot of thinking." Angel tilted her head. "You want to tell me what the one thing is you got perfect?"

You, Heidi wanted to say. She didn't, though. "Maybe you'd rather not, if you think I'm too messy or weird, but I'd love to tell you over some good coffee."

Angel grinned. "You're on. I know—"

"—just the place," Heidi finished, and they both laughed. "Let me give you my phone number."

"Wait here," Angel said. She darted back to the booth and returned to the bench. She handed Heidi a CD. "On the house. My card is inside." She leaned in close enough Heidi thought she might kiss her cheek. "Call me."

Angel stood. She picked up a sprig of lilacs that had been sitting next to the bench. Heidi accepted them and inhaled the fragrance. It took her back to the times she and Angel had kissed, the scent of lilacs in the air and on Angel's skin.

"Thank you," Heidi said.

"Make a wish," Angel urged her.

"That's dandelions, not lilacs." The same thing Heidi had told her ten days ago—or today, depending on how one looked at it.

"I think it works with lilacs on the first day of the Festival."

Heidi shook her head. "I've made enough wishes for a lifetime."

"Fair enough. I'll see you around?"

"Count on it."

Heidi watched her go, the second person tonight to walk away from her. But in both situations, she felt content with the outcome. Heidi collected herself and then wandered back to the stage to listen to the rest of the Leather Anvil's portion of the concert.

***

VI

By the time Heidi arrived at home, all of her children were there. Kate had reheated the previous night's chicken enchiladas and generously shared them with the younger two. They were still sitting at the table, laughing about something Kate was showing the younger ones on her phone. All three of them looked up when she came in.

Kate picked up right away on Heidi's lack of enthusiasm. She stood and went to the stove. "You want some? It's still warm."

"Thank you, but I had dinner at the festival." Heidi set the CD on the table. "I did get this, though."

Max pulled it closer. "This is the band you like, right? Did you see them?"

"Sort of," Heidi replied. "I was distracted for part of the time with other things." She sat, and so did Kate. "Maybe we should talk about it."

"What happened?" Kate asked.

Heidi looked at each one of her children in turn, their expectant postures and open expressions. She rubbed her temples to ease the pressure building there. She had to tell them. "Cass and I broke up."

"Oh, no!" Kate jumped up and wrapped her arms around Heidi. "I'm sorry, Mom."

Heidi patted her hand awkwardly, her arms still pinned to her by Kate's embrace. "It's all right. I think this was building for a while, and I tried too hard to stop it by planning a big proposal. It was a friendly split, something we both agreed on."

Jilly wiped away tears. "I love Miss Cass."

"I know you do." Heidi stood and took Jilly's hands, pulling her up. "Come on. Let's go talk about it. Kate, Max, can you take care of the food and dishes?"

"Sure thing." Kate poked Max until he stood.

While the two of them cleaned up, Heidi led Jilly down the hall to the master bedroom. The sound of Kate and Max bickering good-naturedly followed them until Heidi shut her door. She sat on the bed and patted it. Obediently, Jilly came and perched next to her, but not too close.

"I know you're sad and mad," Heidi said. "But I want you to know that Cass and I both love you. She still wants to be your viola teacher, and she and I still want to be friends. But we can't be your moms together."

Jilly scooched closer and leaned into Heidi's side. "What happened?"

"I'm not sure if I can explain," Heidi said. She thought for a moment, stroking Jilly's hair. "Sometimes two people are both very much alike and not alike at all."

Jilly shifted to frown up at Heidi. "That makes no sense."

"Miss Cass and I are similar in some ways, like how much we love you and how hard we work to do the right things. But we don't want the same things in life."

"Like that poem we read in class about the two paths in the forest?"

Heidi chuckled. "A little bit. But neither of us wants to take a less-traveled road. We simply don't want to be on the same road as each other."

"You promise you're not gonna get mad at each other all the time? Like you and Dad?"

"I think Dad and I have resolved our differences."

"You did?" Jilly squirmed to turn toward Heidi.

"I don't think I'm going to like Jen any better than I did before. But I took Dad a gift for his niece's baptism, and we talked a little about both of us being better at sharing responsibility." Heidi put her arm around Jilly. "It's not the same with Miss Cass. We don't have kids together. So she'll still be your teacher, but she's not meeting us in the park for ice cream after lessons. That's all."

"Are you ever going to get married to someone?"

Heidi sighed. "I don't know, sweetheart. Maybe someday. Right now, I want to try doing better as a mom."

"Okay. Hey, can I have some ice cream?"

"Where'd that come from?"

"You said it. About ice cream in the park. We can't go to the park, but can I have some of the stuff in the freezer?"

"Sure."

They returned to the other room, and both Max and Jilly helped themselves to ice cream. They settled on the couch to watch some cheesy movie with a lot of teenagers breaking into song at school. Heidi glanced over her shoulder. She should talk to Max too, but first she had to speak with Kate. She sat across from her at the table.

Kate was looking over some papers, and Heidi interrupted her. "What's this?"

"Nothing." Kate quickly folded everything and stuffed it into an envelope.

"Training programs at BOCES?" Heidi asked. She'd seen that envelope before, but Kate had kept it hidden.

"Yeah. I got this from school. It's just info." Kate folded her arms.

"It's fine. I know you understand that if you choose not to go to college now, you relinquish your scholarship. You'll have to pay for classes if you decide to go back later. But other than that, I say go for it."

"What?"

"Go for it." Heidi reached for the envelope. "There's some good stuff here. I happen to have a few connections."

Kate's cheeks were red, but she was smiling. "I was so scared you'd be mad, especially if I said I wanted to do what you're doing."

"You want to be a nurse's aide?"

"Maybe." Kate shrugged. "I want to work in healthcare, but I don't know what. And I don't want to waste my scholarship and pay the other half of my tuition to find out I hate whatever I chose to study." Kate met Heidi's gaze. "I don't want to do something I hate because I feel like I'd be betraying my education."

"Smart girl," Heidi remarked. "Where'd you get all that from?"

"What you said about regretting things sank in." Kate tapped her head. "Do you like your job?"

"Some days it's really hard," Heidi admitted. "But yes. I love what I do."

"Do you ever think about going back to school?"

Yes, Heidi had. But if the last ten days—or one day—had taught her anything, it was that she had to decide what her priorities were. Going back to school was low on her list. If she liked what she did, then what difference did it make? People asked her all the time if she "really wanted to be a nurse." Some of her friends who were nurses got asked why they'd never gone on to medical school. Somehow, they were meant to believe they were lesser.

Heidi looked Kate in the eyes and said, "I've thought about it, but I like my job. It keeps a roof over our heads and food in our fridge. It gives me good hours most of the time so I miss as few of your things as possible. I'm happy, and if you want to do one of the training programs, I'll help you select and go from there."

Kate jumped up for the second time that night and crushed Heidi with her hug. "Thanks, Mom!"

"You're welcome," Heidi squeaked out.

Kate let go, laughing, and went to join the others on the couch. When Max wandered out to the kitchen, Heidi decided this was the right moment to talk to him too.

"Do we have any popcorn?"

"In the pantry, there should be a box. I can make it in a sec. Come sit."

Max parked himself in the same spot Kate had left. "I wanna see the rest of the movie."

"You've seen it at least eleven times already. I promise you'll be back before the end."

"Okay, fine."

"I hear you're interested in theater summer camp."

Max sat up straighter. "Who told you that?"

"Kayla's mom. The one who brought you home. She says Kayla does camp, and you wanted to but didn't think you should ask me." Max didn't need to know that conversation happened on one of her other do-over days.

"Yeah, 'cause how're you gonna get me there and back, and it costs a lot..."

"Don't worry about the first one. Kayla's mom and I will discuss sharing the driving. I get done with work before you finish camp, so I'll pick you up. Kayla's mom can drive you there. As for the money, I have some set aside. It was meant for you for when you get older, but if this is what you want, I'll use some of it now." She also thought she might ask if Evan could spare a bit extra so they could split the cost, but if he refused, she had backup. "Kayla's mom says there are still spots, but we'll have to register you right away tomorrow."

"This is so awesome!" Max stood, and Heidi cringed, wondering if she was in for another hug that squeezed the breath out of her. Instead, Max raced for his room, calling, "I'm gonna text Kayla right now!"

Heidi laughed softly. She picked up the CD, still in the middle of the table where she'd left it. Leather Anvil's *Sonic Pixie Dream Girls*. She opened it, and sure enough, Angel's business card was tucked into the case. Heidi glanced at the time. Was it too late to call? Too early, and Angel would still be at the festival?

The kids were still absorbed in the movie. Heidi microwaved the popcorn and brought it to them, to a chorus of "Thanks, Mom!" She smiled to herself. A few minutes of watching, and she figured out where they were in the movie. She had time for a little privacy if she called now. Leaving the kids to watch yet another musical number, she went into her room and closed the door.

Trembling with nerves, Heidi sat on her bed, staring at the numbers on the business card. Her heart hammered as she entered them carefully into her contacts under Flores, Angel. Then she tapped the number and waited.

"Hey, this is Angel," came a friendly voice. Heidi was about to answer when she realized it was the voicemail recording.

At the tone, Heidi said, "Hi, um, this is Heidi...the weird woman from the festival. Um...your card. In the CD case. And I thought I'd try calling, but...um. Anyway, if you'd like to have coffee or whatever with me, um...call me back. Yeah. All right, bye."

Heidi tossed her phone onto the bed and lay back, groaning and covering her face with her hands. Maybe Angel couldn't get to the phone in time. Or maybe she was too busy. She might be screening calls, especially from strange women on park benches.

Just as Heidi sat up, resigned to throw on old pajama pants and a well-loved T-shirt, her phone buzzed. Her breath caught as she picked it up and turned it over. Everything felt like it was in slow motion, even though she was rushing to answer. At last she had the phone to her ear.

"Hello?"

"Hey, Weird Heidi from the park." Angel giggled. "Got your message, and I'd love to meet up. How about the day after tomorrow?"

"I...yeah. Perfect. Equal Grounds okay?"

"That's where I was going to suggest! I'll see you there at four."

"Four. Yes. Uh...goodnight, Angel."

"Goodnight, Heidi."

Heidi ended the call and pitched her phone aside. She lay back again, this time spread eagle. She couldn't help the tiny, triumphant, "Yes!" that escaped her lips.

Day Sixty-Six...

(Or Day Seventy-Five)...and Counting

The smell of coffee from the automatic pot woke Heidi from a deep sleep. She stirred restlessly, vaguely recalling that she'd been dreaming—a definitely not-safe-for-work dream about a woman with dark hair and sparkling eyes. She squinted and peered around. Early sunlight filtered in around the curtains. She blinked, trying to clear the sleep from her eyes, then opened them fully. She switched on the radio on her bedside table, tuned to WNDR 95.5.

"Goooooood morning, Rochester!"

Heidi groaned and rolled over Good god, Angel was cheerful, even at this unholy hour. She sighed when her hand hit the cold sheets, but feeling around, her fingers came in contact with a small sheet of paper. She grinned sleepily and somehow managed to sit up.

The radio was still playing. "How about some tunes to put you in the right mood for your morning commute? We've got the latest from Leather Anvil, followed by another eight in a row of your indie rock favorites."

Leather Anvil's "Dead to the World" began playing, and Heidi muffled her laughter in the pillow. That was a shout-out if she ever heard one. "Thanks, Angel," she said out loud.

When she sat up, she remembered the note in her hand. It read, "Make sure you're listening at 6. Love you!"

Heidi's good mood lasted all the way through her morning ritual. She was in the car by 6:40, with instructions for all the kids and strategic alarms set to remind them. Max had camp; Jilly was spending the day in Cass's studio, learning about different instruments; and Kate was working at Wegmans. None of them had to be up yet, therefore, they were all still in bed when Heidi quietly closed the door.

She kept the note from Angel tucked into her scrubs pocket so she could have it with her all day. On the drive in, she listened to Angel bantering with her co-host. Every now and again, she caught something she was sure Angel had directed at her.

They weren't being secretive about their relationship, though Angel liked to give Heidi a sly radio wink every so often. It was nice, having a bit of an inside joke on her way to the hospital. Neither of them felt the need to hide anything, but they weren't discussing the particulars with their coworkers.

As far as those particulars went, Angel stayed over at Heidi's as often as not these days. She was the first person Heidi had dated since Evan to do so. Most of Heidi's relationships hadn't lasted long enough to reach that stage. Even Cass had always preferred to be at her place, which meant Heidi either had to make arrangements or get home by midnight. Cass's unwillingness to stay at Heidi's—she always said it made her uncomfortable with the kids— meant they only spent Heidi's non-working weekends together.

With Angel, everything was different. She was more than happy to stay, as long as Heidi understood her work schedule meant being up long before the rooster even considered cracking one eye open. Heidi had worked some unpleasant shifts before reaching enough seniority to be on days only. She got it.

It was new, bringing Angel around and having her stay over. When Heidi had introduced her to the family, she'd been a frantic mess of nerves. But everything went fine, and the kids adored her. Jilly called her Auntie Angel, and Max always pulled her into a long discussion about musical theater. Kate had been slower to warm up, but she was also busy with work and preparing for her training program in phlebotomy.

After work, Heidi called Angel. "You coming over?"

"I was planning to, if you want me there. I could bring food so you don't have to cook."

"I see your evil ways, getting my kids to eat vegan shit without telling them." Heidi laughed. "Too bad none of them will be home."

"You caught me. Not just the kids, though. So, dinner?"

"I'll try whatever you cook. And yes, I appreciate not having to make it."

"See you soon."

"Oh, wait...I have to get Max and drop him off at his dad's. Supposedly Evan already picked up Jilly. Can we make it a bit later, like five-thirty? After that, I'm kid-free and all yours."

"Awesome! I'll be there."

They would have the whole apartment to themselves all night, not only for dinner. Kate was sleeping over at a friend's house, and the younger two were going to their father's for the rest of the week. He had some time off, and he wanted to spend it with them. Heidi definitely didn't mind being alone with Angel for a change.

In the past, Heidi might've tried to make the night perfect, without much regard for how the other person might be feeling. As long as it looked like she was organized and had it all together, she considered it right. Angel never cared about that, though. She only wanted them to have a good time with each other. And eat homemade vegan pizza, apparently. Tonight was all about catching up and being together. Heidi forced herself not to have any agenda other than that.

She pulled into the parking lot at the studio where Max and Kayla were practicing. As soon as the clock on her dashboard read 4:00, the doors opened, and kids spilled out into the heat. Max and Kayla bounded over, piling into the back seat and talking over each other to tell Heidi all about the latest happenings at camp.

She listened as well as she could, given that she didn't know anything about theater; she couldn't pick out one sentence from another with both kids talking, and she really had no clue how theater camp worked anyway.

"Mom!" Max broke into Heidi's thoughts.

"What?"

"Are you or not?"

"Am I what?"

"Helping out at the show. Like, they need people to do stuff. Parents."

"It's this weekend, right?"

"Yeah."

"I can help. I'm not working."

"Cool. I have a thingy for you to fill out."

They drove Kayla home, and then Heidi headed for Evan's house. She'd agreed to this week only if Evan was all right with making sure Max got to camp every day. They were performing *Alice in Wonderland*, and Max was the King of Hearts. He couldn't miss rehearsals if Evan failed to understand how important they were.

Heidi braced herself but then deflated. She didn't need to control this. Max would call her if there was any problem, and she was still getting him from camp every day because she had to drive Kayla. Benji knew where Evan lived, and she was fine with picking Max up in the mornings.

When they arrived, Heidi helped Max gather all his things from the back of her car. They waited on the stoop until Jen answered.

"Hey, Max!" she said, and then, more tersely, "Heidi."

"Hello, Jen. Is Evan home?"

Jen pulled her long hair into a ponytail. In the background, Heidi heard the sounds of Melloney playing.

"I can manage to get Max settled," she told Heidi.

"I understand that. I need to speak to Max's father." Heidi took a calming breath. "Please." Jen turned to go, but Heidi stopped her. "Wait."

"Yes?"

"I'm sorry. I know you can handle things with Max and with Jilly. So I'm sorry for coming across as though I don't trust you. I need to speak to Evan about something else. Maybe you'd be willing to listen too."

Jen raised her perfectly sculpted eyebrows. "I'll go get Evan."

When the two of them returned, Heidi motioned for them to step outside. Jilly was happily entertaining Melloney, and Max was probably settling in wherever they'd put him.

"Is everything okay?" Evan asked.

"Yes, of course. We're all set for Max's camp, and he'll probably give you the same volunteer sheet he gave me." Heidi held it up. "That's not what I wanted to tell you."

"Go on."

"I'm seeing someone," Heidi told them. "She's been staying over at the apartment. If the kids talk about Auntie Angel, that's who they mean."

Jen looked annoyed, and Heidi couldn't blame her. She'd gone almost right from Cass to Angel in the blink of an eye. It had taken ages to tell everyone about Cass, and now here Heidi was, only a couple months later, talking about Angel staying over.

"All right," Evan finally said. "That was...fast."

"I know." Heidi paused. "Angel is—"

Jen's jaw dropped. "Wait. Angel Flores? From the radio?"

"You know of her?" Somehow, Heidi hadn't pictured Jen as someone who liked indie rock.

"Evan likes that station." Jen blushed. "I've started listening, but I always feel a little behind, not knowing all the cool bands."

Heidi snorted a laugh. "Don't worry. The three of us will have you covered. You'll learn in no time."

"The...three of you..." Jen frowned.

"That was the other thing I was going to ask. Maybe we could all have dinner sometime, all of us and the kids. I think we could manage a single evening together."

Evan's expression softened. "I'd like that."

"Good. I'm going to leave you to enjoy your time with Max and Jilly. I've got a date." Heidi couldn't help smiling.

Jen and Evan went inside, and Heidi returned to her car. She wasn't likely to rebuild a solid friendship with Evan, and she definitely wasn't going to hang out with Jen on her own. But they could at least get to know one another a little better, for the sake of the kids. It would make negotiating music lessons and theater camp and schoolwork far easier.

Angel was already in the kitchen when Heidi arrived. The apartment smelled amazing, like tomatoes and basil straight out of the garden. Angel was dicing vegetables and throwing them into a pot. When she set the knife down, Heidi came up behind her and wrapped her arms around Angel's waist. She kissed her neck.

"Hi," she murmured against Angel's skin.

Angel turned and kissed Heidi, searing and full of anticipation. "Hi," she said once their lips were free.

"It smells so good in here."

"We're having spaghetti squash noodles with homemade sauce and roasted veggies," Angel said. "Wait until you try it."

"Sounds good," Heidi replied. "So...we have a little time?"

"Not long enough for that." Angel gave Heidi a sly smile.

"That wasn't what I had in mind, but now that you mention it..." Heidi pulled her in for another kiss.

Angel didn't object. She leaned against the counter and pulled Heidi closer. They made out with the sounds of the sauce bubbling in the background. Surely there was enough time for this, at least.

After several glorious minutes, Angel pulled away. "I should check on the food."

Reluctantly, Heidi let her go. She sat at the table. "I told Evan and Jen about us," she said. "How you stay over sometimes."

"Oh?" Angel gave the sauce a stir and joined Heidi at the table.

"When I dropped Max off. I thought they might overhear the kids or one of them might say something. Figured it was better coming from me."

"Well." Angel put her hand on top of Heidi's. "So, what do you wish will come from this?"

"Oh, no. No wishes. I think I've had enough of that for a lifetime." Heidi chuckled.

"I feel you." Angel squeezed her hand. "Let me try again. What do you hope comes next?"

Heidi turned her hand over to hold Angel's. "I don't know what our next step is. I'm used to planning everything out. It's probably why it never worked with Evan or Cass. They're both serious planners too, but our goals never seemed to mesh."

"We don't need a 'next step.' I love you, and this is where I want to be right now. I think that's good enough."

"It's definitely good enough."

Heidi stood and came around to the other side of the table to pull Angel up.

She kissed her and backed her up against the pantry. When Heidi slid her hand underneath Angel's shirt while kissing her neck, Angel gasped. Heidi ran a thumb over Angel's soft sports bra.

"The squash...will...overcook," Angel managed between sharp inhalations.

"So, it won't be perfect?" Heidi murmured in her ear. "I think that's okay."

And it was.

A.M. Leibowitz is a queer spouse, parent, feminist, and book-lover falling somewhere on the Geek-Nerd Spectrum. They keep warm through the long, cold western New York winters by writing about life, relationships, hope, and happy-for-now endings. Their published fiction includes several novels as well as a number of short works, and their stories have been included in anthologies from Supposed Crimes, Beaten Track, Witty Bard, and Mischief Corner Books. They are an occasional host for the Bi+(plus) podcast as well as doing bi+ advocacy work and curating the best-of bi list on the QueerBooksForTeens website. They are a social media contributor for Supposed Crimes, LLC, and they post about news, reviews, and updates for the website. In between, they blog coffee-fueled, quirky commentary on faith, culture, books, chronic illness, and their family.

Passing on Faith

It's a multi-faceted exploration of how culture, religion, gender, sexuality, social expectations, our own personal expectations, experiences, family, friends, and so forth, impose on us ways of living, being and seeing the world. - Debbie McGowan

Following his father's death, Micah Forbes believes he can finally put the family who rejected him and their religious bigotry behind him. In a cruel twist, his older brother calls to tell him he's inherited their father's abandoned vacation home.

Micah discovers the house comes complete with a long list of repairs, boxes full of family secrets, and a handful of quirky neighbors. Despite not wanting to get in too deep, he can't help the spark of interest stirred when the sexy redhead next door offers his help. Everything about the enigmatic Cat Rowland throws Micah off-balance, from his gender-bending sense of fashion to his handy repair skills to his deep spirituality. Before long, Micah is swept up by Cat and his friends, but Cat himself keeps his heart carefully protected.

When Micah's past and his present collide in a painful way, his self-destructive coping habits threaten to overwhelm him. To save himself, he needs to open his soul and let someone in. Cat has the key to unlock him, if he can let down his guard and trust his faith enough to catch Micah as he falls.

Anthem

Trevor Davidson has everything going for him. He's just moved out on his own with three friends, and he's landed a job as music director at a large Boston church. He has high hopes for marrying his long-term girlfriend and settling into a comfortable, devout lifestyle.

Andre Cole has spent the past few years throwing himself into a dead-end job at a Cape Cod-based call center. When an opportunity to move back to Boston arises, Andre believes it will be the do-over he needs to put his past behind him.

A chance meeting in a club on New Year's Eve brings Trevor and Andre together for a brief but steamy encounter. Both assuming that's the end of it, they are unexpectedly thrown back into each other's lives when Trevor's church hires Andre for their website design. While Andre is content at first to move on, Trevor's conflicted feelings bubble over into his songwriting. Before he can stop it, his ode to Andre becomes an inadvertent Christian radio hit.

Unfortunately for Trevor, he isn't the only one who knows the song's hidden meaning. Someone has leaked the story and upended Trevor's life. In order to put the pieces back together, he needs to learn to be honest with his girlfriend, with Andre, and especially with himself.